THE SECRET SOLDIER

THE MAUREEN RITTER SERIES
BOOK 3

EOIN DEMPSEY

This book is for the staff and children of Izieu.

1

London, Tuesday, October 6, 1942

After a tearful goodbye to Christophe, her lover and fellow resistance fighter, on the beach outside Marseille, Maureen Ritter traveled via submarine to the British territory at Gibraltar. The houses in Izieu were both empty now. The Jewish refugees she had harbored since before the war began were all safe in Spain and had already applied to the embassy in Madrid for visas to the United States. Maureen was content in the knowledge that even if they didn't receive the visas, they'd be safe from the Nazis there. The mission her father had given her—to look after the workers from his former factory in Berlin who'd fled Germany because of their status as Jews, was complete. But her part in fighting the Nazis seeking to persecute them was far from over. Maureen had seen too much while living in Berlin for four years and in France for six to return home now. The cause was too important to return to America as her family wanted. She'd set everything she knew in the world aside to fight and was determined to continue until the Germans were defeated. The fire inside her hadn't diminished. It burned stronger every day.

After being dropped off in Gibraltar, Maureen waited for the convoy that would take her to the United Kingdom, a place she'd never been, but had been fighting for in the South of France for almost a year. A British agent had arranged passage to the UK for her. Although Maureen had worked with her in France, and had risked her life alongside her several times, she knew little about her. All she knew was the agent's code name —Monique. She was Maureen's contact in London.

The ship took two long weeks to arrive. Maureen spent the time on the naval base in Gibraltar, sleeping in a bunk for recruits, wishing Christophe had come with her.

The frustrating wait ended when she boarded the British ship and joined a convoy of 60 other vessels bound for Scotland. The journey past the Strait of Gibraltar, into the Atlantic Ocean, up through the Bay of Biscay, and into the Celtic Sea took ten days. The English Channel was too dangerous to sail through. It was full of U-boats waiting to sink ships like theirs and was to be avoided at all costs. So, the vessels took a circuitous route to her final destination of London. Safety was deemed more important than speed. And to remain safe, the convoy was escorted by a British destroyer, three other warships, and a rotating series of air patrols, mainly consisting of American Liberator bombers. Maureen particularly enjoyed watching them flying above their heads. It was something to relieve the boredom of the voyage.

After what seemed like an interminable journey, the convoy docked safe and sound at the Scottish port of Greenock. Maureen nearly despaired when she saw it on the map. It was about as far from London as Paris was from Marseille. Still, she was in the UK, and the trek continued. The first train she took from the port in western Scotland was to Glasgow. The next was to Edinburgh. After a night spent in Scotland's capital city, she took a final train to London—where Monique and service to the British Crown awaited.

~

The South of France, Monday, November 13, 2006

Amy moved her hands down to her swollen belly, gently cradling her unborn baby. It had been weird at first, growing so large. She'd always been slim, but had come to love her new shape. The kicks that bubbled underneath her taut skin were a reminder of what was to come, how her life would soon change. They were her only direct communication with the person who'd shape the rest of her life, and she relished each one.

She sat up in bed and reached for the curtain across the window. Drawing it back revealed dawn over the French countryside. The sky morphed from purple to orange, tinged with red. Clouds piled up on the horizon and then parted to reveal the golden aura of the sun. Amy watched in silence as the beautiful scene unfolded in front of her eyes, wondering if anyone else was watching or if this was just for her.

The house was quiet. Her grandmother was asleep and likely would be for two or three more hours. Ostensibly Amy had come to interview her, but being here offered so much more. Her doctor in New York had given her the go-ahead to make the trip but warned her to return before she hit 36 weeks. That gave her a window of three more weeks—enough to finish the interviews and spend time with Maureen before life turned into something unrecognizable.

Her trip to France offered many benefits, not least of which was the opportunity to get away from the father of her child, her ex, Ryan Smith, but even more so, his mother, Louise.

Back in New York, the spare room in her apartment was already full of the latest gadgets for raising infants. All from Ryan's mother. It was her way of exerting control. Amy had turned down Louise's offer for her and the baby to move into her palatial mansion on the Upper East Side, so Louise used her money in other ways. Amy knew her intentions were sincere. Mrs. Smith was lonely, and her other grandchildren had moved back to Connecticut with Ryan's wife after the divorce, but she didn't seem to know where to draw the line. Perhaps she thought she could replace Amy's mother. Amy reached over to her bag on the bedside table and drew out an old photograph of her parents from her wallet. It was so familiar that it was as if it had been drawn from her own memories.

"I miss you, and so does the baby," she whispered before putting it back.

All the baby clothes piled up in the spare room of her apartment were white or yellow. Despite Louise constantly pushing and cajoling her to ask at every scan, Amy hadn't found out the gender of the baby. There were few enough genuine surprises left in life, and she wanted her child to reveal itself to her in its own time. Amy remembered her last conversation with Louise before she had flown to France the week before.

"Don't you think Ryan has a right to know if he's having a son or a daughter? I wish you'd let him come to one of the scans. He's so looking forward to being a father again. Perhaps you should give him a chance," she'd said.

A chance! The man who had broken her heart and destroyed her career by making sure it was her, not him—the so-important foreign editor—who was let go from *the Times*?

"And he's divorcing his wife for you. He really loves you, and wants to do right by you, Amy," Louise had said.

Amy knew that wasn't true. Ryan and his wife would have divorced either way. It was impossible to tell if Louise knew that Ryan had tried to get back together with his wife at the expense of his relationship with Amy and then changed his mind when that door closed.

But explaining anything to Louise that the older woman didn't want to hear was a fool's errand. Including the fact that Amy already had a boyfriend. Although she wasn't sure that was strictly true anymore.

Mike had said he wanted to continue their relationship, but when she'd left him at the airport on her way to France, she had made it clear he was a free man.

"You're only going for two weeks," he'd said. "Where is this coming from?"

"I don't want you to waste time waiting for me. Everything's going to change soon. I won't be able to go out or do barely any of the normal things we take for granted."

"It's a baby, not a life sentence," he'd said.

"Just have fun."

"Can I call you when you're over there?"

"Yes, of course," she said.

Seeing his face as she'd told him was hard, and she doubted her words at the time and still did, but it was best for them both. He'd left her with a smile and a kind word—a gentleman as always. If they'd met under other circumstances, she was sure things would have been different, but she had her baby to think of now. She couldn't afford to have her heart broken. Not with everything else going on in her life.

It was Maureen, a headstrong woman and incurable romantic, who had convinced Amy to give Mike Nugent a chance in the first place, the opportunity to decide to keep seeing her or not when she'd found out she was pregnant. Amy's first instinct had been to drop him without a word, sure that he'd run as soon as he heard she was carrying another man's child, but Maureen had reasoned that he was an adult and deserved to make his own decisions about their fledgling relationship.

He had stayed with her as her body changed and dealt with her hormone-induced moods without complaint. He'd been there for her when she needed him, and sometimes she even thought of saying she loved him. But suppose he realized he couldn't do this once the baby was born? She was on borrowed time with him, she was sure. And finally, she'd decided it was better to cut ties now than go again through the agony and grief she had felt when Ryan went back to his wife—the same wife his mother claimed he was now divorcing for her.

After a successful attempt to steal a few more hours of sleep, Amy got out of bed and dressed for the day. The mild weather allowed for a loose T-shirt over the sweatpants that seemed surgically attached to her these days. Her grandmother was sitting at the table on the patio outside and smiled as she saw her. Maureen's two dogs scuttled around and ran to jump on her. Amy took a moment to pet the crazy Pomeranian and the sweet bulldog, even though bending down wasn't an easy task anymore.

"Good morning, dear," Maureen said as Amy joined her at the table. The fruit was already laid out, along with fresh bread her grandmother had delivered every morning. The aroma of freshly brewed coffee filled her nostrils, and she poured herself a cup.

"How are you feeling?" her grandmother asked.

"Good," Amy answered. "Relaxed and happy. It's good to be here."

"That's exactly what I wanted to hear. Let me know when you want to start the interviews again."

"I think I'll do a little writing first—gather my thoughts."

"I'll be here when you need me."

"I know that," Amy said, reaching for her grandmother's hand.

Amy was at the desk her grandmother had set up for her in the spare room when her phone buzzed. She checked it. It was a text from Mike.

How are you feeling? New York isn't the same without you.

She picked up her phone, acutely aware of the need to temper her words.

I'm getting the rest I need, and the book is progressing nicely. I don't miss New York at all!

She hit send. It was hard to say if she welcomed the texts she still received from him, but she didn't have the heart not to reply at all. Mike deserved the world. Better than her. She had no intention of hurting him.

Another text came through a few minutes later, Amy reached for her phone expecting something else from Mike, but it wasn't from him. It was from Ryan.

I hope you're feeling well. My mother wants to talk to you later to make sure you're okay. Would you mind talking to her for a few minutes?

She closed the phone without replying and returned to writing—her escape.

2

London, Tuesday, October 6, 1942

Maureen arrived in London on a gray October afternoon. It seemed like years since she'd left the sunny climes of the South of France. Half of Waterloo station was cordoned off, and the sound of construction, of hammers striking and bricks being laid, filled the air. Maureen wondered who had died there when the bombs came. The street outside was in a similar state. The scars of the blitz were everywhere to see. She passed blackened buildings now hollow inside, but life in the city continued. The sidewalks were full of people coming home from work, and many were smiling as if life couldn't have been any grander. Maureen had been told by the sailors she'd met on the journey over about the spirit of the people. It seemed the harder the Germans hit them, the more determined to hold out the British population became.

Alone in a city she didn't know, she found a hotel in Soho and called a phone number she'd been given by her liaison on the ship.

A female voice answered. "Hello, you've reached Burton's Home Supplies," she said.

"I think I have the wrong number," Maureen answered.

"Wait," the voice said. "Have you come from Scotland? We were expecting your call. Where are you?"

Maureen gave her the name and address of the hotel.

"Stay put," the woman on the other end of the phone said. "You'll be contacted in due course."

Maureen nodded and hung up the phone. Apparently, strolling up to the War Office and asking for a job wasn't the done thing. So, she waited.

Waiting wasn't Maureen's strong point, and after two days of reading in her room, she began to grow impatient. She descended the stairs to the main lobby, where she greeted Henry, the young man behind the desk, with a smile.

"Miss Ritter?" Henry said. "I have a note for you."

Maureen walked across to him. "Any idea who left it?"

"No," he said in his strong cockney accent. "It was in the mailbox with the rest of the letters this morning. But this was delivered by hand."

"Thanks," Maureen said as he handed her the envelope.

Maureen felt adrenaline buzzing through her veins as she sat on the bed and opened the letter. It was only a few words.

REPORT TO 57 ORCHARD ST. AT TWO O'CLOCK THIS AFTERNOON. DON'T BE LATE.

MONIQUE

Her idea of going for a walk through the city streets was abandoned, and she returned to her room. A surge of relief flooded her body. She'd started thinking she'd wasted her time coming all this way. Her hands were shaking as she placed the piece of paper on the bed beside her.

She picked out one of her favorite dresses. Red, with black buttons down the front, a belt, and shoes to match. She applied some lipstick as a finishing touch and stared at herself in the mirror for a few seconds.

"You've come a long way for this," she said. "Don't mess it up."

She left the hotel soon after and took the Tube to Marble Arch. Oxford Street, damaged as it was, still heaved with activity, and she stopped to peer in some shop windows as she walked toward Orchard St. She arrived an hour early, located the building, and found somewhere a few hundred yards down the street to sit and have the most insipid cup of tea imaginable. Time seemed to stand still, and her hands were shaking as she lifted the cup to her mouth, but eventually, she found herself standing outside a cream-colored apartment building just before two o'clock. It didn't look like anything special and had no brass plate or sign to signify what might be inside. The intrigue she felt was almost too much to bear, and unable to wait any longer, she pushed the front door open. A stairwell in front of her led her to apartment 57 on the fifth floor. Maureen took a deep breath and smoothed down her dress before knocking.

"Come in," came a voice from inside.

Maureen pushed the door open and was greeted by a young secretary sitting behind a desk. Her brown hair matched the color of her eyes.

"I received a letter to come here at two," Maureen said.

"What's your name?" she said. It was the same woman who'd answered the phone, calling the place "Burton's Home Supplies."

"Maureen Ritter."

The secretary took a few seconds to check a list on the table in front of her and then looked up again. "They're expecting you. You can go inside."

"Who's expecting me?"

The secretary's only answer was a hand gesturing toward the door behind her. Maureen walked over and knocked. A gruff voice from behind the door ordered her to enter, and she pushed it open. Monique was standing at the desk with a man in civilian clothing. He was in his forties with slicked-back graying hair. His handsome face was clean-shaven. He offered Maureen a firm handshake.

"Major Bernard Franks," he said. "And I believe you two are already acquainted."

Monique shook her hand but didn't offer a smile or even a friendly gesture. Maureen might have been insulted if she didn't know her so well. They all sat down.

"So, I understand from Monique that you were one of her most trusted contacts in the South of France,"

"I'm happy to be introduced as that."

"And you're an American," he added.

"From the New York area originally, but my family moved to Germany in 1932."

"To get a job in Berlin. Tell me more about that in your own words."

"My father was unemployed and got a job offer from his uncle to work in his metalworks factory in Berlin. He didn't have much choice. We went from living with my aunt, to owning our own mansion in the space of a couple of years."

"What did the factory produce?"

Maureen had the irritated feeling he already knew but answered as if he didn't anyway. "Metal goods at first, but his cousin, Helga, who was the co-owner of the factory, introduced the idea of making armaments for the Nazi army. And airplanes too."

"And your father agreed?"

"His hands were tied, but yes, he went along with it. It was a gold rush for the armaments industry in the 30s. Leading up to all this."

"Your fluency in German is certainly an asset."

"And French. My family moved back to America before the war started. I stayed on in a small town near the French Alps to evacuate the Jewish workers from his factory in Berlin we'd brought there, as well as some others we picked up along the way."

"I spent some time in Berlin myself before the war. And is your father's cousin Helga still there running the factory?"

"Yes. Factories now. Plural. As far as I know, they're still going. Although she and the rest of the family don't speak anymore. Things were a little tense at the end. She's a loyal member of the Nazi Party."

Major Franks picked up a pencil and pointed it at Maureen. "So, Miss Ritter, what do you know about the Special Operation Executive?"

"I know how it feels to be a part of your operations. I've blackened my face and helped lay explosives on train tracks to derail Nazi trains. Monique has seen what I've done for the cause already. Many times."

"It's because of her recommendation that you're here," Franks said. "I've been with the SOE since it was formed three years ago. We specialize in—"

"Clandestine operations behind enemy lines in occupied Europe. Monique gave me the speech when we first met."

"So, you're aware of the sensitive nature of what we do here?" Franks asked.

"I've seen friends die on missions to slow the Nazi war machine. I'm more aware than most," Maureen said.

"My colleague here has debriefed me on what you went through. But the real question is, are you ready to go back for more?"

"Show me where to sign,"

Franks smiled. "That's good to hear. We know of your work, smuggling Jewish refugees to safety over the Pyrenees, forging documents and performing all manner of anti-Nazi activities. It's our job to hone you into an even more effective weapon."

Monique remained stony-faced.

"In the South of France?" Maureen asked.

"Perhaps," he answered.

"Why would you think about sending me anywhere else?"

Monique interrupted, "It's not guaranteed that you're sent where you want. And there are tests first, to see if you are suitable."

"Tests?" Maureen said. "Blowing up that train wasn't enough? Seeing my friends killed by Nazi soldiers in front of me wasn't enough?" Maureen felt her anger rising, but the two spies didn't react, and seemed to be enjoying the show.

"I'm sure the tests won't present a significant problem to someone as experienced as you," Franks said. "But you will have to pass them to receive an assignment."

"Send me back to Marseille or the Lyon area."

Franks clasped his hands and sat forward. "Why there? You know Paris well. You operated there for several years."

"I want to go back because my fiancé is there. Half of my friends are there. I speak the language. I know the cities and the roads. I've set up safe houses all along the coast to Spain and beyond. The Nazis have choked the life out of the place I love and I want to send them back to hell where they belong."

"I told you." In so far as she ever permitted herself to smile, Monique was smiling.

"Yes, you did," Major Franks said smoothly. "Miss Ritter, you can report for your first test tomorrow."

〜

Kent, Friday, October 9, 1942

A man in a blue suit with an impressive mustache picked Maureen up from her hotel and whisked her from Soho to a manor house outside the city. It was set among the rolling green fields of Kent. Upon her arrival, the man, who didn't say three words if two would do, brought her inside the house to an office where Maureen found herself sitting opposite a gray-haired man in a tweed suit. The nameplate on his table read Dr. Kewell, and he shuffled through some papers on his mahogany desk before bringing his eyes to hers. He introduced himself as a psychiatrist and said this was the first test Maureen had to pass to become an agent of the SOE.

He held up a card blotted with black ink. "What does this look like to you?"

"Like a child spilled a bottle of paint?"

"No," he said. "What do you see in the patterns?"

Maureen squinted and leaned forward, wondering if she was missing something. "Two bugs walking toward a pool of vomit?" He held up another. "Now it looks like the same two bugs have called four of their friends to come help them out with the vomit," she said.

Maureen didn't quite see the use in this test, but was willing to do what it took to return to France. He showed her card after card, but she didn't see any pathway into her soul, just a bunch of bugs scurrying toward a pool of vomit.

"Let's try something else," the doctor said after a few minutes. "Do you love your parents?"

"Of course, what kind of a question is that? You expect me to say no?"

"Did they have a happy marriage?"

"Until my mom died. They had their ups and downs like anyone else and my father remarried in the 30s. What has this got to do with fighting the Germans?"

The doctor didn't answer the question and pressed on with another question after writing down some notes.

"Would you say you were a happy child?"

"Until my mom died. That wasn't what I'd call a joyous event."

"Are you close with your family?"

"I would be if I could be. They're all the way over in New York. It might as well be a different planet for how hard it is to get to these days."

The doctor asked her dozens more questions, asking her opinion on the war effort, nutrition, politics, exercise, agriculture, and even feminine hygiene products. By the end of the test, Maureen was as confused as she was bored.

"Time for the next test," a young woman who walked in said as the doctor closed Maureen's file. Without any idea if she'd done well or not, Maureen followed the woman out to the hallway.

"Change into these," the woman said, handing Maureen a green shirt, matching pants and a pair of boots,

"What are these for?" Maureen asked.

"The obstacle course."

Maureen stepped into a changing room, and when she emerged, she felt like a soldier. She was wearing the right clothes, anyway.

"How well do I have to do on the obstacle course?" she asked the woman.

"That all depends."

Maureen shook her head in bewilderment and didn't ask any more questions. She was confident in her athletic ability. She'd carried kids over the Pyrenees. Voluntarily!

Maureen followed the young woman outside. Two men

were standing by the edge of a sprawling field, wearing army uniforms. The young woman brought Maureen to them and left without saying a word.

"She's not the talkative type," Maureen said. "I'm Maureen Ritter." One of the men introduced himself as Captain Dennis Taylor and the other as Captain Stephen Hendry.

"Nancy's new, she's finding her feet. Welcome," Hendry said and extended a hand to shake hers. "You're the American."

"My reputation precedes me."

"We've heard about you all right," Hendry said.

"So, how did I do in the test? The one with the splotches of paint on the white paper? Did I fail?"

Taylor shook his head and laughed. He had a round head and glasses. "No. There's no passing or failing those tests. They're just an insight into the person taking them."

"And what kind of a person am I?"

"According to the officer who interviewed you in London— a determined, independent and spirited one," Hendry said. He was tall and slim with blond hair and a matching mustache. "As for the test you just took, we'll see when the results come in."

"You could be ideal for our program," Taylor said. "But let's see how you do with the next test first."

They walked along a well-tended stone path until they came to another field.

Taylor opened a gate, and they walked through. "Welcome to the obstacle course," Captain Hendry said.

Maureen took a moment to survey the course before her. Man-made water-filled ditches crisscrossed the area, and platforms with ropes to climb ascended twenty feet into the air. Massive tractor tires were buried in the ground. Rope netting hung over a stagnant pond. There were barrels to crawl through and barbed wire fences to crawl under. At the far end, a man in a similar uniform to hers was climbing a wooden pole to a platform.

"What do you think?" Taylor asked.

"Piece of cake," Maureen said. The men laughed, apparently unable to see how nervous she was. She was desperate to succeed, and there seemed to be so many opportunities to fail.

The man climbing the pole swooped down from the platform on a rope swing and ran over to an officer who was standing with a stopwatch in hand. "How did I do?" he asked the man between heavy breaths. The recruit was the same age as Maureen and reminded her of her brother Michael. He had the same hair and face shape. She was thankful Michael was safe and sound in New York with his German wife, but his last letters had hinted that he'd join up soon to fight against the country he'd represented in the Berlin Olympics.

"You'll be apprised of your results as soon as we tabulate them," the supervising officer said. "Please wait inside and we'll get back to you."

The man traipsed off, looking disappointed.

"Your turn," Hendry said. "Are you ready?"

"As ready as I'll ever be."

The two men smiled and led her over to the starting line. Hendry drew a stopwatch from his pocket. Maureen stood ready, waiting for the word.

"Go!" Hendry said, and she ran forward to leap over a wooden wall. Seconds later she was dancing through the tractor tires. Going from one foot to the other sapped her energy in seconds, and she was breathing heavily as she moved forward. She kept the image of Christophe in her mind as she crawled through the barrels and then under the sheet of barbed wire stretched two feet off the ground. She was a muddy mess when she emerged. The rope swings over water reminded her of summers at the lake outside Berlin when she was 16. Her muscles were screaming, but she kept going, ending up on the same wooden pole she'd seen the man on. The prospect of finishing was the reward she focused on. Not having to do this anymore felt like an unimaginable luxury.

She swung down from the wooden platform, unable to keep the smile from her face. She knew she'd done well, but more importantly, that the course was over.

Hendry and Taylor were waiting at the finishing line for her. She didn't bother to ask how she'd done. "Where do I wait?" she said between breaths.

Hendry answered with a smile. "No, you stay here. We've already tabulated your score."

"And?"

"The maximum was 65 points," Taylor said.

"And you scored 65," Hendry added. "But that's not the end. Not by a long way."

"I just came from France, you know," Maureen said. "The Nazis don't build wooden obstacles for us to climb over or bury massive tractor tires in the mud. They just slit your throat and hang your body up for everyone to see."

Taylor nodded. "These tests are to see what you're made of. We expect a certain level of physical fitness as well as mental acuity."

"When do we learn how to shoot and make explosives? Real skills with practical uses?"

"All in good time," he answered.

Hendry walked back to the manor house while Maureen recovered. Taylor didn't speak to her, just continued jotting notes on the clipboard he was holding. The other instructor appeared again five minutes later with five other men in tow. Each was wearing a backpack, and the instructor handed one to her.

It was so heavy she nearly dropped it.

"What the hell?"

"Rocks," Hendry replied. "Now, do the obstacle course again, as a team with the backpacks on."

Maureen looked around at the five men she'd never met. One was younger than she was and looked about 19 or 20. Another was older, perhaps in his late 30s or early 40s. The rest were about her age—26. Judging by the accents they used murmuring to each other about her, they were all English. And judging by the way they were looking at her, they didn't think she belonged there. Maureen knew she had seconds to make a good impression or lose them. She stepped forward to the man closest to her. He was the older man. He was tall, with a thin beard. As she got closer, she noticed his facial hair covered a deep scar along his jawline.

"Maureen Ritter," she said, offering the firmest handshake possible.

"Howard Mount," the man responded.

"Put the old man with the little girl," the youngest of the men said in a jovial tone.

"Shut your cake hole, Stanley," Howard said. "I was doing obstacle courses like this when you were in nappies."

"Gonna start telling us about the last war, are you, Grandad? You and this bird will make a fine pair!" Stanley said in a thick cockney accent.

Neither instructor interjected. Both were standing back, watching the show unfold in front of them.

Maureen stepped forward to introduce herself to one of the other men. He took her hand but begrudgingly. "Don't slow us down."

"Remember you will be negotiating this course as a team," Taylor said. "Pick a partner, but the collective is what matters. If one member falls behind, the entire group will suffer."

"Your time will be measured against other teams that have gone before." Hendry's face hardened as he spoke. "Make no mistake—your time matters. Do what it takes. Whatever it takes."

The other men paired up in seconds, and Maureen was left with Howard by process of elimination.

Stanley sneered at them until the man he was partnered with reminded them they were being judged as a team. "We've no chance with them!" Stanley said.

Maureen took Howard aside. The other men were younger and fitter. They were going to have to use their heads.

The first obstacle was a wooden wall eight feet high. She pointed down toward it.

"Take off your backpack when we reach it. Stay on top. I'll pass you the packs and we'll get over."

"Should we be taking them off?"

"They didn't say not to."

"Okay."

"The order of the obstacles has been changed," Hendry said.

Taylor took a whistle out of his pocket and put it between his lips. "Get ready!" He blew the whistle. Stanley sprinted ahead with his partner, but they struggled once they arrived at the wall, and with no clear plan to climb it as a team, they lost time. Maureen directed her partner to go first. Howard took off his rucksack and put it on the ground. He scaled the wall with ease, reached back for his pack, then Maureen's, and then helped her over. The other pairs copied their tactics, and all the teams got to the next obstacle together. They swung over a stagnant pond. The weight on her back almost dragged Maureen back in, but she managed to get across.

Stanley ran on once again and reached the tractor wheels in the ground first. He danced through them in seconds and kept on, streaking ahead of his partner and the rest of the group.

Hendry and Taylor were watching them through binoculars. Maureen stuck beside Howard, even though she was faster than him. They reached each obstacle together and helped the others where they could.

Howard struggled on the tallest wooden wall on the course. It was over 30 feet high, and he slowed as he reached the top.

"Come on, Howard," Maureen said from beside him. "Let's do this together. Up and over."

The middle-aged man increased his speed, and when they reached the bottom together, they were only a few seconds behind the rest of the group, except for Stanley, who was far ahead. He was waiting for them as they reached the finish line several minutes later.

"What kept you?" he sneered as Howard and Maureen came in last, albeit by only a few seconds.

Taylor and Hendry didn't hide the satisfied looks on their faces.

The recruits were all bent over, red-faced and panting. Maureen let the rucksack full of rocks tumble to the ground.

"That was excellent," Taylor said. "Good preparation for when we do the course again in the dark—with your legs tied together."

The men laughed, but Maureen wasn't so sure the officer was joking. She stayed quiet. Howard put his hand on her shoulder as he stood back up and offered her a nod. She tapped him back.

"Let's go," Hendry said. "Time for some well-earned supper."

They trudged back to the house as a group and were led downstairs to the basement—the servants' quarters. The recruits lined up for food. They were given beef stew with a slice of bread. The aroma was divine. They took their seats at a large oak table. Maureen sat beside Howard, with Stanley directly across from her.

"Couldn't keep up, could you?"

"Enough," one of the other men said.

"What's your name?" Maureen asked.

"Michael Turner, from Southampton." His brown eyes

were the same color as his greased-back hair. "This is Ted Bailey." The man beside him nodded. Ted had a flat nose and looked like he'd been in more than a few dust-ups in his time.

"And Tom Owen." Owen was tall and broad-shouldered and shook her hand like he could crush walnuts in his palms.

Maureen began to eat. It was the best meal she'd had in as long as she could remember.

"Food's good," she said between bites.

"What are you doing here, anyway?" Owen said. "Is this part of the test?" He didn't laugh, though Stanley did.

Maureen finished the food in her mouth but didn't get a chance to answer before Turner jumped in. "I was in Belgium in '40 with the expeditionary force."

"How did that go?" Stanley said and started laughing again. The other men joined him.

Turner ignored him. "Got evacuated at Dunkirk, but I wanted more. I heard about the SOE through a friend and thought it was for me. What about you lot?"

He looked at everyone but her.

Howard put down his knife and fork. "I was too young for the last war. Too old for the infantry in this one. I heard I could put my skills to use when I heard the SOE was looking for burglars with a conscience."

"You were a burglar?" Maureen asked.

"But with a conscience now!"

They all laughed.

"What about you, Stanley?" Maureen asked, staring at the young man across the table.

"I want to do my bit like the rest of you. Get behind the German lines. I can't wait to punch Fritz in the gob. Churchill said we were to create havoc. Well, I've been doing that my whole life. Figured I was the man for the job."

"The kid for the job," Turner said.

"No. You've made a mistake there." Stanley glared at his fellow recruit. Turner forked some more food into his mouth.

"I can't wait to get to France," Ted Bailey added. "I think I can do some serious damage behind the lines."

"And what about you?" Stanley said to Maureen. "A woman? What use are you going to be? You gonna do hair and makeup? And a yank too! I didn't realize the Special Operations Executive was that hard up for recruits."

No one laughed. The other men didn't say a word to either support her or put her down. Maureen knew this was her moment.

"You've all said how much you can't wait to get to Europe and wreak havoc behind enemy lines. But how many of you have actually been there already?" She looked around the table. The men just stared back at her. "How many of you have planted bombs, or presented a Nazi patrol with fake papers. Have any of you crossed the mountains with Allied servicemen, or kids fleeing for their lives? Anyone?"

"You were in France?" Howard said. "I had no idea."

"None of us have any idea about each other's past. Yet some of us presume to because of where we're from or what gender we are."

"Where were you?" Howard asked.

"I came from Marseille to be here," she said. "I've seen how dangerous it is on the ground with my own eyes. My best friend was killed and strung up on the streets of Lyon this summer. It could just as easily have been me."

The men concentrated on their food. No more words were spoken about where they'd come from or what it might be like in Europe.

Maureen went to bed that night in the female dorm. She was the only occupant. The next morning when they got up to report for duty, Hendry told them Stanley wouldn't be finishing out the course. They never saw him again.

3

Saturday, October 17, 1942

Maureen grew used to the routine of dawn runs, followed by breakfast and then more trips around the assault course. The recruits began getting to know the course so well that they knew the best footholds and routes to overcome the obstacles. Maureen began to relish the challenge of improving on her best time, and each time she finished, she made sure to run to either Hendry or Taylor to find out if she'd broken her previous personal best. It became a game to her. Since Stanley's departure, none of the other men had questioned her right to be there, not outwardly at least. She still felt isolated and alone. The only other women at the house were secretaries.

She kept the people she loved in her mind as she ran through the pouring rain. Imagining herself in Christophe's arms or being led down the aisle, arm in arm with her father, fueled her and gave her the impetus to keep going when every muscle in her body and every voice in her brain was screaming at her to stop.

After a particularly hard run in the freezing English rain, Maureen took a shower and joined the rest of the recruits in a room that seemed like it had once been a library. They were instructed to sit at the desks provided, and once they were settled, Hendry pinned a map of France to the wall. Taylor began to speak.

"If you pass this course, and let me assure you all that is a big "if," most of you will be sent to France. It's the epicenter of our operations behind enemy lines. The population there is willing, and the Nazi forces are so unpopular that we have plenty of safe houses and sympathetic civilians to help out." He picked up a pointer and held it in his hand, walking back and forth. "We've already dropped in dozens of agents with great success. There have been losses, of course, but I assume you are all aware of the risks inherent in this job."

Maureen had assured each of them of the dangers involved in operating behind enemy lines if they hadn't known already.

Captain Taylor looked at them as he moved around the room. "Each of you needs to realize how deadly this assignment you've volunteered for has the potential to be. If you're caught by the Gestapo, you won't receive a quick or peaceful death. They'll put your head between a vise and squeeze until you start talking."

"We'll deal with interrogation and standing up to torture later," Hendry added. "But before we continue, I'd like to offer you the chance to leave. You can return to your former units, or in your case, Miss Ritter, your former life, and we will harbor no judgments. There will be no retribution. This is your chance."

Nobody moved.

"No one?" Hendry said. "Then let's press on, shall we?"

"It's no secret what's going on in Europe," Taylor said. "Make no mistake these are epoch defining times. The work we're engaged in will not just shape our world but that of our grandchildren and into the future. The Germans, in a desperate grab for the natural resources that might win them the war, are stretched all over Eastern Europe and beyond. The battles in North Africa and southern Russia are about oil—the elixir that Hitler needs to drive the tanks that got him this far. But things aren't going as smoothly as our friends in Berlin thought they would. Hitler's minions believe he's infallible after his victories in France. Some of us saw the calamities of 1940 firsthand." He gestured to Maureen and Turner. "Hitler got lucky. The French generals handed their country to him on a silver platter, but that was a fluke. The war in the east was meant to be over a year ago, but the Russians are hanging on. And in North Africa, Monty and the Americans are finding their feet. Things seem dark—I know that. But the Nazis are overextended and outnumbered. Hitler's generals never wanted to fight a war on two fronts but that's exactly what we're going to give them. But only when the time is right. Your job is to create the conditions to give our boys a chance when the invasion comes."

Hendry walked around the room, slapping a piece of paper on each recruit's desk.

"What's this?" Turner held up the sheet.

"Last will and testament," Hendry replied. "Fill in the blanks so we have it on file."

Maureen shifted in her seat as she contemplated the possibility of dying. She filled Christophe's name in as her benefactor and returned the paper.

～

The mountains in the background were just as she remembered, like cakes dusted with sugar rising into the sky. The road turned to gravel and then dirt before the houses came into view. Some kids were playing outside and ran to the car as she pulled up.

Around a dozen other children were on the swings and the seesaw the refugees had built. The plots of vegetables were lined up in neat rows like soldiers on parade. It was all so familiar. Christophe was with her and took her hand as they walked inside together. Maureen turned the corner, expecting to see the other refugees at the dining room table, but no one sat there. When she turned around, Christophe was gone. She ran outside to see a darkening sky. The sound of Nazi aircraft filled the air.

Maureen woke up sweating, her heart thumping. She looked around, taking a few seconds to find her bearings. She was in the women's dorm. The other three beds were empty. A sliver of moonlight knifed in through a chink in the curtains. Unable to sleep, she went to the window to peer out. Thoughts of the Jews in France piled up in her mind.

Most of the people she'd cared about were gone now. The original Jewish refugees from Izieu were safe in Spain. The last she'd heard was they were staying in the hotel near Valencia that she and her old neighbor in Paris had organized for them. Knowing they were happy and free from the grip of Nazi tyranny made her smile every time she thought about it.

Raids against the Jewish population had only increased in France and all over Europe since she'd left. The Nazis were stepping up their efforts to subjugate the Jews they were so obsessed with. Maureen remembered her schooling in Berlin in the 30s when the children were continually warned about the dangers the Jews presented. The students were reminded daily about a sub-section of the population that no one she knew had ever been harmed by and comprised less than 1% of German society.

She got back into bed and spiraled into a deep sleep.

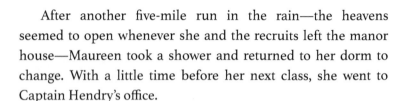

After another five-mile run in the rain—the heavens seemed to open whenever she and the recruits left the manor house—Maureen took a shower and returned to her dorm to change. With a little time before her next class, she went to Captain Hendry's office.

"Can I talk to you, sir?"

"Take a seat." He was shuffling through some papers but looked up at her as she sat. "What can I do for you, Miss Ritter?"

"I've had something on my mind for a while. I didn't know who else to talk to."

"Delighted to help if I'm able," Hendry said.

"I've been disappointed in the apathy in Britain toward the plight of the Jews in Europe. The newspapers do cover some stories about pogroms or other abuses they suffered, but most people on the street seem to shrug their shoulders as if it's a normal part of war to murder hundreds of thousands of innocent civilians."

Hendry's mustache twitched above his lip. "A conundrum indeed."

"There's been little mention of their plight in class here."

Hendry cleared his throat before speaking. "The general attitude is that in order to help Europe's Jews, the Nazis have to be defeated, and all energies must be devoted to that bigger picture."

Maureen cleared her throat. "I understand that, sir, but

various programs could be implemented to evacuate Jews to safe havens like Palestine but the British Government stopped supplying the required number of visas for Jews to move there years ago."

Hendry stood up and went to the window. The rain had stopped at last. "I understand everything you've said and agree with you, but what can I do? The political will isn't there. I don't have that kind of sway."

"Do you know anyone who does?"

Hendry shook his head. "There could be a different avenue, however. Have you heard of the OSE?"

"The O*euvre de Secours aux Enfants*? I dealt with them a little during my time in France."

Maureen had heard of the Jewish humanitarian organization but, without the need of their help, had never approached them directly. They didn't seek to evacuate the children abroad as aggressively as she had, more to hide them until the war ended and the Allies came.

"I respect them and the incredible work they do," Maureen said. "They've saved thousands of children."

"Interesting that Albert Einstein was their first president," Hendry added but pressed on before Maureen had a chance to comment. "The reason I ask is I ran into a representative of theirs in London a few weeks ago and had the same conversation with him we just had. You mentioned the refugees you sheltered in the countryside before—what was the name of the village?"

"Izieu."

"Yes, I remember now. I also recall you mentioning to me that the houses you own there are vacant now."

The houses Maureen's father had bought years ago to shelter Jewish refugees had been empty since the last of the Jews from her father's factory in Berlin had been evacuated to Spain a few months before.

"Would you mind if I called my friend from the OSE?" Hendry said. "Perhaps you and he might come to an arrangement?"

"Please do," Maureen said with a smile.

Captain Hendry picked up the phone and made the call.

"Hello, Pierre?" he began. "I have someone here who might be able to help you. One of my recruits."

Hendry handed her the phone.

"I have two houses available an hour east of Lyon," she began. She took a few moments to explain who she was and who had previously lived in Izieu. The man from the OSE listened for several minutes before telling her what his needs were.

"We have 51 to place altogether. 44 children." Pierre said.

"Are they all Jews? Where are they from?" Maureen asked.

"All over. Some from France, but also Belgium, Austria, Germany, Algeria and Poland. French is our common language. The adults are from different countries too. Life won't be easy but they'll make it work."

Maureen's heart soared. "That's wonderful. I'm so happy someone will use these houses for what they were intended for." Maureen said. "I lived there for years myself. We had over 100 refugees in these buildings in '39, and they all got out safely. Do you have a plan in place to evacuate the children?"

"Not as such. The Italian authorities who rule that zone now aren't bothered with chasing after Jews. They'll be safe from the Nazi lunatics there."

"Izieu has everything the youngsters could want—the fields, the river. It's like an outdoor playground. And the adults can grow all the food they need."

"Sounds ideal for our purposes."

"If you do want to evacuate them, my friend in France is a master forger," Maureen said. "He could provide them with papers to leave."

"Thank you, but that presents a different set of problems. The end is nigh for the Nazis. Dictators always overreach themselves. Russia was Napoleon's downfall and it'll be the same for Hitler. I think the war could be over before you think."

Maureen was amazed at the man's optimism. "The Allies haven't invaded Western Europe yet, and the Russians are holding off the Nazis in the east but they're still thousands of miles from Germany."

"Well, the OSE will make lives for the children in hidden safe houses in the meantime. The decision about whether they stay or go isn't up to me. In fact, once the houses are handed over you should stay away. Permanently. Or at least until after the war."

"I understand," Maureen said. She called out the details of the address and how to get there.

"Thank you," Pierre said. "I'm sure the children will be safe and happy in Izieu. You've done something good."

Maureen thanked him back and hung up the phone.

Though she was happy, she couldn't help but think of the others she couldn't rescue. No matter how many people she helped, there were always thousands more she couldn't. It would be fantastic to visit Izieu when she returned to France and help with the new batch of kids. But really, what could she do for them? She was being trained to operate in the French underground. It would only endanger the children if she got involved.

"Thank you, sir," she said to Hendry.

"Glad to help," the officer answered.

Maureen got up and left with a bright smile on her face.

Several days later, the recruits were ordered to file outside. It was nighttime and pitch-black as they lined up. The temperature had dropped to the point where Maureen was shivering. Maureen remembered Taylor's promise that they'd be attempting the obstacle course again at night, with their legs tied together. The others hadn't believed him.

"Get together with your partners. It's time to tackle our assault course again, but this time with these," Hendry said, holding up a length of rope. He threw it to Maureen. "Tie it tight."

"What?" Turner said. "You can't expect us to do this?"

"I don't expect it. I demand it," Captain Hendry replied.

"I've been in France already," Turner said. "I don't remember seeing the Nazis tie anyone's legs together and make them crawl through barrels. What's the point of all this?"

"You'll be working in pairs. Show us how you work together toward a common goal."

Maureen shook her head and picked out Howard Mount. He'd become her go-to man in these situations. She didn't question her orders, just stood still as Howard tied the rope around her legs. He pulled the ends so she could only hop, and then she did the same to him. Several recruits from other groups they hadn't mixed with before came out to join them. In the end, seven teams of two started the course.

Hendry blew his whistle and the race began. Maureen and Howard did everything with care, in slow motion. He shunted her over the wall, and she waited at the top to pull him over. They held onto one another through the tractor tires and passed the rope back and forth on the swing.

An hour later, the recruits limped back to the manor house, smelly, filthy, and freezing cold. Maureen could still taste the pond water in her mouth. She and her Howard weren't the first to finish but were the only uninjured pair. Turner seemed to have broken an ankle and couldn't walk back without help. His time in the training program was over.

By the time she returned to the house, Maureen wanted to cry from the sheer pain and exhaustion that was overtaking every cell in her body. She was questioning her decision to undergo such a horrible process voluntarily. What sane person would actually volunteer to go through this? She looked at her fellow recruits and had her answer. She wished them goodnight and pushed the door open to the female locker room. It was empty apart from her change of clothes. It felt good to strip off and wash the mud and grime off her tired body. The water was warm, and she stayed under the shower for several minutes, luxuriating in the comfort it provided.

Being clean felt like a renewal of her body and mind, and she changed back into her clothes with fresh vigor. When she emerged from the locker room, Captain Hendry was passing by with a clipboard in his hand.

"Oh, I'm glad I ran into you, Ritter."

"Don't tell me I failed. Don't even—"

"You passed the tests!" he said with a smile. "Welcome to the Special Operations Executive. You're a secret soldier now."

A tidal wave of relief, happiness, and pride washed through her. Yes, she was proud.

"Your training has only just begun," Hendry continued. "We have several weeks ahead of us and it's not going to get any easier."

"I'm ready for it," she answered.

"Good. That's what I thought you'd say. Now, get to the canteen for supper," he said. "The other recruits are waiting for you."

4

Saturday, December 12, 1942

The gift of a rare day off afforded Maureen the chance to travel to Oxford to see some old friends. After getting a train to London, she changed at Waterloo and continued to the medieval city, dominated by the world-famous university it was known for. She thought of the three Bautner boys as she stared out the window at the beautiful English countryside, untouched by German bombs. It had been two years since she and Christophe, with the help of two Allied servicemen they were escorting, carried Rudi, Adam, and Abel Bautner over the Pyrenees to safety in Spain. She shook her head at her sheer audaciousness in trying something so insane as to carry others over those treacherous mountain passes most people couldn't even drag themselves over. Yet, she and Christophe had done it somehow, and the boys had taken a steamer to England and a foster family in the city the train was just about to pull into. She'd kept in touch with them by letter when she could, but that had been impossible these last six months or so.

A flutter of nerves passed through her as the train reached the station. She wished the boys were standing on the platform waiting for her, but their adoptive parents insisted in the letters she exchanged with them that she come to the house. She did as she was asked without argument. Seeing the old town untouched by the ravages of the war that dominated her life was sweet relief. Apart from the rationing, the soldiers in the streets, and the idle searchlights outside the station, the war might not have been going on at all. For the first time in years, she felt removed from it and could push it to the back of her mind to focus on something else. But like logs in water, her thoughts of the war soon bobbed back up. Her longing for Christophe surfaced as she ambled through the picturesque streets of the medieval center. The spires of the university buildings dominated the skyline. Maureen was comforted that they hadn't been flattened by Nazi bombs like so much of London. Some things had to survive this war; otherwise, the life they'd known before it would be lost forever.

A policeman provided directions to the address she took from her pocket, and a young man with a horse and cart acted as her taxi to the boys' house. It was just outside the city on a quiet road. Lush green fields sat just beyond the red brick houses lining the street. It was perfect—exactly what she dreamed of for "her boys" when she was transporting them over the mountains. Being here made it all worthwhile. She rapped on the door as great swathes of nervous joy washed through her. A middle-aged woman with curly red hair and blue eyes answered the door.

"Doreen?" Maureen said.

"And you must be Miss Ritter," the woman replied. "Come in. The boys are dying to see you."

Maureen stepped inside. An ornate mirror sat on the wall, and she checked her hair as she passed. The wallpapered walls were covered in pictures of the boys at the beach, at school, or posing together outside various buildings. Doreen led her into a tidy, well-furnished living room where the three Bautner brothers were waiting. They ran to her, overwhelming her in seconds. "Oh, my. You've grown so much," she said. Buried under an avalanche of joy, she didn't want to emerge for air. Rudi was ten now and almost as tall as his adopted mother. Adam was eight, and several inches taller than when she'd last seen him. Little Abel was seven, as cute as she remembered but not a baby anymore. She took a few moments to hug them each in turn. "I missed you," she said.

"We made cards for you," Abel said in an English accent. Maureen sat down and took a few seconds to look at the hand-drawn cards. Her heart warmed, she hugged each of them again.

"It's so strange that you speak English now," Maureen said with a smile.

"Every day in school," Adam said.

A tall man in an armchair across the room stood up. "Reg North," he said and shook Maureen's hand. "Welcome to our home. Thank you for bringing the boys to us."

"Thank you for taking them in."

"It was our pleasure," his wife said as she stepped forward.

"Come and see our room," Abel said, taking Maureen by the hand.

She stayed for dinner, reveling in the stories the brothers told of childish adventures chasing rabbits and playing hide and seek. Mr. and Mrs. North, who didn't have children of their own, smiled as the boys spoke. It seemed everyone's dreams had come true here.

Maureen was almost finished with her delicious vegetable casserole when Rudi asked her the question she knew was coming. "Any news from our mum?" The boys knew their father was dead, but their mother was still missing in the

German camp system. Maureen looked across at the boys' adoptive parents before bringing her eyes back to Rudi.

"I'm sorry," she said. "Not yet. Wherever she is, I know she's missing you."

Mr. and Mrs. North gave the boys permission to stay up extra late that night, and Maureen read each of them a book before bed. Beatrix Potter—an old favorite.

She tucked each of them in and kissed them goodnight. The fact that Rudi wiped it off only made her laugh.

She sat and drank tea with the Norths in their living room after the boys had gone to bed. They talked long into the night. They promised to keep in touch, but Maureen wondered how, for she was going to France soon. She didn't mention anything about it, and the couple seemed to know better than to ask. They talked about the boys, accepting each other's gratitude once more before Maureen retired to the spare room, wishing a world existed where the Bautner brothers never met her or the wonderful people who'd taken them in and were tucked into bed every night by their real parents.

~

Training continued. Maureen noticed her body changing. Thick ridges of muscle lined her shoulders. Her skin was tougher. Her mind was a library of lethal information, from making bombs to organizing militia units. She was almost ready to return and knew the word would come soon. Still the only woman in the manor house, she was alone in her dorm when the week's mail delivery came.

"Letter for you, Maureen," the secretary who dealt with mail said as she handed her a letter.

"Thanks, Lizzy."

She waited a few seconds until she was alone and then opened it. It had been sent through Spain and redirected to England from there—the only way to get mail through to Nazi-occupied Europe. It had taken two weeks to reach her.

JANUARY *18, 1943*

MY DARLING MAUREEN,

WINTER IS AN AFFRONT TO THE GOOD CITIZENS OF LYON, AND I FEEL AGGRIEVED TO HAVE TO BEAR IT. LUCKILY, I RARELY SEE THE LIGHT OF DAY DUE TO MY ACTIVITIES. OUR NEW OVERLORDS HAVE MADE THEIR PRESENCE FELT IN THE CITY AND ALL OVER SOUTHERN FRANCE SINCE THE CHANGEOVER IN NOVEMBER. I WELCOME THEM WHOLEHEARTEDLY, AS DO THE REST OF THE PEOPLE HERE. THE SWASTIKAS FLYING OVER EVERY PUBLIC BUILDING IN THE CITIES MAKE QUITE AN INTERESTING CHANGE FROM THE TRICOLORS THEY REPLACED.

I MISS YOU WITH EVERY INCH OF MY BEING. I LONG FOR YOU THROUGH THE DAYS AND DREAM OF YOU WHEN I SLEEP AT NIGHT. I JUST HOPE YOU'VE FOUND WHAT YOU WERE LOOKING FOR, BUT EVEN MORE THAT YOU WILL RETURN TO ME SOON. WHEN ARE YOU COMING HOME?

WITH LOVE,

CHRISTOPHE

She folded the letter and placed it back in its envelope. Apart from taking down the Nazis, what drove her most was the thought of being with Christophe again. It had been more than six months since she'd seen him, and the few coded letters they'd been able to send one another offered little insight into what was actually going on in each other's lives. He knew what she was doing in England, however, and most of the questions in his correspondence were to do with when she was coming back. She longed for him, thirsted for him as if she were dying in the middle of the desert. His multiple marriage proposals gave her pause and kept her awake at night. Part of her agreed with her decision to delay giving him the gratification of her hand in marriage while the war was raging, but something deeper regretted not giving him that affirmation. It would have been so simple. They loved each other; why shouldn't they be man and wife? Because they couldn't have a wedding with her family? She'd done everything without them since '39. She knew he'd wait for her and spent much of her free time gazing into her daydreams of marrying him surrounded by everyone they both loved. She would make it up to him someday. A sparkling future awaited. Getting to it would be the problem.

Thursday, February 18, 1943

The training was drawing to an end. Of the six recruits that had started, only she, Tom Owen, and her friend Howard Mount remained. The others had succumbed to injury, or in the case of young Stanley Jenkins, to a "paucity of team spirit," as Taylor put it weeks after the man left. Maureen sometimes wondered if she'd been placed with the group to see how they'd react to working with a woman. The instructors never said so, but she was convinced Stanley had been sent home because of his caustic reaction to her presence. His idiotic comments hadn't bothered her, however. They were nothing she wasn't used to. It puzzled her why certain men were so threatened by the thought of a woman performing a role they perceived as theirs. To her, the important thing was winning the war, not who did the job.

Maureen was back from the morning run—ten miles now, instead of the previous five, when Hendry saw her in the hallway.

"Report to my office after you've cleaned yourself up, Miss Ritter."

She nodded and went to the shower. As she was emerging, wrapped in a towel, she noticed a bag on one of the other beds in what had been her private dorm. A woman was in the corner. She was tall with dark curls and striking blue eyes. Maureen smiled.

"Hello."

"Nice to meet you," the woman said. "Nancy Baker."

They shook hands.

"Good to have another woman around here," Maureen said.

"Yes. I thought I'd be the only one."

"No," Maureen answered. "And I'm sure more are coming."

With little time to talk, Maureen changed as quickly as she could and reported to Captain Hendry's office, where the officer was sitting behind his desk waiting for her.

She saluted as she entered. "At ease," Hendry said. "You can sit down." Maureen did as she was told without speaking. "Any idea why I chose you for this training school?"

"I thought Monique recommended me."

"Oh, she did, but that didn't mean I had to take you on. I take a small percentage of the people who apply, and as you've seen not all those who come here finish the course."

"Women can travel more easily in the occupied territories. I was a courier for a while in southern France. We can pass through checkpoints without arousing as much suspicion."

"All true." Hendry sat forward. "But that's a reason for any woman to come here. Why you?"

"I don't know, my experience?"

"The reason I was so excited was your background. I knew everything about you before you came here, Maureen. You were the daughter of a rich arms manufacturer in Berlin, yet, instead of living the good life with the other fat cats you fled Germany and joined the resistance. You could have returned to America with your family before the war, yet you decided to stay. Why?"

"Because I had people relying on me, and I had debts to settle with the Nazis."

"Had?"

"Have."

Hendry sat back in his seat with a satisfied smile. "That's why I took you. Well, that was one reason. The other was to prove my fellow officers wrong. I know you won't let me down."

"You have that right, sir."

"Let's talk about your assignment, shall we? As you know, things in France are a little different from when you left."

"I am aware, sir."

The occupying German forces had invaded southern France in November 1942, breaking the terms of their own armistice. Hitler had ordered the expansion himself after the

Allied successes in North Africa. Determined not to show a soft underbelly to the enemy, the dictator moved the Wehrmacht south, and France was one now. The occupied and free zones were no more. All of France was under the yoke of Nazi occupation. Petain and the other puppets the Germans had put in place were rendered irrelevant.

The only area treated differently was one Maureen knew well. The Italians had been given permission by the all-powerful Nazis to occupy the region of France beside the Swiss and Italian borders—an area that encapsulated a hamlet few paid attention to called Izieu.

"Are you also aware of the Auvergne region west of Lyon?"

"Not intimately, sir. I've been on a couple of day trips to the forest there, but I couldn't profess to knowing the area well."

"It's become a safe haven for men fleeing the Nazis. Not just resistance fighters on the lam, but ordinary citizens sick of being pushed around by the invaders. A certain group has come to our attention there. A ragtag bunch of misfits, but hardened ones, living in the forest under the leadership of a local resistance leader called Henri Sella. Your job will be to organize the rabble Sella has gathered together into a fighting force worthy of taking on the Nazi invaders."

"How many men does he have?"

"Not entirely sure. About 150."

"Are they armed?"

"No. Not to the level they'll need to be in order to take on the Germans, but we'll take care of all that after you make contact. The War Office is prepared to give you whatever you need to transform them into your own private army. You will run the day-to-day operations but London will be in touch regularly. We're sending in a radio operator with you."

"I can work the wireless."

"I know, but I want you to concentrate your efforts on more important matters. Leave the technical stuff to someone else."

"Okay."

"Have you read Robin Hood, Ritter?"

"I saw the movie."

"Well, this band of outlaws isn't quite stealing from the rich to give to the poor, but with a little training and direction they could give the Nazis quite a black eye. The invasion of France is coming. I don't know when. Nobody does, but we need to be ready. The more Germans we kill between now and that day, the fewer of our troops will die on the beaches, and the sooner we can all get back to our regular lives."

"Why me, sir?"

"Why did I choose you to go into the woods and train a bunch of mechanics, cooks and farmers? Because you're the best we have, Maureen. I chose you because it's a difficult task, and you're the right person for the job. I know you've had to work harder at every turn just because you're a woman. No one else came to this house with such a deficit of respect among their peers to make up. It won't be any easier in France. You'll have to do it all again. But your power to overcome the obstacles here has convinced me you can do it there, and that you'd do a better job than any of the other recruits."

A warm swell of pride filled Maureen's chest.

"Thank you."

"Just don't let me down."

"I won't." Maureen asked Hendry a question that had been swirling around in her head for weeks. "What did you do before the war, sir?"

Hendry's lips curled upward into a smile. "I had a washing machine factory in Dorset. My brother's running it now. And the sooner we wipe the Nazi scum from the face of the planet, the sooner I'll get back to it, and my family."

5

Tuesday, November 14, 2006

Amy clicked the stop button on her tape recorder and
pushed out a breath in amazement. Her grandmother's matter-of-fact way of telling the most amazing
stories she'd ever heard constantly amazed her. Maureen's dogs
approached the patio table. Amy reached down to pet them.

"I wonder if they've noticed anything different about me,"
Amy said.

"They're very perceptive."

Amy had long since stopped expressing wonder at her grandmother's heroics during the war. Out loud, anyway. It was better
to treat them as source material, to stand back and examine them
with objectivity and due diligence. That was the way Maureen
liked it too. She had no desire to be fawned over—quite the opposite, in fact. She'd never been recognized by any government and
had never won any medals for what she'd done to counter the
Nazis and save those most vulnerable. It was time she was
acknowledged for what she'd done and for all she sacrificed for

others during those tumultuous years. Recognition or reward had been the last things on Maureen's mind when she'd risked her life so many times for others. Amy was sure that the walls in her grandmother's house would be full of medals and plaques had she sought them out after the war, but she had none. It seemed she'd just returned to ordinary life once the fighting ended.

"I have a question for you, when was the last time you saw the Bautner boys?"

"Not for many years. Long before you were born."

"What happened to them? Do you know where they ended up?"

"The last I heard they were living in England. Rudi married a lovely woman with Adam as his best man. They sent me a photograph. Let me see if I can find it."

The older woman disappeared for a few minutes before returning with the small leather-bound chest. She laid it on the dining room table and popped open the lock. She spent a moment shuffling through old photos, showing Amy pictures of her parents in the 60s and 70s, before coming across a black and white picture near the bottom of the pile.

"Ah, here it is," she said. "Didn't Rudi look handsome? He was 22."

Amy took the photo in her hand. Rudi stood in his wedding suit with his new wife. Adam was beside them, beaming a satisfied smile.

"Was Abel there?"

"Of course! Here he is."

Maureen handed her a photo of a young man in his late teens, equally as handsome as his brothers.

"We fell out of touch after that. It was harder back then without computers and with phone calls being so expensive. I do think of them from time to time. Even still."

"Where were they living when he got married?"

"In Oxford, but his wife's family was from the south coast and they moved there soon afterward."

"Did the other boys go with them?"

"Adam did, but Abel stayed in Oxford to attend the university. He was always such a clever boy. I have no idea where they are now."

Amy gently prodded her grandmother for any further information about where the Bautners could be now, but the older woman didn't know. It was no use. Searching through her memory box didn't provide any clues either. The brothers seemed lost in the mists of time, but Amy knew someone who could help. She excused herself and got up to look for her phone. It was in her bedroom on the dresser. A message from Ryan's mother about how she was feeling awaited her. She gave it minimal attention and replied that she was fine before texting Mike. It didn't seem right to string him along by reaching out to him, but she didn't want to lose him as a friend. He was too important to her.

I might need to employ your skills in finding people soon. Some kids from my grandmother's past. She hit send, but a sudden wet feeling sent a shiver through her body and drove her to the bathroom, where she saw dark red blood in her underwear. Feeling no pain, she walked back to her grandmother.

Amy tried to remain calm, but her voice was quaking. "Grandma, I think I need to go to the hospital."

"What is it?" Maureen said and rose to her feet.

"I'm bleeding—a lot."

Her pants were wet now, stained from the inside.

"Can you drive?"

"I don't think I should."

Without another word, Maureen picked up her phone and called one of the neighbors. She spoke rapidly in French, seeming to argue with whoever was on the other end before hanging up. "I called Armand. He's on his way over."

Amy felt cold and weak. Her legs seemed to give way, and she flopped onto the patio chair.

"The baby!"

Maureen hugged her. "It's going to be all right. Have you had much bleeding before?"

"A few spots here and there, but nothing like this."

Her grandmother held her as they waited for Armand to arrive. The five minutes it took him seemed to take hours.

Maureen ordered him to pick Amy up and take her to the car, where she laid down towels on the back seat. Amy was conscious of bleeding on the poor man but realized that wasn't as important as her baby's welfare and wrapped her arm around him, and he cradled her. Maureen sat with her in the back seat. Her conversation about the books and her war stories helped distract Amy from the horrific thoughts polluting her mind.

It was a ten-minute drive, and Armand pulled up outside the emergency room. He ran inside and emerged a few seconds later with an attendant pushing a wheelchair. The hospital worker helped Amy into it and wheeled her inside. Amy thanked Armand. He waved to her, wishing her luck before getting back into the car. Maureen followed them but was soon left behind.

Amy was brought into an empty cubicle where a nurse asked her several questions in French she didn't understand.

"*Ma grand-mère est dehors. Elle sait trauire,*" Amy said.

The nurse nodded and went out to get Maureen to translate.

Happy to have her grandmother with her, Amy recalled what had happened. The nurse examined her. A few minutes later, a doctor arrived, and Maureen translated again.

"Is it serious?" Amy asked. "Will I lose the baby?"

The doctor, a young woman with curly red hair, shook her head. "We need to perform some more tests."

Another attendant brought Amy through to a different room for an ultrasound. Hearing the baby's beating heart brought tears of joy to Amy's face.

"The baby's alive," she said. Maureen hugged her, gripping her hand.

An hour later, Amy was back in the cubicle when the doctor came back.

"The ultrasound clearly shows you have a condition called placenta previa. It's where the placenta blocks the cervix. It's a complete blockage in this case. You say you haven't had much bleeding to this point?"

"No."

"That's unusual," the doctor said. "But by no means unheard of."

"What does this all mean? Is my baby going to be okay?"

"Yes, but you said you live in New York? You won't be able to travel until the child comes, and you'll need to rest until then. No lifting anything heavy. No strenuous exercise of any kind. I'd recommend bed rest most of the time."

Amy almost cried with sheer relief. She could handle sitting in bed while she wrote. As long as the baby was okay, nothing else mattered.

"Due to the high risk of bleeding during birth, you'll be required to have a caesarean delivery."

"I can do that."

The realization that she would have her baby in France and leave behind her doctor, friends, and brother, Mark, was nothing compared to the relief she felt.

Her grandmother gripped her hand. "It's going to be fine. I'll look after you."

Amy nodded. She reached down to her swollen belly, trying to process that she'd be having the baby in a foreign country where she didn't speak the language.

The doctors kept her in for observation overnight but found nothing else to concern them. The next morning Armand came back to pick Amy up.

"Thank you, so much," she said to him as she got into the car from her wheelchair. The Frenchman nodded with a slight smile and sat behind the wheel. Her grandmother sat beside her in the back. The older woman would be her constant companion until the baby arrived, when Amy would swap the company of a 90-year-old for that of a newborn.

"The doctor said I'd be in France until a month after the baby comes," Amy said.

"Stay as long as you want. I'm so happy to have you, dear."

The moments Amy had been dreading since she'd found out the baby was okay the day before came later that afternoon. She gave herself an easy start and called her brother in Boston first. He was concerned and offered to fly over, but she didn't think that was necessary and told him to hold off until the baby came.

She was in bed and looked over at the view of the French countryside through her window before calling Ryan. Much to her relief, the phone went to voicemail. She left a long message, giving him every detail she could remember so he wouldn't have to call her back. Her plan didn't work, however. Ten minutes later, Louise Smith's name flashed up on her phone.

"Are you okay? Is the baby?"

"Yes, Louise. Did Ryan tell you?"

"Yes, but I just had to call. I'll be over on the next flight I can find."

Amy felt her heartbeat quicken at that thought.

"No. Please don't. I need rest. My grandmother is with me."

"A 90-year-old woman?"

"Don't come over. I'm fine. I have work to do. I can do it from the comfort of my bed. Rest assured I won't strain myself in any way."

"You're in rural France. You trust them to deliver the child? Their health system—"

"Is one of the best in the world. I'll miss my doctor, but I'll find another. Believe me, everything is going to be fine. Come over with Ryan when the baby comes. In the meantime, try to relax, like I will be."

Getting Louise off the phone wasn't as simple as that, and they talked in circles for another ten minutes before Amy earned the right to hang up.

"I need to go, Louise. I have to get back to work."

Amy cycled down through her texts. An unread message from Mike stuck out. She wanted to tell him. She wanted to call him, but knew she couldn't.

Amy put the phone down and picked up her laptop once more. The mission would be to get the book finished before the baby came. She brought her fingers to the keyboard and began to type.

6

Wednesday, March 3, 1943, the Pyrenees Mountain range.

The seas around Marseille were too dangerous now, so Maureen took a train from Gibraltar to Barcelona and then to the French border. Her guide across the mountains was a middle-aged hunter named Pedro. French was their common language, but he only spoke when he had to, and they spent many hours in silence, concentrating on placing one foot in front of the other on the punishing mountain trails. With all the difficulty they faced traversing the Pyrenees back into France, it was nothing compared to when she'd taken the journey in the opposite direction back in '40. That was when she and Christophe, with the help of two refugees from the Nazis, had carried the three Bautner boys, aged 3, 5, and 8, across the mountains to safety in Spain. From there, the boys got their ship to England and were sent to Oxford.

Pedro held his hand up in a fist to signify they were taking a break. Maureen sat down on the side of the trail. It was almost night, and she could see her breath pluming out in front of her already. Her legs were aching, and she unlaced her boots to check her feet. Her socks were worn and stained. She took them off and tossed them aside before reaching for a fresh pair in her backpack. After taking a few moments to tape up her feet, she slipped on new socks—her third pair that day. Pedro was smoking a cigarette, staring into space in front of him. She took that as a sign she had a few more minutes before they had to set out again and reached into her rucksack again for some food. She chewed on some meat and dried fruit.

Pedro stood up. It was time to leave. She was still munching her food as she hefted the rucksack onto her back. The Catalonian didn't say a single word. He just walked ahead of her up the mountain trail.

Maureen followed her guide through the night. Her body was stronger than it had ever been, but even so, the hike was about as much as she could bear. They stopped for a few minutes at a time, forgoing sleep in favor of walking when the Nazi patrols were seen the least. The security in the border areas was much tighter now than when she'd left. Marseille was an occupied city, and its port—which had been a hub of resistance activity before the occupation—was now run by the Wehrmacht. France had no more free ports. The Germans were in total control.

Pedro said about seven words in the entire time it took to traverse the mountains. It was dawn on the third day when he finally opened his mouth. He pointed to a river valley in the distance.

"See down there? France."

Maureen smiled and clapped him on the shoulder. She could almost feel Christophe in her arms already, though she had a lot more to do than just get reacquainted with her fiancé when she arrived.

Christophe had continued in his role of forging documents for refugees and escaping Allied servicemen. He'd demonstrated his talents when they needed them most in Paris the year before when extricating the master forger Adolfo Kaminsky from the hell at the *Vel' d'Hiv*. Maureen often wondered what had happened to the poor souls she and Christophe hadn't been able to rescue in the short time they had. Thousands of Jews were taken away in the ensuing days, never to be heard of again. Her resolve to destroy the Nazi war machine had never been stronger than after that.

They walked for a few more hours until Pedro dropped her off just over the French border. A man with a coal truck was waiting, and Maureen hid among the bags in the back just as she had with Christophe and the boys when they'd crossed back in '40. The driver brought her to the beautiful medieval city of Perpignan, where she stayed the night in a safe house, readying herself for her return.

~

Saturday, March 6, 1943

After taking two days to recover from the travails of trekking across the Pyrenees, she boarded a train at Toulouse. The omnipresent Nazi flags in the previously free city were a reminder of what had transpired since she'd left. The idea that Vichy France had been free in any way, shape, or form was risible, but at least the French authorities had retained some semblance of control over the people. Now that was gone, along with any lingering doubt about who was calling the shots for the people. Though things had changed, this still felt like a homecoming, even though she had little idea of where home was now. America was the country she was raised in, but Germany had shaped who she'd become. France was where she'd become an adult and started to act upon the lessons she'd learned as a child. Christophe often laughed as he asked where she was from. It was hard to say. She was a citizen of the world —a vagabond with a mission.

The false identification papers the British War Office provided her were as good as she'd seen—on a par with what Adolfo Kaminsky produced. Today she was traveling as a farmer's wife from just outside Lyon, but hidden in a secret compartment in her bag were documents identifying her as a doctor's secretary from Marseille and a teacher from Toulouse. Her identity changed depending upon what her needs dictated. This chameleonic life was nothing new to her. She'd had several different identities before she left France to join the SOE. She'd worked as a courier for Monique before she went to Britain and had transported numerous refugees to the border and the port in Marseille to escape France.

Hiding her American accent was the most difficult part. Nothing was more likely to get her stopped at a checkpoint than if the police, or now more usually German soldiers, detected it. It was essential to get everything straight in your mind before talking to someone who could have you arrested and interrogated on a whim, so she spent the first few minutes of each day traveling under an alias, practicing as that person. Today she was Geneve Dupont, farmer's wife and mother of three.

The police had already checked her papers at the station. Her anger toward the French police was undiminished. Their part in the evacuation of Jews to Germany was unforgivable. But she didn't reveal her feelings and handed over her papers with a polite smile.

She did the same thing with the two German Gestapo men in brown trench coats once she'd taken her seat on the train. The man who asked her was bald and looked like a boiled egg with glasses and a hat.

"Papers, Mademoiselle," he said. She complied without speaking. Without any reason to believe they were looking for her, she remained calm. The men might not have been after anyone specific. For all she knew, they were just trying to intimidate the citizenry on the train. They'd be looking for anyone jumpy or who talked back. It was best to smile and pretend she loved having her papers checked by a foreign secret policeman.

"Ah, you're a Madame not a Mademoiselle," he said with a smile. "I'm disappointed."

"I have three children," she answered.

"What are you doing so far from home? Shouldn't you be looking after them?"

"They're with my sister for a few days. It's our aunt, you see. She's sick and the poor old woman has no one to look after her. All the cousins are taking turns to check in on her. This was mine."

She'd used the same line so many times she could have said it backward.

The Gestapo man hesitated for a second, then handed her back the papers. "Have a pleasant trip," he said and moved to the next person.

The train was delayed almost an hour as the Gestapo agents worked their way through. That was nothing out of the ordinary. Everything stopped at the behest of the Nazi invaders. A jolt of excitement shot through Maureen's veins as the train finally started moving. Christophe didn't know she was coming, and picturing the look on his face as she walked in brought a smile to hers. He had been living in Lyon since she left, unable to return to his home city due to their botched mission to destroy two U-boats in Marseille the summer before. Monique, the British spy who'd recruited her, had organized it, but unbeknownst to her, it was a sting operation by a lone Gestapo agent. Monique killed him on the dock, and they'd gotten away, but it was too dangerous for Christophe there now. He had no direct connection to what had happened, but the Gestapo wouldn't care about that. They'd torture him until he talked. So he'd lived in the Lyon area under an assumed name ever since Maureen left. His business as an art dealer was on hold, as was his relationship with his father, who ran his own shipping business through the port in Marseille.

The train left the city to reveal the beauty of the countryside. Maureen began to think of the people she knew who'd already died—Jean Villiers, the resistance head whose life was snuffed out in an instant by a German bullet to the forehead. And Gerhard, her old friend she'd met in Paris before the war. He and Maureen had tried to organize a coup against Hitler in Germany through Gerhard's father, a general in the Luftwaffe, before the ruse was discovered and his father was executed. Gerhard was dead now, too, killed trying to save his informant girlfriend when the Nazis came for her. She shuddered as she thought about how their bodies had been strung up in the center of Lyon for every passerby to see. It was a horrific end for someone so brave, honorable and kind.

Her grief hung heavily for a few moments before the image of Christophe appeared in her mind like sunshine through a cloudy sky. It was amazing in such horrific times that there was still so much joy to be had, but she'd found it in him. He's asked her to marry him more times than she could remember, but it was always the wrong time. He always accepted her replies that she wanted her family at the wedding and travel from America was out of the question. Apart from the danger of the U-boats under the water, securing passage on one of the few available ships was nearly impossible. She cursed the Nazis and what they'd done to siphon away what should have been the happiest years of her life.

Who would she be if the Nazis had never invaded or if Hitler had never come to power in Germany? She'd thought about it many times, and the answer was always the same—she'd still live in Berlin, probably married and working as a doctor. She never would have known France and the people she'd met here. She never would have loved Christophe. It was hard to regret the path she'd taken. She thought of it like that.

The train arrived at the station in Lyon just before six o'clock in the evening. No one other than the resistance fighters she was to train knew she was coming. Maureen stepped onto the platform, hoping somehow Christophe was there waiting for her with a smile and a bunch of flowers. She shook her head at the ridiculous notion that he might somehow have guessed when she was coming back. She hadn't told Christophe any specifics in her letters for the sake of security and surprise.

Maureen hefted her bag onto her shoulder before joining a line for the latest police checkpoint.

Stepping out onto the street in Lyon felt like returning to the scene of a crime. Several German soldiers were outside the station, smoking and chatting under a massive Nazi flag fluttering in the breeze. Maureen strolled past without making eye contact or reacting to the wolf whistles directed at her. She kept Christophe in her mind as she walked. The city was like Berlin now, except without the pride Hitler had instilled in the people there. Signs of the Nazi invaders were everywhere, from their flags to their posters, to the anti-Semitic slogans written on every blank surface. Several people walked past with the Star of David on their chests. And the Wehrmacht seemed to be everywhere she looked. Sitting outside cafés and loitering on street corners. On patrol and standing guard outside public buildings. She was a long way from London now.

Her excitement grew as she neared the address Christophe had sent her, and a smile spread across her face as she counted the numbers on the street until she came to his. She walked up three steps and looked at the names on the apartments, almost whooping out loud as she saw his pseudonym—Thierry Chabal. Struck by the thought that she hadn't checked her makeup since her journey from Toulouse, she drew a small mirror out of her bag. Unsatisfied with how she looked, she reached for some lipstick and applied some. After checking herself again, she pushed the door open and walked up two flights of stairs until she came to a wine-colored door. She closed her eyes and smiled before knocking.

The 20 seconds it took him to answer the door seemed to take weeks, but when he appeared, all plans she had, all lines she'd prepared, disappeared, and she jumped into his arms. He held her, seemingly unable to believe she was back. The feeling of his kiss was greater than all the loneliness she'd felt when she was away. Her heart blossomed and bloomed.

"Well, I would have dressed up if I'd known you were coming!" he said.

"I think you look wonderful, my darling," she said and kissed him again.

They were still in the hallway, and Christophe laughed as he picked up her bag and led her inside.

Maureen looked around the apartment. It was tidy, but the furnishings were basic and old.

"It's a bit of a step down from my place in Marseille, that's for sure," he said. "But I haven't worked since you left, and being a vital cog in the resistance doesn't pay much."

"I love it," Maureen said.

Christophe placed her bag down in the corner. "The balcony's worth seeing," he said, walking out. It was large enough for a table and two chairs. Several people walked along below. A small café a few doors down provided color and character to the street.

She put her arm around him as they looked down together. After spending a few minutes in each other's arms, she returned to the kitchen table.

"It's not wise to talk outside," she said.

"You're trained now? I assume they accepted you in the SOE?" She nodded with a smile. "I'm engaged to a lethal weapon," he said. "A woman who can kill Nazis with a swipe of her hand."

Maureen laughed though there was some truth in what he'd said. One of the things she'd excelled at in training was hand-to-hand combat, and she was confident in being able to take down a man with her bare hands if the need arose.

Christophe led her into the kitchen, and she watched as he prepared them a simple meal of potato cakes and vegetables. He was even thinner than when she'd left. Every person she'd seen on the street on the way here in Toulouse and Lyon had the same hungry look he had. The entire population seemed as skinny as greyhounds.

"It's not much," he said. "Again, if I'd known you were coming..." he said as he chopped onions with a large kitchen knife.

"It's not the food, it's the company that counts," she said and reached her hand over to his.

"What have you been doing while I was away?" she asked.

"I've found my niche as a forger for the resistance. I have a little basement apartment I use just outside the city—just like Gerhard had. I'm not as good as our friend in Paris we rescued, but I'm getting there."

"I was hoping you'd say that. Part of the reason I'm here is to step up the evacuation efforts."

"Was that what your superiors in London ordered?"

"No, that's more of an extra-curricular activity I'm planning. Are you creating passports?"

"Whatever the need is."

"I think this is the beginning of a beautiful friendship," she said with a smile.

"What's your actual mission here?" he asked.

"To organize the resistance into a fighting force to be reckoned with. London is committed to backing them and will supply whatever they need to give the Nazis a black eye. The invasion is coming. Nobody knows when, but if we can drain enough resources and dampen the Nazis' morale enough it will make a substantial difference."

"And where will you be carrying out this work?"

"Much of the resistance has gathered in the forests in the Auvergne region."

"Seems like a good place to hide."

"Yes. Ideal for fighting guerilla warfare. It's crossed by deep rivers and lacks major roads so the Germans can't move in their armor. We could hide an entire army in there, and the Wehrmacht wouldn't be any the wiser."

"And that's what you intend to do, isn't it?"

"Yes."

"A life in the woods, eh? It's not what I'd envisaged for you when we first met at that fancy ball in Paris."

"Me neither, Christophe," she said. "I'd much rather stay in the city with you, but what I want to do doesn't really factor into it."

"The powers that be in London probably aren't overly concerned with your love life."

"Not so much," she said and stood up. She walked around the table and sat on his lap. "But I'm here now."

"I don't suppose you'll have the need for an expert forger, or an art dealer when you're out in the woods teaching butchers and bakers how to shoot Nazis?"

"No," she answered. "But I'll be back in the city every so often and I'll be availing myself of the services you provide."

"Oh, I love it when you talk about forging official government issued documents!" Christophe laughed and kissed her.

After taking some time to get reacquainted, they returned to the balcony. The coffee he brought her was so awful that she would rather have had water, but she didn't want to hurt his feelings and drank it anyway. The evening was setting in over the city.

"Don't count on the streetlights coming on," he said. "The situation here isn't any better than it was in Marseille before you left. Rolling power cuts most nights. Apparently, our Nazi friends don't pay the electricity bills on time."

"The Germans don't care about running the place. Just conquering it."

"There's something else I have to tell you," she said. "About the houses in Izieu."

"They're empty now."

"Not anymore. I was in contact with the OSE in London. They're appropriating them for some Jewish refugees."

She told him the details of the new occupants of her father's houses.

"New refugees? It's sad the need's there, but I'm glad you can still help."

"Jewish children from all over Europe."

"Excellent. I'll drink to that!" he said, holding up his coffee mug.

"Interesting that Hitler let the Italians take over part of France," Maureen said. "I never thought Hitler would reward Mussolini's loyalty with such a valuable prize."

"I wouldn't count on it being a permanent arrangement. Snakes like Hitler aren't known for keeping their word."

"Do you have any wine? This coffee tastes like a pond I fell into a few months ago."

"I won't question you about that," he said with a smile.

He walked back into the apartment and returned with two glasses of Merlot. They sat together, drinking wine and watching the street below. Maureen hadn't felt happiness like it for longer than she could remember.

~

Sunday, March 7, 1943

Waking up beside Christophe was as wonderful as it was familiar. He was faced the other way, lying on his side. The morning sun was peeking in through a chink in the curtains illuminating dust particles in the air, spinning them into pure gold like some celestial alchemist.

Inevitably, thoughts of what she had to do in the next few days began to intrude. Her duty. She tried to push them out, to savor this moment with the man she loved.

She got out of bed and went to the window, drawing back the curtains to wake Christophe. They had so little time. She didn't want to waste another second of it.

"I was having a dream about the old days, back in Izieu," he said as he opened his eyes. "We were together with all the refugees from Berlin, but happy, without the Nazi sword of Damocles hanging over us."

"We had some good times out there," she said and walked over to the bed. She sat down next to him, cupping his cheek with her palm. "I'm glad the refugees are safe now. I couldn't sleep if I'd left them behind."

"Is the new batch there now?"

"I think so."

"Do you have time to take a trip out there, before you become "Maureen of the Forest?""

"How long did it take you to come up with that name?"

"Just came up with it now. I have the car. It's parked outside the city. We could make the trip today if you have time."

Maureen took a few seconds to ponder traveling out to the houses her father had bought years before to house Jewish refugees from his factory in Berlin. No matter how much she was tempted, she knew her orders.

"I've been told not to get involved," she said. "I have so much to do with the resistance, it would be dangerous. Not just for me either, for the kids too."

"Spend one more night with me, anyway."

"Okay," she said with a smile. "I'll travel to the forest tomorrow."

"And we can spend one more night together before you begin sleeping with hundreds of dirty men. They'd better keep their hands off you!"

"They will if they know what's good for them."

After a leisurely breakfast of fresh bread, butter, and jam Christophe had purchased on the black market, they went for a bike ride around the city. Christophe hefted a satchel onto his back before mounting his bicycle. Maureen felt like every German soldier on the street was staring at her and that it was only a matter of time before they recognized who she was. But none stopped her, and other than the usual checks, they passed through the city streets with no difficulties.

Even fewer cars were on the roads than when she'd left the previous year.

Christophe rode north and over the river toward the 1st Arrondissement. She followed without questioning where they were going. He ducked down a small street she didn't know and pulled up behind him as Christophe stopped at a small wooden door. Maureen knew better than to ask questions on the street and waited as he knocked. A woman with curly black hair who looked about 35 answered and looked Maureen up and down.

"Who's this?" she asked.

"Don't worry," Christophe replied. "She's my fiancé. I trust her more than any other person on the planet." He took the bag from his shoulder and held it up. "Can we come in?"

The woman threw daggers from her eyes at Maureen.

"It's okay, Celine," Christophe repeated.

Celine relented and opened the door. Maureen followed Christophe inside. She felt awkward but knew he was doing all this for a reason.

"How are they?" he asked as they entered the woman's living room.

"Fine. No problems."

"Maureen's an expert in these kinds of situations," he said. "She's going to help us decide what to do."

"There's no decision to be made," Celine said. "They're fine here. The Gestapo will never—"

"Let's just see." He pushed past her, motioning Maureen to follow.

Christophe walked through the kitchen and down to a dark basement full of old furniture covered in gray sheets. They were alone now. Christophe walked over to an old gas stove in the corner without saying a word. "Help me with this."

She did as he asked, and they shifted it back to reveal a barely discernible trap door. He knocked and lifted the handle. "All right down there? Only me, Christophe."

Maureen peered into the hole and was met by five pairs of eyes looking back up at her.

"You can come up and stretch your legs for a little bit," he said. A teenage girl climbed out. She was dressed in a gray sweater and pants. Another younger girl followed her, and then another and another. Within a minute, five girls stood in front of them, aged between about 11 and 16.

"Maureen, may I introduce you to Michelle, Naomi, Celeste, Vera and Simone Belmont. Five sisters who've been hiding here for several weeks now."

The girls all had long brown hair in pigtails. Michelle, the oldest, was strikingly beautiful and held out her hand to greet Maureen. "Pleased to meet you."

Christophe reached into the bag he'd brought for bread, cheese, pickled vegetables, and a couple of cans of spam. The girls didn't wait to eat it, attacking the food like they hadn't eaten in days.

"What's it like down there?" Maureen asked.

"Not as bad as the last hole we hid in," Michelle said between bites.

"How long have you been hiding?"

"Six months. Since our parents were taken."

Maureen walked over to the hole. It was big enough for them all to sleep in, and there was a table and three chairs in the corner beside a pile of mattresses.

"Where are you from?" Maureen asked.

"From Warsaw originally, but we moved a few years ago," Michelle said in perfect French. "Our mother was from Lyon."

They stayed with the girls for a few minutes before Celine arrived down from upstairs.

"That's long enough," the woman of the house said. "They have to get back in now. If the Gestapo comes knocking, they'll all be taken."

Maureen said goodbye to the girls and watched as they climbed back into the hole. None complained.

Christophe closed the trapdoor and moved the oven back into place. The three adults went upstairs to the kitchen.

"What's your plan to get the girls across the border?" Maureen asked.

"This again?" Celine said and turned to Christophe. "I've had this argument with him before and I'll say the same to you. To where exactly?"

"Switzerland is two hours away by car."

"By whose car? And to climb the mountains? And where would they go once they reach Switzerland? The girls are safe in the basement. This Nazi madness won't last much longer. It's just a matter of waiting it out."

"For how long? They'll go crazy down there."

"It's safe. Trying to climb the mountains into Switzerland is akin to a death sentence for these kids. They've never done a hard day's work in their lives," Celine said.

"My friend here is a forger," Maureen said.

"I can make passports or other travel papers. Enough for everyone," agreed Christopher.

"How much time would that take?" Celine asked.

"That depends on what types of papers you need."

"We don't have any money to pay you, if that's what you're after."

"You won't need any. What we will need are photographs of the girls. Once I have them, I can start."

"I don't know," Celine said. "I'd like to run this past the OSE leadership before we do anything rash."

Maureen suppressed her frustration, focusing on breathing in and out before she spoke next. "How long do you think that'll take?"

"To send a coded letter back and forth to Switzerland?" Celine answered. "Several weeks."

"And they're so close," Christophe said.

"I've had enough of this," Celine said. "The girls are under my care. I've been charged with the responsibility of looking after them. I won't be pushed into making life or death decisions by anyone, especially a stranger."

Maureen bit her lip. She was just about to speak when Christophe cut her off. "I'll be back in a few days with some more food. You know how to contact me if something comes up."

Celine nodded and walked them to the door. She shut it behind them without saying goodbye.

Maureen was livid as they reached the bikes. Christophe took her in his arms. "I know what you're thinking but she's right—they're safe. For now, at least."

"Does everyone connected with the OSE think the war's about to end? Are they all delusional?"

"No, they're not. Celine is a little eccentric, but she's been harboring Jews for over a year now. She sent a family over the Alps a few months ago. They didn't make it. I suppose she's a little overprotective now."

Christophe got on his bike.

"How many other Jews do you deliver food to around the city?"

"About 20. Most of them are kids."

"And they're all hiding in squalor? Should we send them to Izieu?"

"No. We have to stay away from the houses. At least you do, anyway. Izieu is out of our hands now."

"Come with me." They cycled to the river. Lyon was set up at the confluence of the two major waterways of the Rhône and the Saône and had been a major trading post since the time of the Romans 2000 years before. They parked their bikes by the vast expanse of water and sat on the grass.

Christophe said the words she knew were coming.

"You can't save everyone. What they do is their decision. I'm just trying to keep them alive until the decision does come down to evacuate them. Everyone on our side wants the same thing. It's just they don't agree on how to do it. There are thousands of Jewish children sheltering all over France alive thanks to the OSE."

Maureen picked up a stone and tossed it out into the Rhône. "I know, I just can't believe what that woman said. The Nazis are coming," she said as they stared at the water winding south toward the Mediterranean. "Can you manufacture papers for the girls and the other Jews in hiding around the city?"

"Not without photographs, and certainly not without the consent of the adults looking after them. And I'm barely able to keep up with the demand of the Allied servicemen passing through. I sleep about 4 hours most nights."

"I knew you'd say that," Maureen said.

He put his arm around her, but it offered little comfort. They sat there until the sun faded and the air grew colder. Maureen tried to accept what Christophe and Celine had told her, but she'd seen what the Nazis were capable of. She knew they'd come for the children in hiding sooner or later, and not because of what they believed or what they'd done, but because of the blood running through their veins.

7

Tuesday, November 21, 2006

Amy was in bed watching TV when the pain came. Shock struck her like a bucket of freezing cold water. It felt like something had broken inside her, and she cried out. The baby! She reached down to touch her belly as the agony came again like a red-hot dagger plunging in and out of her stomach. She tried to raise herself to her feet as if it was a cramp she could walk off, but her legs failed her, and she fell back down on the soft cushions of the bed. Realizing this was an emergency, Amy called out for her grandmother. The TV was still playing, and she picked up the remote control to switch it off before shouting again. This couldn't be. Her pregnancy wasn't meant to end like this. But then she saw the flush of red blood on her pajamas and screamed. Thoughts of her grandmother and everything she went through flashed across her consciousness. Amy dialed 112 on her phone–the emergency number in France, but it didn't connect. Her American phone wasn't set up to make calls in France, only text messages.

She tried to get up, but the pain forced her back down. The only position that didn't bring burning torture was sitting back on the bed with her arms spread across the back cushions, but she couldn't stay like that. Taking a few deep breaths, she forced herself to her feet. Screaming helped with the pain. Walking was almost as difficult as getting off the bed, but she forced one foot in front of the other and made her way toward the door.

Maureen arrived at the door in her nightgown.

"Something's wrong!" Amy shouted.

"Sit down, for goodness sake!"

Amy did as she was told.

"I tried to call for an ambulance but my phone didn't work."

"I'll call. But don't move!"

Her grandmother walked out to the telephone in the hallway as quickly as her legs would carry her.

Maureen sat holding her hand as they waited for the ambulance to arrive. It wasn't far to the hospital, and 25 minutes later, Amy was being wheeled in. Terrified and in a foreign country, her grandmother was her only comfort. Lots of people called out in French. Amy understood a few words until one nurse approached her, speaking perfect English.

"The baby's coming tonight," she said.

"Is it going to be okay? I'm in so much pain. I have placenta previa."

"The doctors know all that. How many weeks are you?"

"33."

"We'll bring you in for surgery in a few minutes."

"Can my grandmother come in with me?"

"Is that what you want?"

Amy nodded.

They prepped her for surgery and gave her an anesthetic. She was still holding her grandmother's hand as she succumbed to sleep.

Amy opened her eyes and felt a different kind of pain. She was in bed, still in the hospital. The baby wasn't in her anymore, and she tried to sit up, but the agony in her stomach slowed her. The nurse who spoke English appeared with a smile on her face.

"Congratulations, Mom!" she said. "You have a beautiful baby girl."

"Where is she?"

"In the NICU, the neonatal intensive care unit."

"Is she okay? I want to see her."

"She's small—only two pounds. She's on a respirator right now to help her breathe."

"Is she going to be okay?"

"It's early. She's very tiny and only a few hours old. I'll get the doctor and you can speak to her. She'll answer all your questions."

"What time is it?"

"It's just after four in the morning," the nurse said with another smile. She was pretty, with blue eyes and blond hair.

"When can I see my daughter?"

"After the doctor comes. I'll bring her over right away."

"Where's my grandmother?"

"She went home to get some rest. She was in the operating room with you and knows what's going on."

The few minutes between the nurse leaving and the doctor returning seemed like days and were filled with grisly thoughts of what might happen to her little girl. A girl. She was no longer an abstract notion of a human being growing inside her. She was out and in the world. Her daughter was on the floor below her. People had touched her. Held her. The fact that she hadn't been able to yet gnawed at her, and the desire to see her baby was like nothing she'd felt before.

It was 10 o'clock at night in America. Amy looked around

for her phone. She had to call Ryan and her brother. But did she have her international calling card? It wasn't just a case of dialing a number. Her grandmother had tossed her wallet into the overnight bag she'd had ready, and Amy reached in to find the card. But the doctor interrupted her.

"Congratulations, Amy," the doctor said in excellent English. Her face betrayed little emotion.

She was in her late thirties, with an olive complexion and brown eyes. She looked how most Americans thought every French person would, and she had the name to match.

"Thanks, Dr. Bardot. How is my little girl?"

"We're still finding out. She's doing well, but it was a difficult birth and she came early."

Amy couldn't help herself and started bawling. The doctor kept her composure.

"I'm so sorry to tell you that, but we don't know enough yet. Her little lungs weren't fully formed so we've hooked her up to a ventilator."

"When will we know if she has any permanent damage?"

"Hard to say, but it's only a possibility. The chance that she didn't suffer any ill effects is just as good."

"So, you're saying it's 50-50?"

"I'm not saying that at all. I'm saying that she's getting the best care possible and that we're monitoring the situation as closely as we can. Her heart is strong. She's just going to need to get used to things outside the womb. We're here to facilitate that."

Amy nodded, using a handkerchief to wipe away the tears. "Is she in any danger?"

"The first 24 hours will be important. And as I said before she's in the best hands. I can't say too much more now." She paused for a few seconds as if letting what she'd said sink in. "What's her name?"

"Marie," Amy answered. "Marie Maureen Sullivan. After her mom and her grandma."

"It's a beautiful name. Stay strong for Marie. You can come see her now." Amy sat up too quickly and felt the tug where they'd cut her open. The doctor lunged forward to catch her, but Amy had already retreated to the pillow. "Be careful. You're a bit more delicate than usual. I'll get a nurse to wheel you to the NICU to visit. You'll need to take it easy for a few days."

"Thank you," Amy said. The powerlessness she felt was almost overwhelming. All she could do was sit and wait for the nurse to come.

Getting off the bed wasn't easy, but she would have crawled through barbed wire to see her baby. The nurse helped her into a wheelchair and they left the room.

"You'll be fine in a few days," the nurse said as Amy grimaced in pain. Amy had no regard for her own well-being. Everything had changed in the last few hours. She was like a different person. She didn't feel nervous or hesitant to see her baby like she'd thought she might. She just wanted to take care of her.

The nurse brought her to the window at the NICU, but Amy didn't want the first time she saw her child to be from twenty feet away.

"Can we go inside?"

"Let me make sure."

The nurse disappeared for a few minutes before returning to Amy with a smile. "You won't be able to hold her yet, but we can go see her."

She pushed Amy through the door. The NICU had about twenty beds in it. Some were open, but most were self-contained incubation units. Amy tried not to look at the other babies until she reached Marie. She wanted her daughter to be the only one she saw. Amy burst into tears as she saw her tiny baby with a white hat on, hooked up to a ventilator and with a feeding tube through her nostril. Her skin was pink and blotchy, and her eyes were closed. She was the most beautiful thing Amy had ever seen, and she had to hold herself back to keep from blubbering.

"Hi, Marie," Amy said to her daughter. "It's me, your mommy. I'm so happy to meet you."

She reached up to touch the glass. Marie didn't move. "I love you, my darling."

Amy sat there for 30 minutes, staring at the little girl, before the nurse returned to take her back to bed.

She still hadn't called Ryan. No matter how inconvenient it was, he was Marie's father. It had taken a while to stop loving him after their breakup, but she was sure she was there now. The voices pushing her toward him were silenced now, and any affection she once had for him was dead. Once more, it was her grandmother who'd helped her through. Her advice had been key. Forgiving him was all it took. It hadn't been easy, but once Amy was able to let go of her grievances toward him, she could focus on their future—raising their child together.

She took out her phone and, knowing it didn't make calls, texted instead.

I had the baby last night. It's a girl. Sorry it took me so long to tell you. I was in surgery and then fell asleep. Marie is in the NICU now. The doctors don't know much. She's on a ventilator, but I think she's okay. I'll tell you more when I find out.

She waited with the phone in her hand for a few minutes, but when he didn't respond, she copied the text and sent it to his mother.

Amy returned to her room, where a nurse helped her change. After putting on a fresh pair of pajamas, a dressing gown, and a pair of slippers, Amy waddled down the hallway as best she could toward the elevator to the NICU. Her stitches from the operation to draw Marie out of her were still raw and sore. She'd only looked at them a couple of times and didn't intend to again for a while.

Her heart melted once more as she sat down beside Marie's ventilator. Amy sat there for hours, staring at her baby, watching her chest expand and contract in time with the breathing tubes.

Her phone was buzzing as she returned to her room. She saw the name and took a deep breath.

"Hello Louise."

"I got your text. How is the baby?" she said.

"Everything happened so quickly. I'm sorry."

It felt strange to have to answer to this woman but no less than being tied to her son, someone she would otherwise never have spoken to again for the rest of their lives.

"I would have liked to have been there," Mrs. Smith said.

Amy wasn't surprised at the woman's sentiment. She was sure Mrs. Smith would have wanted to have been in the delivery room with her, intruding.

"I'm sorry," Amy mumbled because it was the easiest thing to say. She didn't want to have to explain herself to Ryan Smith's mother right now. She was too tired.

"So, how's Marie?" Mrs. Smith asked. Amy had no doubt her concern was genuine, but she wished she could have spent this time with someone else, like her own mother. She hadn't even called her brother yet, and here she was talking to this woman.

"Holding steady. I was just down in the NICU with her. She's the most beautiful thing I've ever seen."

"I'm so excited to meet her. Can you hold her yet?"

"I don't know when I'll be able to. She's too little, too fragile."

"My poor granddaughter."

Amy relented, realizing it wasn't Mrs. Smith's fault that her parents couldn't be here today. It wasn't her fault that she and Ryan hadn't worked out. It wasn't her fault Amy was alone.

"Do you want to come to France to meet her?"

"I'll be there tomorrow," Mrs. Smith said.

Tomorrow was very soon, but was no use arguing with her. "I should be here for another couple of days myself."

"It's just such a shame Ryan isn't with you," the older woman said, shaking her head. "I haven't even been able to speak to him yet."

Amy made her excuses and hung up. She called her brother, Mark, from a payphone in the hallway. He was as shocked as she expected and promised to get a flight from Boston later in the week to meet his new niece.

Amy spent much of the next hour or two chatting with her friends back home.

Talking to other people distracted her from her worries. Her heart and her mind seemed to be in different places, however. Her heart felt only the immense, almost overpowering love for her daughter that colored everything now. Her mind ran in thousands of different directions, but her heart was like the ocean current, strong and steady on one course. It was as if the two parts of her body were battling one another for dominance over Amy's soul.

Her mind cycled through every permutation of Marie's health, asking questions constantly. Would she recover? What if she'd sustained permanent brain damage? What if her lungs were affected? What if she'd just been born too soon and never made it out of here?

Her heart's course was different. It seemed to exist only to love the little girl. That was its only concern.

It was time to call Mike. She had to clear her heart. It was only fair to both of them.

He picked up on the third ring.

"It's me," she began. "I had the baby."

"What? Boy or girl?"

They talked about how she was feeling and Marie's condition for a few minutes before the feeling building inside her mind came to the surface.

"I can come over if you need some help," he said.

"No, you don't have to do that. It's just a little awkward when you're not the father."

Mike paused for a few seconds. She didn't want to hurt him, but couldn't stop herself.

"Yeah, you're right. I'm not the father. I just wanted to see you."

"I'm sorry," she said. "I didn't mean it like—"

"You're right. Ryan Smith is Marie's dad, but I thought since we were together you might want to see me."

"I do," she said. "But I'm just not sure this is the right time and place."

"Yeah, you're right," he said, his voice falling flat. "I just thought you might like some company."

"I appreciate your offer Mike, but really, where is this going?" The words came out of her mouth like someone else was saying them. Inside, her heart was breaking.

"What do you mean, us?" he replied. He seemed amazed. "I never cared you were pregnant by someone else. You know that."

"It's a massive part of my life. Nothing else matters. I just don't know if you're ready to take on someone else's child. You turn girls' heads everywhere you go. You should be out enjoying yourself. I can't give you that life anymore. I have Marie now."

"What part of our relationship for the past six months has led you to this conclusion?" he said. "I don't remember dragging you out to clubs until four in the morning. Our usual Friday night usually involves sitting on the couch while you look at my beer as if you'd kill someone to be able to drink it."

"Yes," Amy said. "It's been great, but I just don't know if I have space in my life for a relationship right now."

"I understand," Mike said.

"You're a great guy, but I have to focus on Marie right now. She needs all of me."

"Yeah," he said under his breath. "How long have you been feeling like this?"

"I think I just realized. You'll thank me in a few weeks when you're back enjoying the freedom you'll never have with me."

"I'll thank you for breaking up with me?" he said. "I look forward to that. Please let me know how little Marie does."

"Of course," she said. "We can still be friends."

"I never wanted to be just your friend, Amy." He pushed out a deep breath. "Hug that little girl for me," he said and hung up.

Amy cried. Tears were her heart's voice, but she knew in her mind she'd done the right thing. Mike was going to leave her sooner or later. No matter what he said, he'd never want to raise someone else's child. Her body was wrecked after the surgery, and there were too many younger, prettier girls in the city. She was doing them both a favor. She only did it because she loved him. All that mattered now was Marie. Her own heart's desires would have to wait.

Her phone buzzed beside her. Ryan's name appeared on the screen. She picked it up, ready to do her duty.

8

Amy woke from a sleep dominated by dreams of her daughter and immediately felt the lack of her. Amy was back in Maureen's house. Leaving Marie behind when she'd checked out of the hospital the day before had been one of the hardest things she'd ever done. The doctors were less concerned than when Marie was first born, but she wasn't gaining weight yet, and the prospect of her jumping from two to four pounds seemed like a distant one. The worst part was not being able to hold her. Marie was likely to be here, in France, for weeks. What would Amy do with that time? She had to start getting her life together, for her daughter's sake, as much as her own, but how could she when all she wanted to do was sit in the NICU and stare through that glass at the little baby that had already changed her life beyond recognition? Every lens she viewed the world through was colored by that little girl now.

Ryan and his mother had been in the hospital with her when she checked out and were due to visit Marie again that afternoon. This level of contact was acceptable while Marie was in the NICU, but Amy couldn't handle anything approaching it in the future. Still, it was comforting to know how much they cared.

Amy's obsession with her baby hid the hurt she felt from her breakup with Mike. Even though her mind was almost wholly occupied with thoughts of Marie, part of her still pined for Mike. But that was her heart talking. Now wasn't the time to be distracted by selfish notions. Everything had to be focused on her baby's well-being, no matter what she might have wanted. Mike had texted her a few times since their breakup, mainly inquiring about Marie's condition. Amy had replied each time. It was difficult to quit him, and she didn't want to be rude, but to continue talking to him seemed pointless. The relief at not being stuck with her was probably sinking in for him now, and he'd doubtless stop contacting her for good in the next few days. Their time together had been a wonderful distraction, but she had more important things to focus on now. That little baby was relying on her, and she was determined to meet her every need.

After taking a little time to pump some breast milk with the contraption the hospital supplied, Amy walked over to her dresser. She looked tired and drawn. It was little wonder. She'd barely gotten a decent night's sleep all week. Her hair was losing some of the luster she had loved so much during her pregnancy, and her skin wasn't as soft to the touch as it had been a few days before. But a little makeup worked miracles, and Amy smiled back at her reflection in the mirror. The thought of seeing her daughter again lifted her heart, but seeing the empty bassinet beside her bed where Marie should have slept the night before sank it like a stone once more. Amy took a deep breath, trying to draw courage from Maureen's experiences during the war, but it was hard. She felt so helpless. All she wanted to do was run to that hospital and pluck her little girl out of that ventilator. She hadn't even held her yet.

Her laptop was sitting on the table in her room. Amy walked over and opened it up. The manuscript shone white on the screen. Her grandmother's story wasn't finished.

A knock interrupted Amy's thoughts and Maureen appeared around the door. "I ordered a taxi. Almost ready to go, dear?"

"Give me a few minutes to get dressed. Don't forget we're meeting Ryan and his mother today."

"And Mark and Conor are coming in the next few days. Your brother and my brother. It's exciting." She smiled and shut the door.

Amy dressed in the smartest clothes she could fit into, wary of judgments from Ryan and Louise. A wool sweater and comfortable jeans were the best she could come up with.

"It'll have to do," she said and walked out to join her grandmother.

It was a dull, cold day, and Maureen wore a coat to protect against the scything wind that hit them as they stepped outside.

Ryan and his mother were waiting in the registration area and stood up as Amy and her grandmother walked in. Amy had seen them both the day before, so she let her grandmother take center stage.

"It's a pleasure to meet you," Ryan said to Maureen. "Amy mentioned that she was working on your biography."

"She's a wonderful writer. It boggles my mind that the newspaper ever thought to let her go," Maureen said.

"We had to make some painful cuts in the past few months. Amy was only the first."

"I don't think we need to talk about that now," Louise added.

Ryan spoke about his work, and Maureen asked him some questions about interviews he'd done with various world leaders, but Amy was only half-listening as he spoke. Her mind was on Marie. The only question she wanted to ask him was when his other children were coming to visit, but she knew now wasn't the place or time.

It felt strange to be with him, to see him and Louise conversing with her beloved grandmother, but she knew it couldn't be from now on. She was tied to this man, likely for the rest of their lives. Rightly or wrongly. They would have to work it out for their child's sake, and fighting wouldn't benefit anyone. She turned around and asked a question herself. It felt like she was feeding his enormous ego, but she did it anyway.

They rode the elevator together, discussing the birth and reiterating what the doctors said.

"It's been a while since I've been to France," Louise said as the doors opened.

Maureen hung back as they entered the NICU. Amy knew how excited she was to see Marie, but also that Ryan was the father and should go first. Only two people were allowed to visit a patient at a time, so Maureen sat by the window with Louise as Amy brought Ryan inside.

"She's so tiny," Ryan said as they sat beside her incubator.

"She hasn't put on any weight yet, but the doctors say we need to be patient."

"All of mine lost weight before they gained it," he replied.

She wasn't sure if she approved of his phrasing but remembered her idea to keep things with Ryan as smooth as possible for the baby's sake.

He pulled up two chairs for them. It felt strange to have him beside her. This was her place. Watching Marie's chest expanding back and forth in time with the respirator was her thing, but reality had just arrived on the plane from New York. *This is the rest of our lives in a microcosm,* she thought to herself.

They sat by Marie's bedside for 20 minutes, talking about

nothing other than her. Long periods of silence punctuated their conversation.

"My mother is dying to get in here," he said after several minutes of quiet.

"I'll leave," she said and stood up.

He looked across at her with a fond smile and held out his hand to take hers. She shook it as if meeting him for the first time—not what he'd wanted from her.

"Amy, you're doing a great job."

"Thanks," she said and walked out to sit with her grandmother.

Louise thanked her and went into the NICU with a bright smile.

"How was it with him?" Maureen asked after she left.

"I'm trying to keep your advice in the forefront of my mind."

"About forgiving his past misdeeds to concentrate on the future?"

"Yes."

"It's the best way forward," her grandmother said. "But don't forget what else I said—forgiving doesn't mean starting over. When someone shows you who they are, take note."

"I'm not getting back with Ryan, Grandma. I just want things between us to be as civil as possible."

Ryan and his mother emerged 30 minutes later, and Amy led her grandmother inside the NICU.

"This isn't quite how I pictured this," Amy said as they approached Marie's incubator.

"Almost nothing in my life has turned out the way I first pictured it," Maureen said. "All we can do when the gales start blowing is adjust the sails, otherwise we go under."

Her grandmother had tears in her eyes as she sat down. "She's the most beautiful girl I've ever seen, just like her mommy."

Maureen's words were like icy water on the flames threatening to consume Amy's heart. They sat together, marveling at the miracle in front of their eyes, before Amy began to notice tiredness bringing itself to bear on her grandmother. She always had to be on the lookout. Maureen never complained, but that could be detrimental to the health of someone who'd be 91 on their next birthday.

"I should get you home," Amy said.

"Already? We've only just arrived."

"It's been almost an hour."

After a few seconds of going back and forth, Maureen agreed, and Amy helped her out of her seat.

"Goodbye little one," the older woman said. "I love you with all my heart."

Ryan and his mother were at the door. They made small talk about Marie for a moment before Amy made an excuse and whisked her grandmother away.

"That could have been a lot worse," Amy said as they entered the elevator.

"What about Ryan's children? Do they know yet?"

"No. He hasn't told them yet."

"He's going to have to reveal her to them sooner or later. And himself too."

"What do you mean?"

"Revealing Marie would expose a part of him he doesn't want them to know about, but concealing it will be far more painful in the long term. Imagine what his children will think if they discover the truth themselves? He's dug himself a hole. The only way out is by telling the truth."

"I hope Ryan's mother tells him that—he might listen to her. It'd be so special to have Marie's half-siblings come visit," Amy said.

The elevator reached the first floor, and they walked to the taxi rank. They got straight into a waiting cab.

"How about you, Amy? How do you feel now?"

"That I'm a mother?" she replied. Her grandmother nodded. "Like a different person. It was like some celestial hand came down and flicked a switch in my brain the minute she was born. It's hard to fathom being so different so quickly."

"But it happens. When do the doctors think we'll be able to hold her?"

"Maybe tomorrow, but we'll see. I'm dying to, but I don't want to hurt her. She's so delicate."

"Even little ones like her are tougher than you might think."

A pause in the conversation brought a latent subject to the surface of her mind. "I had to break up with Mike," Amy said.

"You had to? I'm not sure I understand. Did he do something to necessitate that?"

"No. Nothing. I just don't have room in my life for a relationship at the moment, particularly with someone who isn't Marie's father."

"Did he show any signs of rejecting the child?"

"No, not at all. He called me to ask how she was doing."

Her grandmother looked puzzled. Explaining why she'd dumped Mike wasn't easy, but in her mind, she knew it was for the best. Ryan had hurt her so badly. She couldn't leave herself open to that again.

"You seemed so happy with him."

"I was for a while, but he's going to have his head turned by the next pretty young thing that crosses his path. I see the way girls look at him."

"I never thought being handsome was a character flaw," Maureen said.

"I was protecting myself and Marie. Both of us. If he'd broken my heart...." She trailed off.

Her grandmother was quick to pick up the slack in the conversation.

"So, you've made the decision for him? That he didn't want to be with you long term?"

"I made a preemptive call. It wasn't easy. It broke my heart, if I'm honest about it."

"Because Ryan hurt you, am I right? And other men before?"

"Things are different in my life now, and yes, I'm learning from past experiences."

"But nothing's changed between you and Ryan? You still don't want to be with him?"

"Never."

Maureen nodded and peered out the window. Her tiredness was apparent in the way she moved and her silence. She spoke little for the rest of the taxi ride. They pulled up outside her house ten minutes later.

The dogs jumped up as they walked in, but her grandmother was too tired to play with them and almost fell into her bed. Amy tucked her in and let her sleep. With little else to do, Amy returned to her computer. She reread the last chapter she'd edited. It was good. The entire book was. But it was unfinished. She sat back in the chair and peered out the window at the sprawling French countryside.

"This story's no good if it doesn't have a conclusion," she said out loud.

It was dark by the time her grandmother woke up. Amy had dinner ready when she emerged from the room. They sat down together to eat red snapper with rosemary washed down with Cabernet Sauvignon.

Amy waited until they'd finished the meal to ask the question that had been on her mind these last few hours.

"Can we start again? You and I have unfinished business," she said.

"I didn't think you'd be focused on that with all that's going on."

"If not now, when? Things are only going to get more hectic once Marie gets home. And I have to return to New York sometime. We might not get a better chance. As much as it pains me, she's going to be in the hospital for another week or two."

Maureen nodded. "It's going to be a lot to go through again."

"Are you sure you want to tell me? If it's too much—"

"I'm positive. I've been thinking about those times more lately. I'd buried them for years. They were too painful to touch. But I'm ready now."

9

Tuesday, March 7, 1943

Maureen was thinking about Christophe as she lay in the dirt. It was a clear night, and a blanket of stars twinkled like diamonds spread on black velvet above her head. She looked at her watch. It was almost ten o'clock. The plane was due any minute. The two resistance men beside her in the bushes watching over the drop were silent as the dead. She couldn't even hear their breathing. She'd met them a few hours previously at a designated safe house just outside the town of Massiac, three hours east of Lyon. They were her escort here and were also tasked with helping her load the supplies they were waiting on.

Massiac was set between two huge forests she would call home until London decided differently. The faint sound of the plane cut through the night air. Maureen signaled to the two men, and after double-checking they were alone, all three held up flashlights. The outline of the airplane came into view against the lighter sky above. Maureen and the other men held up the lights for a few more seconds, waiting for the sound of the plane's engines to dissipate before putting them away. Deliberately attracting attention felt wrong, and it was with some relief that Maureen placed her light back into her backpack, where it clinked against her pistol.

"See? There!" Maureen said as she spotted the first parachute.

The two men nodded but didn't move from their prone position. No one made a sound as the parachutes came down. The first was a packing crate that fell to the ground with a crump. The second was the same, but the third was something altogether different. Maureen got up as she saw the man land in the field and ran out, reaching him as he unstrapped the parachute from his shoulders. He turned around to her as she greeted him in English with a whisper.

"The French enjoy this time of year," she said, using the code words.

"Yes," he responded. "Not too hot. Not too cold."

"Good to meet you, I'm Maureen," she said.

"Charles," he said in an upper-class English accent. He was about six feet tall, with an angular face and a mustache. London said he was the best radio operator they had.

The two resistance men arrived beside them a few seconds later.

"This is Serge," she said. Charles shook his hand. "And Phillipe."

The two Frenchmen helped Charles with his parachute as Maureen ran over to where one of the packages had come down. She pulled a crowbar from her backpack and opened the crate. Charles's radio was inside. The other drop was at the end of the field, several hundred yards from where she was standing. She scanned the tree line for suspicious movements, ran to the second crate, and dug into it with the crowbar. The moon-

light revealed two dozen Sten guns—a gift to Sella to show
what the British could deliver if he played ball. The crate was
too heavy to move, so Maureen rested against it until the other
three men arrived to help out.

"Your radio," she said to Charles.

"Yes, it's a good one," he replied.

The other crates contained submachine guns to kickstart
her friendship with the men she was to train.

Serge reached into the container to pick up one of the Sten
guns but came back with a handful of grease instead.

"They're packed in Cosmoline to keep them in good shape.
It wards off cold, heat, dirt and moisture. They won't work until
they're scrubbed clean—not an easy process."

They each took a corner and lifted the heavy crate. It took a
few minutes of exhausting work to move it to their coal-
powered truck. Once they'd loaded it, they went back for the
other one. Charles took his parachute with him to bury it later
somewhere far from here.

"Welcome to the Auvergne," Serge said to Charles as they
stowed his radio into the back of the lorry. "The free French
under Henri Sella still rule this place."

They set out in silence. The further they drove into the
Auvergne Forest, the rougher the terrain became. Maureen was
beginning to understand why the resistance referred to this
area as the "Fortress of France." The truck climbed higher as
the hills turned into mountains. Serge mentioned that many of
them were over six thousand feet. The road soon became a
meandering dirt track that Maureen would have had no idea
how to navigate. They looped through seemingly endless
plateaus and around volcanic rock formations, occasionally
drifting perilously close to gorges whose bottoms were invisible
in the dark. Wooded slopes sprang up on all sides, and the road
softened beneath a blanket of pine needles. It was the perfect
terrain for the resistance to wage guerrilla warfare. They hadn't

seen another living soul, let alone a German patrol, since setting out.

It was after one in the morning when the truck pulled off the road into what seemed to be a makeshift camp. A guard with an old WWI Lee Enfield rifle slung over his shoulder looked at them with suspicious eyes before waving them through. Maureen gazed around in amazement. The place was like a parking lot. At least 30 cars sat with tents between them. Dozens of men were still milling around despite the time of night. Some were armed with old rifles, but most were setting up tents or tending to fires.

"This is Camp du Montagnes I," Serge said.

"I heard there were 150 men here. Have you done a recent count?"

"No. People come and go."

Charles looked at Maureen. The powers that be in London had told her she would have her work cut out here.

"Where did all the cars come from?" Charles asked. "I thought they were rarer than hen's teeth."

"Stolen," Phillipe said. "You saw the terrain on the way up here. No other way to travel."

They got out of the truck.

"Is Sella still awake?" Maureen asked.

"Probably," Serge answered. "He doesn't sleep much. Let me check."

The resistance fighter left Maureen and the radio operator standing by the truck for five minutes before he returned.

"He'll see you now."

They followed Serge as he moved between the cars and tents. The irritating sound of snoring was everywhere, and Maureen wondered how anyone could sleep. Serge stopped outside a large tent at the edge of the camp and directed Maureen and Charles to enter. She pushed back the fabric over the door and walked inside. Three men were sitting at a table playing cards by candlelight. None looked up. Maureen cleared her throat to get their attention.

"A woman in camp? Who are you?" one man said.

"London sent us," Maureen answered. "Which of you is Henri Sella?"

One of the men placed his cards on the small round table in front of them. A small pot of banknotes sat in the middle.

"I'm Sella," the man said. He was in his mid-forties with a thick mustache. His worn complexion told of a life spent outdoors.

"Can we talk?" Maureen asked.

"Of course," he said and dismissed the two men he was playing poker with.

A few seconds later, they were alone.

"Who's she?" Sella said to Charles. "Your wireless operator? It won't be easy having a woman in camp."

"He's the wireless operator," Maureen said. "I'm the contact."

The Frenchman looked like he'd tasted something awful before his lips spread into a smile. "Is this some sort of joke? They sent us a woman?"

Maureen knew this was coming. The instructors in England had said as much. Hendry had called it a "deficit of respect." She'd been coming up against the look in this man's eyes her whole life and hadn't backed down yet. She wasn't about to start now.

"I'm here to reorganize the band of bakers, cooks and postmen you've assembled and turn them into a fighting force."

"You?" Sella said.

Charles stepped forward, but Maureen put her arm across his chest to stop him. "The War Office is committed to the partisan cause in the Auvergne and beyond. They'll provide you with what you need, but only if I approve. Charles here, is a communications expert. My skills lie elsewhere."

"I'm sure they do," Sella said with a crooked-toothed smile.

"All communications with London will go through me. Similarly, all weapons orders will too. Food and everything else you will need can be dropped from the sky, but only if I give the word. Not him," she said, pointing at Charles. She stepped toward the resistance leader. "I'm not here to share anyone's bed. I'm here to rid this country of the Nazi cancer. I'm here to train you, to arm you, to save your lives. The sooner you realize that we're partners the better, because from what I can see, a company of Wehrmacht troops could wipe out your forces with their eyes closed."

"You have no idea what my men are capable of. We've been up here for weeks without anyone's help."

"But what could you do without the weapons and training you need? The Nazis have whatever they need. It's not a fair fight. Have you run drills with the men?"

"No," Sella answered. "The few weapons we have are from the last war, and bullets are so rare that we only use them to hunt game for the pot."

"What's your goal for the men here?"

"To live free from harassment and to take potshots at the Germans when we can."

"That's all about to change," Maureen said. "Training starts tomorrow."

"And what will we drill with? Baguettes?" Sella sneered.

"Come with me," Maureen said.

The camp was quieter as they walked back through the tents and cars. Everyone except the guards seemed to be asleep now. They came to the truck, and Maureen directed Sella to climb inside. She handed him the flashlight, and his eyes glowed as he beheld the weapons.

"And this is just the start," Maureen said. "I give the word and you'll have all the guns you want."

Sella got out of the truck and shook her hand, his

demeanor toward her unrecognizable from what it had been just a few minutes before. He looked like a child on Christmas morning. "We'll smash the Boche," he said with a smile. "They killed my son in the first days of the war, and my wife died soon after. I've been waiting for my revenge ever since."

"And you shall have it," Maureen said.

Back in the tent, Sella gestured to the small table he'd been playing cards on. "Join me and let's talk." He cleared off the cards and put the money in his pocket. "You want some wine?"

Maureen didn't feel like drinking at this time of night but accepted anyway. Charles did the same, and soon they were all sitting at the table with a glass of light-bodied red that was far better than she'd expected. Sella lit up a cigarette as Maureen began.

"How many men do you have here?"

"About 250, but it grows every day. More and more are coming from the cities and towns."

"Any army veterans?"

"I'm pretty sure we have a few."

"Find these men and bring them to me in the morning. Anyone with experience with weapons will be invaluable," Maureen said. "And I'll call in the order to London to get the weapons we need. We just have to sit down and figure out how many first." She picked up her wine glass and took a sip.

"The first thing we need to do is divide the men up into squads, if possible, led by one army veteran. These squads will stick together, living away for days or weeks at a time, but keeping in contact with basecamp. They'll hit the Germans and fade back into the forest."

"Our knowledge of the area is our only advantage over the invaders, but a lot of the men don't even have that."

"Where are you from?" Charles asked.

"Not far from here," Sella answered.

"We'll try to get one or two men who know the local area in

each squad. We'll isolate each recruit's skill set and mix them up to maximize the effectiveness of our force. But not before we train them in the basics. That starts tomorrow. Do you agree?" Maureen said.

"I agree." The sneer on Sella's face was long gone.

10

Wednesday, March 8, 1943

The sound of the camp coming to life woke Maureen after what she estimated was a little less than four hours of sleep. In an attempt to shield her from the desperate men in the camp, Sella had given over his tent to sleep in. Her back was stiff from the cot, and she raised her arms above her head to stretch out her aches and pains. It was cold, and she put her coat back on and buttoned up the front before standing up. Ravenously hungry, she searched the tent for food but found nothing other than a few empty wine bottles and some cigarette butts. She turned over the flap on the inside of the tent and stepped outside. Two men dressed in work clothes stopped in their tracks, their eyes stuck to her like limpets. She nodded to them and walked past, expecting them to wolf-whistle. They didn't, but only because they probably thought she was Sella's new girlfriend.

Dozens of men were milling around. A few had old weapons of the same type the guard who'd greeted them the night before carried, but most had nothing. The smell of something cooking over a campfire led her through the slew of cars and tents toward two men cooking meat and eggs over a fire. They looked at her as if she was a different species.

"Good morning," she said in French. "Any chance of some food?"

One of the men nodded, almost as if he was afraid to talk. The other just smiled and stared. Every man who passed did the same. It was as if they'd never seen a woman before.

The fresh venison was delicious, and she thanked them and left after she finished.

With nothing else to do until Sella woke, Maureen climbed into the back of the truck and began to inventory and clean the weapons. It was a laborious, disgusting task, but by the time Charles found her, 11 Sten guns were ready for use.

"First day on the job, eh? Never easy," he said. He mentioned nothing about her being a woman, but the connotation was there.

"I'll have to prove myself, as any leader would, but I'm confident."

"Good for you." He sat beside her, insisting on helping clean the weapons before having something to eat. They finished the job in less than an hour and stacked the guns.

Maureen brought Charles back to the men cooking over the fire. Several others had joined them.

"This your boyfriend?" one of them said with a sneer.

"My wireless operator. He's hungry. Can you spare any more?"

They gave Charles some leftovers, which he accepted with thanks. She and Charles left the men by the fire and went to scope out a possible firing range near the camp.

Sella appeared an hour later. The morning light revealed the scars on his face the night had hidden. Several crisscrossed his forehead, and one lined his neck just below his Adam's apple.

"Had breakfast yet?" he asked.

"Yes. We're ready to begin," Maureen said.

"I'll set up my radio," Charles said, wishing Maureen all the best with a silent look she understood. She nodded back to him.

"I'll gather the men," Sella said.

A few minutes later, more than 200 partisans were gathered in the middle of the camp. The men ranged in age from about 16 to 50, but most were in their 20s. They looked malnourished and dirty, but they were all she had. Many whispered and laughed as she stood up in front of them. She and Sella were standing on the back of an open-top trailer, looking down.

Sella quieted the crowd and began to speak.

"You know me. Some of you have been with me for weeks, but we need support. Almost all of you have been crying out for weapons and training. So, the War Office in London sent this woman to help us." Several men guffawed, and a few made crude gestures in her direction. Sella ignored them. "She will direct your training and supply us with the arms we need to kill Germans, because, after all, isn't that what we're here to do?" The men cheered. "This is Maureen," he said and stood aside.

"I have been sent from London on a mission to...." She trailed off. Many of the men were talking among themselves now. Some were openly jeering at her.

"What can a woman teach us about killing Nazis?" called a man from the back.

Sella went to step forward, but Maureen stretched out her arm to stop him. "How many of you have lost loved ones to the Germans?" she asked.

Nothing. Not one man moved.

"Seriously? None of you? You've had it easy!"

A few hands went up, then a few more.

"I have too. I left this country after four years to learn the skills I needed to take the fight to those Nazi animals. I've been hiding for long enough. But I need your help. And every man here owes me."

"What do we owe you?" one of the men asked.

"Five dead Nazis."

Many in the crowd laughed.

"And I will keep tally. Every man will sign their name on a board and we will mark off the number of kills to their name. When you reach five the debt will be paid."

The crowd was silent now.

"How many of you are ex-soldiers?" About 15 men raised their hands. "Excellent, please stay behind after the others leave. You will be my drill sergeants. We need to make sure every man in this company is able to clean and handle a weapon. I brought two dozen Sten guns—the latest in military equipment to assist in your training. More are coming. Rifles, grenades, mortars, whatever I ask for. I intend to start hitting the Germans hard within a few weeks, but you need to be ready first."

"And what about you?" one of the men sneered. "Where will you be once the fighting starts?"

"Right by your sides. I'll never ask you to do anything I wouldn't myself. We start training this morning. And we will get organized. The tally board will be last. First to kill five Nazis gets a bottle of whiskey or cognac, whatever you please."

The men cheered.

She dismissed the crowd. Only the army veterans stayed. She took them aside and told them about her plans for training the men. Several volunteered to write down the names of the men here and those coming. All were visibly excited about the tally board.

Half an hour later the men were called back. They were ordered to line up. She and Charles set up desks and wrote down the name and hometown of every man there. They also asked what particular skills each man possessed. Some were carpenters or cooks. Some spoke other languages or had been athletes before fleeing to the forest.

Once the names and skills of the men were documented, Maureen and Charles set about dividing them into squads of 12. Brothers and friends were put together, and many of the squad leaders were ex-soldiers.

After each squad spent a longer-than-usual lunch together, Maureen, with the help of the French soldiers, took them to the designated firing range she'd scoped out earlier that day. Three trees served as targets, and soon they began the arduous task of teaching the men to shoot straight. Many of the partisans were arrogant, thinking that because they'd fired a shotgun on their father's farm, they could do the same with a modern assault rifle. They were all wrong.

Their leader arrived later. "Let me show you how it's done," he said.

"Be my guest," Maureen answered. "But how about we have a bet?"

"You want to take me on?"

The men laughed.

"Yeah. How about whoever loses has to clean the guns when we're done?"

"Okay," Sella said with a sly smile.

They stood back ten yards from the target. The men stood back with expectant grins on their faces. "I'm looking forward to this," a fighter beside Maureen said.

"How about we let your esteemed leader shoot first?" Maureen handed him the machine gun and selected the semi-automatic mode. "Ten bullets. Let's see who does best."

Sella plucked the gun from her hand and took aim. He missed the first shot. "Must be faulty," he said to the crowd's amusement. "That's more like it," he said as the next one hit. He didn't miss again. The men cheered as he finished.

"Nine hits!" He handed the gun to Maureen.

"Impressive," she said. "I don't know if I'll be able to equal that!"

The crowd began to jeer her.

"Okay! Okay! Let me shoot and we'll see." She took aim and hit the target in the middle. "Beginners' luck?" she said as she turned to Sella. He returned her grin. She leveled the Sten gun and hit the target with each remaining shot.

"Clean that up for me, will you?" she said, handing him the weapon. The Frenchman burst out laughing and shook her hand.

By the end of that first afternoon, she and her lieutenants had shown each man the basics of firing, loading, and cleaning the Sten guns.

The wooden targets she'd erected on the trees were riddled with bullets. Sella came to her as the last squad left the shooting range.

"I underestimated you," Sella said.

"Occupational hazard," she replied.

"The men took a giant leap forward today."

"Rome wasn't built in a day, and neither was any army, but it's a start. We'll soon have the men paying off their debt to me. I was impressed by their spirit and that's half the battle."

"Have you done anything like this before?" Sella asked.

"This is what I was trained to do. These men will be Nazi killing machines when I'm done with them. Now, you've got a job to do." She smiled and pointed to the Sten guns.

The resistance leader laughed.

Maureen invited half of the squad leaders to dinner, with the rest to join her the next night. She, Sella, Charles, and the ten men sat down together to eat venison and the wild berries the men had gathered.

"The meals are good, but we're going to need a steady supply," Maureen said.

"Perhaps one squad could be dedicated to hunting and gathering food for the rest?" Armand Croix, one of the squad leaders, suggested.

"And other logistics in their spare time," Maureen added. "Not a bad idea. I'll see who volunteers for the job. I'm sure there are plenty of hunters among the group, and enough game in the forest to feed us."

They talked for an hour. Maureen's excitement never wavered. This is what she'd trained for all this time. It had seemed like this day might never come, but now it was here, and it was even more exhilarating than she'd imagined.

Once the sun set and the temperature dropped, Maureen retired to Sella's old tent—now her quarters. The resistance leader had moved his personal items out that afternoon. Being the only woman in the vicinity had certain disadvantages past being stared at all the time. The southwest corner of the camp had been designated as the latrine, but she wasn't about to use it. Her facilities were random spots in the woods she found whenever she felt the urge to go. The trick was finding somewhere she could be alone. Luckily her tent was beside the woods, at the very edge of the camp.

Maureen poked her head out. Darkness had fallen, and most of the men seemed to have retired to bed. The few she could see were huddled around campfires or patrolling with the new Sten guns strapped over their shoulders. Her bladder was about to burst, and she ducked out and ran into the woods. Whatever light the moon had provided vanished, and she was engulfed in black. It took her a few seconds to get used to the dark to the point where she could just about make out where she was walking. *How did I get myself into this?* She thought to herself as she found a likely spot and then squatted to relieve herself. The sound of a stick snapping behind her caused her to stand up and pull up her pants in one movement. She was about to turn around to see what had caused the sound when she felt a hand over her mouth. She tried to scream, but it came as little more than a muffled groan.

"Keep your mouth shut," a ragged voice said in her ear.

The voice wasn't German. That would have been understandable if not forgivable. To her horror, it was French.

The man grabbed her with his other hand, pulling her back into the black void of the forest. Maureen knew no one was coming to save her. Fear gripped her body. She elbowed him in the stomach, but still, he maintained his iron grip on her. She hadn't seen his face but could smell his foul breath.

Her body and mind kicked into action, and she kicked him in the shins, but it didn't seem to have any effect. He had her right arm pinned and had his hand over her mouth. She couldn't scream, and he was dragging her farther from the camp with every step. She bit into the man's hand. He yelled out, and she could taste his blood in her mouth. He stumbled away, cursing the pain. He looked like a demon in the dark, his features blurred in the inky black.

He lunged at her again, and she caught him with a fist to the throat. He raised his hands to cover the spot, making a strange gurgling sound before coming again. She deflected his blow with her forearm before landing another punch in the same spot as before, then dropped to her knees, searching in the dark for something hard. She almost smiled as she felt a round stone about the size of a baseball. She stood up again. Ready.

The man charged her, grabbing her by the throat and forcing her down. He reached into his pocket for a revolver. She brought her arm back to deliver a blow with the rock. She caught him in the side of the head. The gun flew off into the dark forest as he flailed his arms. He howled in pain, stumbling backward, but she wasn't done yet and struck him again. He fell to his knees, his head a bloody mess. Not in the mood to take any chances, she hit him once more. Her assailant collapsed on the forest floor.

His pistol was gone, so she went down on her haunches, trying to peer through the darkness of the trees, searching for some light to lead her back to camp.

Several fraught seconds passed before she saw a twinkle of gold through a chink in the trees. It was a campfire, and she had to walk around her attacker to get to it. The man was stirring a little, but she could see his eyes were still closed. Maureen gave him as wide a berth as she could, keeping her eyes on the spot of light as she went. Only as she walked did she realize her back and arms were hurting from where he'd grabbed her. She hadn't noticed before when the adrenaline was pumping through her veins.

Running through a dark forest could lead to broken ankles or worse, so she trod carefully while maintaining her speed until she broke through the tree line back into the camp. Two men were sitting by a fire—the one she'd seen from the woods. She ran to them.

"Where's Sella?" she asked.

They seemed to recognize she was in distress. "Are you all right, Madame? You look—"

"I need to speak to Sella."

"I saw him by one of the trucks a few minutes ago," the partisan said. He stood up and jogged over with her.

Sella was sitting with two other men.

"I need to speak to you," she said as she reached him.

"Okay," he said and got up.

"I was attacked by one of the men in the woods," she said in front of the other two. "I fought him off but he's still back there on the ground."

"Are you all right?" he asked. She nodded. "Can you show us where he is?" Sella said.

"I think so," she answered.

"Come on," he said to the others with him.

They didn't hesitate, and soon all four were running back to the edge of the camp. The other two men were carrying pistols and drew them as the group entered the forest. Finding her way back to the spot was difficult, and she took several wrong turns in the darkness before finally arriving. But the man was gone.

"This is where it happened?" Sella asked.

"He was right here, I swear," Maureen said.

"There's a little blood on the leaves here," one of Sella's men said from his haunches.

"He must have bolted into the forest," Sella said. "Go back and get a party together. A dozen men at least. All armed. We'll find this degenerate tonight." The two men left before Sella turned to her. "We'll take it from here. This man won't escape justice. I can promise you that."

"I want to come with you," she said.

Sella paused for a second before putting his hands on her shoulders. "Go back to your tent. You've been through enough." She began to protest, but he stopped her with surprising tenderness. "I know you want to prove yourself to the men, but enough's enough. You'll win them over in time, if you haven't already. But tonight, let us do something for you. Let us prove ourselves to you. This isn't a one-way street."

She nodded.

"Go back to your tent."

"No," she said. "I want to find out who this man is. Someone knows."

Word of the attack spread through the camp like fire through a wheat field. Maureen and Charles began questioning the men. It wasn't long before she got the answer she was looking for.

"I think I know him," a young man aged about 20 called Olivier told her. "I share a tent with a man called Giles Bertrand. He's a real talker. Never stops. Goes on about the places he robbed, women he had. Told me he takes them by force if he has to."

Maureen took a deep breath. "You didn't think to tell Sella this?"

"I've only known him a couple of weeks. I didn't know he was telling the truth. He said he thought you were something to look at, but a lot of the men did. I didn't think much of it."

"What do you know about him?"

"He's about 30. From Issoire. Spent some time in jail. That's about it."

"When was the last time you saw him?" Charles asked.

"Not for hours," Olivier said.

"He must have been scoping out your tent, waiting for you to leave," Charles said.

"Thank you, Olivier," she said and stood up.

Sella was gathering a posse of 20 men to hunt her attacker down. Maureen and Charles found them at the edge of the camp.

"His name is Giles Bertrand," she said. She told him everything they knew about him. Several men in the group knew him and concurred with Olivier about what type he was.

"I'm coming with you," Maureen said.

"No. You stay here. This is our territory. This should never have happened. Let us do this for you."

"Okay, good luck." She turned back to the resistance leader after a few steps. "Sella? Make sure your men bring him back alive."

"Of course," he replied.

She and Charles trudged back toward camp.

"Let's get a glass of wine, shall we?" Charles said.

"Sounds good."

They sat down in front of one of the bonfires to drink. Maureen was wary of showing too much emotion. Men were quick to tar women with the brush of being too driven by feelings. So, she talked about discipline and the need to train the troops instead.

Two hours passed with no sign of the 20-strong search party pursuing Bertrand.

"You're tired," Charles said. "You should get off to bed."

"Yeah," she replied.

Maureen didn't want to admit in front of him that she was scared to return alone. Going back to the tent felt like the hardest thing she'd ever done, but she forced one foot in front of the other. She couldn't show any weakness. Her body was taut as a steel wire. She lay down on her cot and closed her eyes but could only see Bertrand's face in the dark. She reached for her gun and curled up into a ball with it in her hand, ready to face the night alone.

After a restless night's sleep, Maureen woke a little after dawn. Her heart was racing, and she dressed and prepared for the day. The camp was quiet as she left the tent. Two men ran past with rifles, stopping as soon as they saw her.

"We heard about last night. We're so sorry," one man said.

Maureen had never spoken to him before and was touched by his kindness.

"We were out with the search party last night," he continued.

"Any sign of the criminal who attacked me?" she asked.

"Not yet, but we were just about to head out again. Some think he might have fled south. A few of the men are on their way toward his farm too. He—"

The partisan was cut off by a ruckus from behind them as a crowd appeared. Another man was stumbling in front of them with his hands bound. Dried blood coated his brown hair, sticking it to his head.

"They got him!" one of the men said.

They probably expected her to smile, so Maureen complied. She forced herself forward.

Sella emerged from the crowd shoving the man onward. Bertrand stumbled onto the ground. The closer Maureen got, the more she was able to make out his bruised and swollen face.

Everyone in the camp seemed to run over, and Maureen had to push through the throng to reach the front. Sella saw her and picked up Bertrand. Her attacker looked away, refusing to make eye contact with her.

"He fired on us, when we caught him," Sella said. "One of the men took a bullet in the leg. Is this the man who followed you into the woods last night and tried to assault you?"

Sella picked up Bertrand's chin. "Look at her!" he ordered.

Her attacker brought his dark eyes to hers.

She nodded. "That's him," she said in the loudest voice she could muster. The crowd roared.

"Have you anything to say for yourself?" Sella asked him. The man said nothing, averting his eyes once more.

Sella commanded the attention of every person there. "Every man present listen up and listen well. Any attack on one of us is an attack on the group as a whole and will not be tolerated. He also fired upon us when we pursued him. Sentence must be carried out."

The crowd cheered. Several men nodded and patted her on the shoulder. It felt good.

Sella shifted the rabble of partisans watching and dragged Bertrand to the flatbed truck he and Maureen had spoken from the previous night. Two other men helped him push her assailant up onto the platform. Bertrand fell to his knees, glaring at the crowd forming before him. Maureen was just a few feet away, and Sella kneeled down to her. He had a revolver in his hand and pushed it into hers.

"Time to show the men what you're made of," he whispered.

She looked at the gun and then into Sella's eyes. Several

men nudged her, whispering that she should do it. She had to be stronger than any man sent to lead them. If she showed any sign of weakness, she'd lose them. Maureen took the pistol and stepped up onto the platform. She looked out at the crowd and then at the man who'd attacked her. The gun felt heavy in her hand. Charles pushed his way to the front, but only as a mark of support. He didn't say anything to stop her. Bertrand looked up at her with a snarl. Sella nodded. She held the gun to the partisan's head and pulled the trigger.

11

Wednesday, May 19, 1943

The training was progressing well. The men were now proficient with small arms, grenades, and even mortars. The powers in London had been as good as their word and provided the partisans in the Auvergne with all the weapons and supplies they needed. Maureen and the two French army veterans she had installed as her lieutenants, Chirac and Clerc, had taught the ever-swelling numbers of men under her command how to use all of it. The only difference between her troops, the men of the Golden Horde, as they called themselves, and the average German soldier was that the Nazis had air support, artillery, and tanks to call upon. But the depths of the forest negated those advantages. Here, her men were equal to any enemy they faced. Charles was in regular contact with the War Office, and her superiors were happy, but Maureen knew the time had come to step up their operations. The tally board of dead German soldiers was still blank. It wasn't the men who were reticent, however. Maureen knew the blame lay at her door. She wanted to wait until she was sure they were ready. She'd lived with these men for two months now. They tipped their hats to her as they passed her in camp and referred to her as "the governess" behind her back, and "Madame Maureen" to her face. She was happy with either name.

The recruits were as ready as they would ever be. The real question was whether she was ready to risk their lives. They hadn't lost a man yet, but she knew that would all change when the proper operations began. Many of the soldiers she'd trained would die, but she had to let that go. This was war. She had to focus on the mission—to create havoc behind the German lines and open the way for the invasion to liberate France.

Sella was outside his tent, drinking wine and eating some bread and cheese with Chirac and Clerc. The three men looked up as she walked over.

"It's time," she said, pulling up a crate.

"For what?" Sella asked.

"For us to put our training to work," she answered.

The men nodded.

"Have you anything in mind?" Clerc answered. He was 30 and was tall with muscular shoulders and brown eyes. He was from Lyon and had been a Captain in the French Army before it was disbanded after the German invasion. Chirac was smaller and wore a full beard. He had been a sergeant but had excelled in training the men. The two men were involved in most of the planning now.

Maureen poured herself a glass of wine. "I've been in contact with London about this for the past several weeks. The German 92nd Infantry Division was deployed in this area last month. Based in Clermont-Ferrand."

"My home city," Chirac said. "I got a letter from my mother last week. They're making their presence felt."

"The general in charge of them, Erich Halder, is a veteran of the eastern front. His division got a pummeling in Russia on the way to the Caucuses and were sent here to reform," Maureen said.

"And to take care of the likes of us," Sella said.

"No doubt." She took a sip of wine. "It seems our friend, Herr Halder, has made himself at home in Clermont. He has a regular routine. London wants us to send a message."

"You want to hit this general?" Sella said. "Who do you have in mind for the job?"

"Well, me for one..."

"Count me in," said Chirac immediately.

She smiled before continuing. "Then we'll need three more."

"I'd like to," Clerc said.

"So, two more," Maureen said.

"Me also..." Sella offered.

Maureen shook her head. "No, I don't want to involve our entire leadership in case something goes wrong. Maybe the next operation."

Sella nodded, but the look on his face didn't mask his disappointment.

"So, how do we do this?" asked Chirac.

"Halder goes for lunch in one of two or three places every day. His driver waits outside in an open top car to take him back to his house afterward."

"So, we watch the various cafés, and set up outside and wait," Chirac said.

"Sounds easy, doesn't it?" Maureen said. "It won't be. The town is crawling with Wehrmacht. We'll need to plan it out in intricate detail if we don't want it to end up as a suicide mission."

"When are you planning on carrying this out?" Clerc asked.

"I think we should be ready in a week or two," she replied. "I'll visit my contacts in the city in a few days to set things up."

"I'll go with you," Chirac said. "I know the place."

"Why are we even contemplating this?" Sella asked. "It seems like a massive risk for little reward."

"We're here to unsettle the Germans," Maureen said. "Assassinating such a high-ranking officer would do just that."

"And bring an ocean of unwanted attention to our band of inexperienced fighters," Sella countered.

Maureen could see the older man's point, but London wanted this done, and orders were orders. She countered with the best argument she could think of because the War Office didn't explain their intentions, just demanded results.

"Our men are guerilla fighters, yes?" Maureen asked. "You agree that we can't engage with the enemy on their own terms on open ground?" All three men nodded. "The Germans either don't know or don't care about us at the moment. They aren't coming into the forest. We haven't fought the Nazis on our terms yet. This operation will give us a chance to do exactly that."

"With all due respect, I don't understand," Chirac said. "We're not assassins and certainly didn't train the men for urban combat."

"What will happen once we kill Halder?" Maureen asked.

"The Germans will hunt us down," Sella said. Maureen could see the realization hitting him. "And they'll come into the forest."

"But they won't have their tanks or their air support. And our squads will have already been deployed and will pick them off like grouse." Maureen smiled and looked at each of the men in turn. "This is our chance to start affecting the war."

"What about retribution?" Sella asked. "Against the civilian population?"

Maureen paused before answering. "I've thought of that many times. That's beyond our control." She remembered seeing her friend Gerhard shot down on the street in Lyon. "But we can't let their terror tactics stop us from defeating them. We all know who our enemy is. The Nazis are savage beasts."

"Easy for you to say when your family is safe on the other side of the ocean," Sella said.

Maureen controlled the flash of anger she felt. "You don't think I've lost people?" she said.

"Yes, her family is in America, but she's here," Chirac said. "Maureen could be safe thousands of miles away, yet she's in the forest with us."

"I'm not questioning her commitment, just her tactics," Sella said.

Maureen resisted the temptation to tell these men that this wasn't her plan and that it had come from the men in London who only knew the situation on the ground here from what she told them. Telling them that would have only engendered suspicion toward her superiors. The Anglo-French alliance wasn't a natural fit. The two powers had been enemies for hundreds of years before the signing of the *Entente Cordiale* in 1904, and their disparate cultures didn't make for easy bedfellows. The last thing Maureen needed was the men of the Golden Horde questioning London's authority.

After the discussion was over, Maureen issued the orders. "We'll let the troops know the camp is being dissolved in the next few days, and the various squads will go their separate ways. We'll give each one their own territories within the forest. They're ready. And when the fight comes over the next few weeks that tally board will move faster than we'll be able to keep up with."

∽

Thursday, June 3, 1943

Maureen and her hand-picked squad of assassins had been in the small industrial city of Clermont-Ferrand for several days. The need for secrecy had prevented her from telling all the men what they were planning and made finding the last two volunteers for the mission harder, but Chirac had recruited two soldiers from his own squad to make up the numbers. They were young, excellent soldiers, and loyal—exactly what Maureen wanted. The men they'd left behind had been sent out into the forests to wait for the Germans to pursue them. Each squad had been dispatched to different regions of the Auvergne, including the volcanic area, a popular tourist spot before the war. None were too far away from the base camp she'd established in the woods, and all had been ordered to report back periodically to update her on their progress or to rearm.

Their safe house was outside the village of Nohanent, a few miles from the city center. It was run by a childhood friend of Chirac's who had tried to move to Paris before the war to become a writer and had only returned to the farm to look after his ailing mother before France became segmented. His name was Theo, and he brought Maureen and her four comrades a carafe of wine as they sat at his kitchen table, poring over a map of the city. Chirac and Clerc were puffing on cigarettes, the grey smoke swirling over their heads. The two new men, Danty and Barlot, stuck to wine instead. Both were from Clermont-Ferrand. Maureen didn't-ask them their ages, neither looked older than 21, but Chirac had confidence in them, and that was good enough for her.

They were sitting at the kitchen table in the modest house when Maureen asked the question.

"Are we all ready for this?" Each man nodded. "Does anyone have any doubts? Any questions?" No one spoke.

They had spent each of the last four days in the city studying General Erich Halder's habits. He favored three cafés in Clermont-Ferrand for lunch and alternated seemingly on however the wind blew that day. Other things he did were more predictable. He never dined alone, always with his driver and one other man—a lackey from his staff. The three men were armed at all times and when they left, they returned directly to the military headquarters Halder had set up in the town hall in the open-top Mercedes the Wehrmacht had supplied. All questions of the merits of the mission had long since been dismissed. The only focus now was on killing Halder and getting out alive. No one wanted to die on the streets of Clermont-Ferrand.

"We'll split up into three groups. The three cafés are here, here, and here," he said, pointing to a map."

"One of us is going to be alone?" Barlot said.

"Yes, but not far from the others," Chirac said. "Café Central and Café Luigi on Rue Lagarlaye are so close that if we post one person to watch them he can walk over and warn the other two scoping out the other one. Café Annique on Rue Lecoq is farther away. If Halder goes there, the two watching will likely be on their own."

"He takes lunch at noon, usually arriving a few minutes after. He and his men usually take a seat outside, but sometimes by the window," Maureen said. "The question is do we take them while they're at lunch or in the car?"

"I say we take them in the Mercedes as they leave. Too much risk of hitting innocent civilians eating their lunch if we start spraying bullets at the café," Clerc said. "We're going to have to take all three of them out, and I'm not leaving anything to chance. I plan on emptying my ammunition clip into them."

"I agree, for that reason and others," Maureen said. "We don't want some young couple who've saved up their ration cards for a quiet lunch together getting in the crossfire. And if we hit them in the car, we can use our grenades."

"We throw them into a moving car?" Chirac said. "That would be quite a shot."

"Less so if the car's stationary," Maureen answered. "If we roll a grenade underneath, Halder and his men won't stand a chance."

"What about the other Wehrmacht presence in the city?" Clerc asked. "We've all seen German soldiers strolling around. They're all armed and won't take kindly to us blowing up their leader."

"I'll abort the mission if it's too dangerous and you all need to be prepared to do the same. If a platoon of German soldiers walks around the corner, just leave your guns in your pockets and get out of there."

Clerc stubbed out his cigarette. "Did you hear that, boys?" he said to Danty and Barlot. "This isn't a suicide mission. If the odds are against us, we retreat and live to fight another day."

Both of the younger men nodded.

Theo returned to the table with more wine. Maureen put her hand over her glass. She wanted to have a clear head for the next day. She almost said something as the other four men signaled for their host to fill their glasses but decided to keep her comments to herself. She leaned forward after Theo walked away. "Clerc, you watch Café Central. Danty and I will watch Café Luigi, and Chirac and Barlot will take Café Annique on Rue Lecoq. The general and his men usually dine for about an hour, so no matter where he shows up, we'll have time to get the others."

"What do we do when he emerges?" Danty said.

"Two men will sit in the café itself," Maureen said. "Two others will wait on the corner, and I'll be having a romantic liaison with one of the other men on the street opposite."

"Now you're talking!" Danty said with a wide grin.

Maureen shook her head and smiled. "Don't get any ideas, kid!" The other men laughed before she continued. "When they come out, we surround him from the side and the front and let him have it with our Sten guns and grenades."

The men sat back. The quiet determination and nervous tension were plain to see in each of their faces. Maureen just hoped they couldn't see how terrified she was. She retired to bed in Theo's hayloft a few minutes later. She was still awake as the men entered the barn almost two hours after. Soon, they were all asleep, snoring in the cots below her. She was alone above them. Always alone. She thought about Christophe as she lay there as she always did in moments like these. Dark thoughts that she'd never see him again appeared in her mind until she eventually succumbed to sleep.

12

Friday, June 4, 1943

The assassins cycled into the city two hours before Halder and his men went to lunch. Maureen had inspected each of the bikes before her men took them. They would be their only transportation, and a loose chain or a flat tire might cost a life. With so many German troops around, there was little room for error. Maureen wondered about the men on the journey into the city. Would any of them panic and freeze when the time came to kill the general and his staff? There was really no way of knowing, not until the moment came. She had confidence in her men but had never been in battle with them before. She had killed before when the need arose and knew that her training would kick in when she needed it most, but niggling doubts about her men, particularly the younger soldiers, Danty and Barlot, gnawed at her consciousness.

The French police who checked their papers on the outskirts of town didn't search them, just cast lazy glances over the fake documents Christophe had made before handing them back. Full searches were rare due to the sheer number of people passing through the checkpoints each day, but Maureen still breathed a massive sigh of relief as they left the checkpoint behind and entered the city.

They cycled into the city and to the safe house, an empty apartment Theo kept for sojourns with his various mistresses. The weapons were stowed there, hidden in a closet. They armed themselves with Sten guns and grenades before making their way back downstairs with the weapons hidden under their clothes. They split up without a word. Maureen and the other two men cycled ahead while Chirac and Barlot biked across the city to watch Café Annique on Rue Lecoq.

Two German soldiers sitting outside a café sent shivers up her spine as she cycled past them. But they were soon left behind. Clermont-Ferrand wasn't exactly crawling with Wehrmacht, but they were around, particularly if you looked for them. Fading into the crowd after the assassination would be key to surviving this day. The thought that this was all insane and that they should just turn around and return to the forest where they were masters of their domain flashed across her mind, but she pushed it aside. She didn't have time for that. Not now. It was too late for doubts.

Clerc offered a subtle wave before he sped away, leaving her alone with Danty. They parked their bikes and looked around for somewhere to wait. Café Luigi was 25 yards away, across the street. The traffic was almost exclusively bikes and some horse-drawn carts. No German soldiers were visible, and only a few people walked by. She and Danty ambled across to take a seat at a table outside Luigi's. Waiting anywhere else would have looked suspicious. They ordered weak coffee. It was more like muddy water.

Clerc was sitting outside the Café Central, sipping red wine in the dull spring sunshine. Maureen was glad it wasn't too hot.

The coat she wore to conceal her Sten gun would have left her sweltering on a hot day.

Danty was a handsome boy with blue eyes and a tanned face. Maureen tried to chat with him, to calm his nerves and to make it seem more natural, but the young man didn't offer more than one word responses to any question she asked. She gave up after a few minutes.

Though she tried not to, she couldn't help but look at her watch every few seconds. After what seemed like days of sitting outside the café, noon came, and she gestured to her comrade to get up. They stood and strolled across to a bench on the other side of the road. Maureen put her arm around the younger man. He calmed. All communication between them was as if they were lovers.

A few minutes later, two Wehrmacht troops appeared around the corner, carrying sidearms.

"What are they doing here?" Danty whispered in her ear.

"It might be nothing... Let's just see." She watched the two off-duty soldiers as they walked into a barber shop. "Just a haircut, then." She looked at her watch. It was 12:05. The café was half full of lunchtime patrons now. "Maybe Halder went somewhere else today."

"I don't think so," Danty jerked his chin towards the street.

The general's Mercedes convertible had just pulled up outside.

The driver got out and walked around to open the door for Halder and the other men riding with him. Maureen could hear them chatting in German as they stepped onto the pavement. They were talking about ski season in Austria. They took a table outside Luigi's between two other crowded tables. Maureen assessed the crowd, wondering whether to abort the mission or not. The two other Wehrmacht soldiers were still inside the barbershop, three doors down from the café. If they came out at the wrong time, things could get hairy.

"I see our friends have arrived," Clerc whispered as he stood behind the bench. Neither of them looked back.

"We could have a problem," Maureen said and explained to him about the troops getting their hair cut.

"Okay," Clerc responded.

"Go get Chirac and Barlot," Maureen said. "If the soldiers are still inside when the general gets back in his car, we'll have them stand outside to take them out while we kill Halder and the others."

"You make it sound so easy," Danty said.

"Why isn't it?" Clerc replied. "Three will be more than enough to take out the Mercedes, and the other two can run security."

"Then we drop the weapons, fade into the crowd and meet back at the apartment," Danty said.

"Exactly," Clerc said.

Maureen nodded. "Okay, head over to Café Annique for the others. You should be there and back in less than 20 minutes," she said.

Clerc nodded and left.

"Go over and check the barbershop," she said to Danty. "Walk around the block and come back to me."

The young partisan did as he was ordered and returned just as Clerc arrived with the other two men. Suddenly, Maureen felt very conspicuous. They pretended like they were friends and greeted each other with kisses. She looked at her watch. It was almost one o'clock.

"The two soldiers are still in the barbershop," Danty said.

At the café, the general raised a finger to the waiter, who returned a few seconds later with the bill. Maureen had only seconds to make the decision. "Where are your bikes?" she asked Chirac and Barlot.

"Ten yards away," Chirac answered.

"Near that barbershop?" Maureen asked. The man nodded.

"Okay, two Wehrmacht soldiers are in there. As soon as they hear anything they're going to run out. When they do, let them have it, all right?"

"Got it," Chirac said.

He gestured to the younger man. They crossed the street together and walked past the café toward the barbershop.

Maureen watched them for a few seconds as they stopped outside the barbershop. Chirac reached into his pocket for a pack of cigarettes, taking the maximum amount of time to draw it out. Then Barlot began to hunt through his coat for matches. She wondered if the young man was making too much of a show of not being able to find them as the waiter returned to the general and his men outside Luigi's. Halder took his change and deposited it into his wallet before standing up with the other two men. Maureen's breath quickened.

"You ready?" she whispered to Clerc and Danty. Neither answered, but she looked at them both and was reassured. "We take them in the car as they get in. Once they're dead, we get on our bikes and meet back at the safe house."

The driver left first and walked to the green Mercedes with Nazi flags above each headlight. He opened the back door as the Nazi general and the other man sauntered over.

"Now," Maureen whispered.

She walked away from the bench, 30 yards away from the car. The two men were on either side of her. Danty paced ahead to take his place on the pavement. The driver looked up. Maureen smiled at him, and he brought his eyes back to the general, who was in the car now alongside the other German officer. Maureen's heart was pumping adrenaline through her body, electrifying her veins.

Danty was on the pavement, and Clerc stopped to take his firing position. The driver walked back around as if in slow motion. He opened the door and climbed in.

Something caught the periphery of Maureen's eye, and she

looked over at the barbershop. The door opened, and the two Wehrmacht soldiers emerged. Chirac threw down the cigarette in his hand and reached under his coat. He drew the Sten gun as the German soldiers stood transfixed, but it jammed. Halder looked around as the two soldiers reached for their sidearms. Barlot drew his, but the German soldiers beat him to it and fired, hitting him in the arm. Then Chirac went down, his chest bloody red. The other citizens on the street ran for their lives.

"Drive!" Halder shouted as Maureen stepped into the middle of the road. She raised her weapon and opened fire. Her bullets tore into the Mercedes, smashing the windscreen. Clerc was firing too, riddling the car.

Barlot fell back, firing and hitting one of the German soldiers. The barbershop window shattered. Danty fired at the other soldier and dumped him on the pavement like a ragdoll. Maureen was still shooting. A bullet struck the driver in the face, and he slumped over the wheel. The car came to a halt in the middle of the street, 20 feet from where she was standing. She caught sight of the general, but her gun clicked—out of bullets! Cursing, she reached into her coat for another clip.

Halder stood up, aiming his pistol at Barlot. He fired, and the resistance man fell to the pavement beside Chirac. Clerc reached into his pocket and took out a grenade. He pulled the pin and rolled it under the car just as the general and the other officer jumped out. The blast threw them forward onto the pavement, and Danty followed.

Maureen reloaded. She couldn't see Halder and the other man, but another shot rang out, and Danty collapsed to the pavement. She ran to the front of the car and opened fire. Clerc tossed another grenade, but it bounced off the Mercedes and exploded harmlessly a few feet away.

She knew they had only seconds now. The general was hiding behind the car. She had no idea how badly wounded he was, if at all. She looked over at Clerc. Halder raised himself up and fired. The bullet missed Clerc, but he had to hide behind a thick iron lamppost.

Maureen fell to the street and looked under the car. Seeing the Germans crouched down, she leveled her Sten gun inches off the ground and fired. The bullets connected with shins and knees and brought screams of pain. Seeing her chance, she leaped up and ran around the car. Halder and the other man were sprawled on the pavement, blood running from their lower legs but otherwise unhurt. Halder was on his back and caught eyes with her. She just had time to recognize the terror on his face as she aimed her weapon at him. He tried to raise his pistol to fire at her, but she was too fast and stitched three rounds across his chest. Clerc arrived behind them and put a bullet in the other man's head. The two Nazi officers were still, eyes open. Maureen ran to Danty but recognized that he was gone before she reached him. Clerc checked the other two men.

"Chirac's still alive," he said and helped their friend to his feet. His chest was stained crimson.

"I can make it," he gasped hoarsely.

Maureen hustled him along. "We have to get out of here right now,"

The bikes were ten yards away, but Chirac couldn't ride one, and the safe house was 20 minutes away on foot. A truck rolled around the corner. Maureen held up her gun, aiming it at the driver.

"Get out!" she roared.

The man, who seemed to be a delivery driver, put up his hands, whimpering as he climbed out.

"Get Chirac inside!" Maureen ordered.

Clerc walked him to the passenger seat and helped him in. Maureen was about to join them when she spotted three German soldiers running toward them. They stopped to take firing positions about 50 yards away. Maureen beat them to it, sending a hail of bullets in their direction, hitting one man and scattering the other two.

Clerc was behind the wheel of the truck now. Maureen couldn't believe their luck. They'd only seen about five commercial vehicles on the street all morning. Clerc backed up and turned around. The German soldiers were still firing as they drove off, and Maureen could hear the sound of their bullets hitting the back of the lorry. But they made it around the corner.

"We're going to be pretty conspicuous in this thing," Clerc said.

"Stop outside the safe house and get Chirac inside," she said. "I'll get rid of the truck."

Two minutes later, they arrived outside the safe house. People on the street saw the two men get out. Maureen shook her head. If someone talked, the safe house would be anything but that. Several civilians had seen them stumble inside, but this wasn't a city or an area where the Germans meshed easily with the population. Collaborators here were treated with extreme prejudice. She'd seen several hanged. Maureen was confident no one would give them up to the invaders.

She drove up the road and around the corner, dumping the lorry off a few blocks away. She hid her Sten gun under her coat and jumped out. No one on the street seemed to pay her any more attention than she was used to, and the only sign of the Nazis was their ubiquitous flags flying from several buildings.

Taking a moment to steady herself and slow her breath, Maureen jogged in the wrong direction before doubling back. The sound of an emergency klaxon sounded over the city. She moved faster. The Nazis would come looking for them soon, but how could they move with a wounded man? She could have walked away, dumped her weapons, and left the city, but she didn't. Maureen returned to the apartment block she'd left her comrades in and opened the door. A truck packed with German soldiers flew past as she walked inside.

She ran up the stairs, pausing to clean off spots of blood as she went. The apartment was on the second floor of the three-story building.

She knocked, and Clerc answered.

Chirac was on the couch.

"How bad is he?"

"I can make it," Chirac said. "I think the bullet just passed through the flesh."

He pointed to his side. He might have been right. The bullet hole was at the bottom of his ribs on the right side. If it hadn't hit any major organs, he might just live through this.

"You're going to need a doctor, and soon," she said. "You're from here aren't you – do you know anyone?" she asked him.

"My best friend's father is a doctor…"

"Who is he? Can we trust him?"

"His name is Dr. Emile Rives. He runs his practice from his office in the city. It's the best I can do. Mention my name. He's a patriot. He'll help…"

"How far away is he?"

"About ten minutes away on foot. Give me the map, I'll mark it…."

Maureen looked at Clerc. "Did you hear the klaxon sounding?"

"I think everyone in Clermont-Ferrand must have."

"Don't open the door to anyone but me, and if the Germans do come…." She trailed off and gestured toward the machine gun on the coffee table.

"They won't take us alive," Clerc promised.

～

The city wasn't in lockdown yet, but she knew getting out would be harder with every hour they remained. The original plan was out the window now. Maureen kept her head down as she paced through the streets. Another truck full of German soldiers zoomed past. They seemed to be going to Rue Lagarlaye, where their general had been shot. Speed was paramount. If they were to escape, it would have to be in the next few hours. Once the Wehrmacht locked the city down, escape would be nearly impossible, and they might have to hide for days in that apartment. The soldiers would come knocking soon enough.

People were still on the streets going about their business, but the atmosphere around the place was unmistakable. A sense of foreboding seemed to hang in the air.

As she reached the clinic address, Maureen looked at her watch before she went inside. It was just after two in the afternoon. It had only been an hour since they shot the general, but everything seemed changed. She opened the door to the doctor's office. The middle-aged woman at the desk greeted her with a polite turn of phrase.

"I need to see the doctor immediately," Maureen said in a low voice, stepping up to the desk.

"You need an appointment—"

"It's life or death and you're wasting my time." There were two doors off the waiting room, which was full of patients, and she opened one, then the other, as the receptionist chased after her, protesting.

Inside the second room, the doctor had his stethoscope pressed to the thin chest of an elderly man. He looked around in surprise.

"What's the meaning of this? I have a patient with me."

"I tried to stop her, Doctor Rives..."

Maureen shut the door behind her, cutting off the receptionist's voice. "Can I speak to you for a few seconds, Doctor?"

"Who are you? Get out of my office!"

"Daniel Chirac sent me. He's in desperate need of your help," she said. She made sure her words were crisp and even. Acting like an insane person wouldn't help her cause.

"You can't just barge in here like this," the doctor said, though his tone was much softer now.

"Please. I'm begging you. Daniel needs help. I can't go to anyone else."

Doctor Rives, a stout man in his late fifties, brought his hand to his face, rubbing his black beard.

"It's life or death," Maureen repeated.

"Give me a moment, please."

She stepped outside the office again. The waiting patients were all agog, and the receptionist was standing with her hands on her hips, with a face like thunder. Two minutes later, the patient who'd been with the doctor left, tipping his hat to Maureen as he went. Dr. Rives called her inside.

"Daniel's been shot," Maureen said. Time was of the essence. "I don't know how bad it is."

"Can't you take him to the hospital?"

"The Nazis will finish the job if we do, but not before they torture him first."

Dr. Rives looked at her for a few seconds as if evaluating what to do next. "I suppose I should get my bag."

"Please do."

He picked up a black leather briefcase before taking a moment to explain to the people in the waiting room that he had an emergency situation.

"I don't have a car. Not anymore," he said as they reached the street. "Just a bike."

"Do you have one for me?" she asked.

"You can take my receptionist's."

Maureen took the lead as they cycled across the city. More and more German troops were gathering. The door-to-door search would begin soon. They reached the apartment block within five minutes. Maureen made sure to bring the bikes inside, figuring having one might come in handy later. She ran up the stairs with the doctor behind her.

"Dr. Rives," Chirac said as they entered. "It's been too long."

"I was hoping to see you in rather better circumstances than this," Rives said. He got down on his knees beside the couch and examined the wound. Chirac was drinking wine from a bottle. "It's for the pain," he said to Maureen as he tried to smile.

"You're a lucky man, Daniel," the doctor said.

"I don't feel too lucky right at this moment," Chirac replied.

"The bullet passed through. You're going to need blood, fluids and plenty of rest—after I stitch you up."

"He's not going to be able to rest," Clerc said. "We need to get out of Clermont-Ferrand tonight."

"I thought you might say something like that," the doctor sighed.

"I'm blood type O." Maureen started rolling up her sleeve.

"Good, because he'll die without a transfusion. He's lost a lot of blood already."

The couch was soaked red, and a pile of bloody sheets and towels sat on the coffee table.

"Give me a few minutes before we attempt anything together. Do you two mind stepping into the kitchen?" the doctor asked.

Maureen followed Clerc. She turned to him once they were alone. "We need to get out in the next hour or two or we won't make it at all. The Germans are going to start bashing down doors soon. They won't stop until they find us."

"I know but moving Chirac might kill him."

"Not moving him might kill us all," she countered. "So, how do we get out of here?" she asked. "We can't exactly stroll out onto the sidewalk."

"Come with me," the partisan said.

He led her out to the stairwell and shut the door behind him.

"I checked things out while you were gone getting the doctor," he said.

They hurried up to the top floor. Two closed apartment doors stood next to one that led to the roof. Clerc opened it onto the flat roof. Several lawn chairs sat on the paved surface. Maureen walked over to the parapet. The rooftops were so close they were practically touching. She stepped onto the neighboring parapet and ran across the next roof. She was able to travel several hundred yards before the block ended. A fire escape led down to the ground.

"So, what do we do once we reach the end of the block? We're still in the city."

"The roofs will get us clear of this block once the Nazis come knocking. It's up to us to walk the rest of the way back to the safe house in Nohanent."

"How far is it?"

"On foot? About an hour, but much of it is through parks and the countryside. Once we're over the roofs we don't have much of the city center still to cross."

"But we'll have a wounded man with us," she said. Clerc didn't seem to have any answers to that problem, so she took a few seconds to think. "Let me talk to the doctor once he's done with Chirac," she said. "We might just be able to find a way out of this."

They walked back across to their apartment building and back down the stairs. Dr. Rives was stitching up Chirac's wound when they arrived.

"It's quite clean," the doctor said. "Hopefully we can avoid infection."

A few minutes later, Dr. Rives set up the blood transfusion, and soon Maureen's blood was flowing into a bag he'd brought for the occasion. Once it was full, Maureen went to the window. Relieved to see the searches hadn't begun on their street yet, she turned to the doctor.

"When can we move him?"

The doctor's pained expression told her all she needed to know. "We have to get out now," she continued. "Can you get a wheelchair for him?"

"For Daniel?"

"Do you have a better idea for how we move him?"

The doctor shook his head. "I have one in my office. I'll go back and get it once the transfusion is done."

Maureen went to the window. A Nazi truck pulled up at the end of the block, and a dozen combat-ready soldiers jumped out. She whirled around.

"How long until we can move?" she asked. "We have company. They'll probably be at the door in about five minutes."

Maureen's blood was running down the tube into Chirac's arm, but he looked no better.

"It'll be a few minutes at least," Rives replied.

"Can we deal with it from here?" she asked.

"I suppose," the doctor answered. "As long as you keep the bag elevated."

"I'm on it," Clerc said. He took the bag and stood over Chirac.

Maureen went to the doctor. "Leave now and get the wheelchair. Don't come back to the apartment." She pulled a map out of her pocket. "Can you meet us here in about an hour?" she said, pointing to a spot at the edge of a park that led to the outskirts of town.

"How are you going to get Daniel there?" the doctor asked.

"Leave that to us," she answered. "Get going before the Germans smash the door down. You might still be able to slip past them if you go now."

They still hadn't explained how or why Chirac had been shot, but the medical man knew not to ask questions.

"All right," Rives said. He went back to Chirac and took his hand, wishing him well. The partisan thanked him with a smile, and the doctor left. Maureen watched from the window as he walked out the front door to the pavement. He hurried away without being too conspicuous. The German soldiers were on the other side of the street, knocking on doors, harassing the people who answered before charging inside.

"Patch him up," Maureen said. "We're out of here in two minutes." She ran over and picked up the bloody sheets and towels before hiding them inside a suitcase in one of the bedroom closets. She went back for the stained rug and rolled it up, stowing it in the same closet. Chirac was sitting up as she came back. He was pale as fresh milk but ready to move.

"Get him up to the roof and wait for me," she ordered Clerc.

He nodded without speaking and lifted his friend off the couch. The fresh bandages the doctor had left to apply to Chirac were already stained with his blood. Maureen knew even if they did get him out of the city he wasn't guaranteed to survive. If they left him here, the Nazis would torture him to death. So, that was no choice at all.

Clerc staggered through the door with Chirac, taking most of the wounded man's weight over his shoulders. Maureen was alone. She turned over the couch cushions and covered them with a clean blanket from the closet. She looked around the apartment for anything incriminating. It was surprisingly clean, although anything more than a cursory glance would no doubt reveal what she hadn't been able to clean up in the short time she had. The men had brought the guns with them. Satisfied that she'd done everything she could in the limited time she had, Maureen ran out, locking the door behind her.

The men were already on the roof as she emerged. The sun had come out, and it was warm now.

"We're moving. Let's go," she said. She got on one side of Chirac with Clerc on the other, and they continued toward the next building. The gap between the two apartment blocks was only a few feet, but Chirac wasn't in any condition to jump. A wooden plank served as a bridge, and they shuffled across.

Maureen went last, picking up the plank for the next gap. She ran ahead to place it and returned to help the other two men. Before reaching them, she ran to the edge of the building and looked down—the Wehrmacht combat troops were entering the apartment block they'd just fled.

"We need to pick up the pace," she said. "The German soldiers will be on our tail in about two minutes."

The two men shuffled along faster in response. Maureen ran back and helped with Chirac. Five exhausting minutes later, they reached the last building at the end of the block. Maureen knew they had only seconds now and just hoped no Germans were waiting for them on the street below. She peeked over the edge—it was clear.

"They haven't made it this far yet," she said. "Down we go."

Walking down the steps was more demanding than on the flat surface of the roofs, particularly with how tired they were now, but they put one foot in front of the other. Chirac never said a word, though he must have been in severe pain.

Maureen looked back just as they descended the first few steps and saw the Germans emerging onto the roof.

"We need to go! They're coming," she said.

They quickened the pace and made it to the street, where they were greeted by the stares of several amazed onlookers.

"It's about three blocks to the park where the doctor is leaving the wheelchair," Clerc said. "How do we get there?"

"Walk! How else?"

They struggled on, hoping against hope not to run into any Germans. But they were on the outskirts of the city now, in an old working-class area dotted with tiny houses. The Germans were too busy searching the city center to make it out here—for now, at least. Every muscle in Maureen's body was screaming as they reached the park, but the doctor was standing there with the wheelchair, just as he'd promised.

Chirac was weak and slumped into the chair. "He needs to rest," Dr. Rives said.

"We can't," Maureen replied.

"That wheelchair will only take you so far through the park," the doctor said.

"He's right. It's more a patch of wild land walled off than a city park," Clerc said. "The paved road ends halfway through."

"Then we'll carry him the rest of the way," Maureen said. "If we stop now we're dead."

"Some of my patients live around here," Dr. Rives said. "Good patriots who might hide you."

"For how long?" Maureen asked. "Hours? Days?" The Nazis are going to swarm this area like angry bees. Our only chance to stay alive is to get out now."

"She's right," Chirac said. His voice was hollow and weak. "We go now, or else we all die."

The distant sound of a klaxon reinforced his words. The doctor bent down and hugged him.

"Travel safe, Daniel. Come see us again when you're better."

Chirac smiled and hugged the older man.

"Thank you for everything," Maureen said.

"Get going. The Germans will be here soon."

Clerc pushed the wheelchair into the park. It was deserted. The whole area was. Everyone seemed to be bracing for the Nazi backlash.

The paved area of the park gave way to a bumpy dirt trail. After a few minutes of pushing Chirac over the smoothest parts they could find, Maureen admitted defeat. They folded up the wheelchair and hid it behind a tree.

"I'll come back for it later," Clerc said as they each put an arm across Chirac's shoulders. Soon, the trail ended, and they were back in the woods.

"Thank you," Chirac said as the sun began to fade.

"Thank me by filling out that tally chart when we get back to camp. The Germans aren't going to forget today in a hurry."

After another hour of struggle, the safe house finally came into view. Somehow, Chirac was still alive and just about able to walk. They burst through the door without knocking. Theo, the poet who owned the farm, ran to help them as Chirac collapsed on the floor. Maureen stood back as the two men lifted Chirac and moved him to a bed upstairs. She walked over to the couch and flopped onto it, unable to get up even to quench the raging thirst in her throat.

13

Tuesday, November 28, 2006

Holding Marie was the single greatest pleasure Amy had ever experienced. Nothing could have been more beautiful or perfect than her sweet little girl. Amy couldn't help the tears as her baby looked up at her. Marie loved her milk and was putting on weight at last—several ounces in the previous few days. Her strength was growing all the time. Amy's mind cast her far into the future to crawling, walking, and even the first days of school. The longing she felt for what most people considered banal was like nothing she'd ever known.

"So you want to hold her?" she asked Maureen.

"Always." She smiled as she cradled Marie in her lap. "I can't believe how much she looks like your mother."

"Does she really?"

"It's like looking into the past."

Amy's brother, Mark, was standing at the window. He'd flown in two days before. Having him there meant even more than Amy thought it would. Her bachelor brother loved his new niece and had been a valuable foil to Ryan and his mother, who were standing beside him at the window.

Amy wanted to preserve this moment, to stretch it out somehow and spin it into forever, but of course, it didn't last. The time disappeared, and soon it was Ryan's turn to hold his daughter. Amy and her grandmother walked out. The issue of telling his children about Marie was still a thorny one. Amy had raised it several times in the preceding few days, but as of now, he still had no answer as to when he would bring them to meet their new sister. Amy tried to see the beauty in Marie being held by her father as she and her grandmother stood on the other side of the glass, but it was hard to rouse the enthusiasm she wanted to feel. It was like Marie had two opposing forces in her life already.

Amy stood alone as Mark and their grandmother chatted. It had been years since they'd talked, but they were getting along well. Maureen was telling him about her brother Conor's upcoming visit from Florida. She was excited. Mark wouldn't meet him. He was going home to Boston the next day. Amy was going to miss him.

"Have you a lady friend at home?" Maureen asked him.

"I have lots of friends," he said with a sly smile.

"No one special?"

"Not yet," he answered. "I do want to get married and have kids someday. I just haven't met the right woman yet."

Amy let them chat, waiting in silence by the window for ten agonizing minutes. All she wanted was to be back inside with her baby. When the agreed time expired, it was Ryan's mother who emerged.

"Go inside," she said. "Let Marie sit with both her parents."

Amy's first thought was to say no, but a more practical, reasonable side of her nature made her agree.

Ryan's mother hugged her and held the door as Amy returned to the NICU. She greeted some of the other parents as she passed them. Some of the other babies were much sicker than Marie and reminded her just how lucky they'd been.

Ryan was still holding their baby and looked up with a smile as she sat down.

"She's so beautiful," he said.

"My grandmother said she looks just like my mother when she was born."

"I hope she looks just like you when she grows up," he said. "You're going to be gorgeous, just like your mommy," he cooed to Marie.

He handed the little girl back, and Amy held her against her chest. Soon, Marie began to nuzzle against her. One of the nurses noticed and appeared over Amy's shoulder. Amy knew her and greeted her with a smile.

"I think she's hungry. Are you breast feeding her?" the young nurse said in English.

"I've just been pumping so far."

"Would you like to try to get her to latch on?"

Amy looked across at Ryan and then down at Marie. Having him here felt inappropriate. This should have been a sacred moment between mother and daughter. She wished he would offer to get up and give them the time, but he didn't move.

"I'm not sure," Amy said with a watery smile. "I wouldn't know what to do."

"It's easy," the nurse responded. "Let Marie guide you." She looked at Ryan. "Maybe you could give Amy a little space, just for her first time?"

"Oh, of course," Ryan said and stood up.

"Thank you, Ryan," Amy said. "I'm sure you understand."

"Good luck," he whispered and left.

Marie latched in seconds and was soon feeding like they'd been doing it for weeks. The bond between them grew even greater. To Amy, it felt like they were one.

Ryan and his mother were gone as Amy emerged from the NICU a few minutes later with a broad smile on her face.

"Don't worry, I averted my eyes—not a pleasant sight for me," Mark said.

Amy smiled. "Just feeding my kid. Now, how about us. Shall we go get some lunch?"

The others agreed. Amy had been spending several hours a day in the hospital and the rest of her time interviewing her grandmother. Amy was wary of tiring her out but her grandmother never complained or asked to stop.

"Do you want to go back to the house and take a nap before we start talking again?" Amy asked her.

"That would be lovely," her grandmother replied.

The café across the street from the hospital served as a suitable venue for lunch. The canteen was better than she'd expected, but Amy didn't want her visitors to spend all their time in the hospital. She, Mark, and Maureen sat down for lunch and talked about fun times in the past and the sparkling future ahead.

The topic of the book came up at the end of the meal.

"I can't believe what you did during the war," Mark said. "I had no idea."

"I kept what happened back then to myself for too long. I'm gaining just as much from telling my story as Amy is from hearing it."

"I'm honored to be related to you," Mark said.

Maureen reached across the table and took his hand. As she drew it back, she knocked her plate, sending it cascading to the floor.

"Oh, no," she said, but her voice was weak.

Amy stood up. "Are you all right, Grandma?"

The older woman seemed to be gasping for breath. Amy repeated her question.

Maureen could barely speak. "My chest hurts. I can't..."

"Get her across the street," Amy said.

Mark took her arm, but their grandmother only grimaced more.

"Get her. She needs help now!" Amy said.

Mark picked her up and jinked through the restaurant before running across the street with Amy a few feet behind. Mark didn't hesitate and sprinted into the ER. He shouted for assistance, and several attendants appeared. They struggled with the language barrier before a nurse who spoke English appeared.

"What happened?" the nurse asked.

"She was complaining of chest pains and collapsed in the diner across the street."

One of the attendants produced a gurney, and Mark laid Maureen down. Her eyes were closed as they took her away. Amy and her brother stood helpless, watching as the nurses pushed the doors open. They heard them shouting for help, and then the doors shut, and it was silent once more.

Amy turned to Mark and hugged him. Her tears wet his shirt. He had left his jacket in the diner. They both had.

"I don't know what I'll do if she doesn't make it," Amy said. "I've only just found her again. I need her."

"She's a tough old bird," Mark said. "You know what she's been through. If anyone can weather this storm it's her."

Amy walked over and sat in one of the plastic chairs in the waiting room. The two most precious people in the world to her were in this hospital. Everything seemed to be in the balance.

Mark walked back across to the restaurant and returned a few minutes later with their jackets and her bag.

"Anything?" he asked as he sat beside her.

She shook her head.

Her phone buzzed inside her bag as he handed it to her. Amy picked it out, wondering if she should call Maureen's brother. She wiped her tears away and blew her nose before flipping her phone open. A text from Mike.

Hey, how's the little one? I just wanted to check in and see how you both were.

It was the first time he'd contacted her since she'd broken up with him the week before. She closed the phone and placed it back in her bag. Thoughts of Mike had flitted in and out of her mind during the few quiet moments she'd had over the last week. Her grandmother hadn't mentioned the breakup, but Amy knew the older woman disapproved. Amy was surprised at the text. She thought he would have forgotten about her and all the baggage she came with the moment she set him free.

Why couldn't she text him back? Didn't he at least deserve to know how Marie was?

Amy reached into her bag once more and drew out her cell phone. Mark was staring into space beside her and didn't ask what she was doing.

Marie's doing much better. I held her for the first time earlier today. Unfortunately, my grandmother collapsed earlier. I'm in the ER with my brother. We don't know anything yet.

The reply was almost instantaneous.

Oh, no! I'm so sorry. I know how special she is. Hang in there. I'm here if you need me.

Thanks, she responded and closed her phone.

Two agonizing hours passed before the doctor emerged and motioned for them to come with him. He had blue eyes and sandy brown hair. He was handsome, but his face betrayed the stress he was under. He brought them into a separate waiting room in the ER, where he sat them down.

"How is she, doctor?" Amy asked.

"Your grandmother suffered a heart attack."

"But she's still alive?" Amy blurted.

The doctor nodded. "She's about the strongest 90-year-old I've ever seen. We moved her upstairs to intensive care."

"Is she going to be okay?" Mark asked.

"Hard to say right now," the doctor responded. "The first 24 hours will tell us a lot. She's in the best hands. It was lucky she collapsed so close by. Any farther away and she might not have made it."

"Can we see her?" Amy asked.

"In a while," the doctor answered. "I'll send someone down as soon as we get the all-clear for visitors."

He nodded and left.

Hours passed with little news. Amy returned to the NICU to feed the baby, but her mood was the polar opposite of what it had been earlier. She tried to draw comfort from the fact that her grandmother had held Marie and, when she was finished, cycled through the photographs the nurse had taken, wondering if they'd be the only ones of Marie and Maureen she'd ever have. She stayed with her daughter for a few minutes longer, staring at the most beautiful thing she'd ever seen but unable to dispel the deep sorrow in her heart.

A text message from Mark brought her back into the moment.

The doctor came back. He has news. Come back down.

Amy blew her baby a kiss and leaped out of her seat. She hurried out of the NICU and toward the elevators. Mark was in the ER waiting room with the same doctor they had seen before.

"How is she?"

"In a serious condition, but fighting hard." Amy's heart swelled in her chest. "She's an amazing woman."

"I knew that already," Amy said with a smile.

"What she's been through is all the more serious for someone of her age, but she's responding well to the treatment so far."

"Will she need a transplant?" Mark asked.

"No. The operation would kill someone of her age. The best we can do is to work with what she's already got."

"Can we see her?" Amy asked.

It was almost six o'clock. It had been about five hours since Maureen collapsed.

"She's asleep now. I think it's best if you both go home and get some rest and we'll see how things stand tomorrow."

"Okay," Amy said. A beacon of hope shone within her. The doctor seemed to recognize as much.

"I have to warn you that this is an extremely serious condition, and with your grandmother's advanced age.... you should prepare for the worst. Her surviving the afternoon was close to a miracle. It might be time to begin getting her affairs in order."

Amy's heart sank like a polished stone. She nodded, trying to fight back the tears. The doctor left. They went back to their grandmother's house without her.

Mark did his best to console her and even made dinner. But it was no good. He didn't know Maureen as well as she did. He hadn't come to rely on her like she had. Amy had no idea what she would do without her. Unable to eat, Amy retired to bed.

∼

After a restless night's sleep, Amy woke with the dawn. She checked her phone for missed calls and breathed a sigh of relief when she noticed there weren't any. Any news was likely to be bad news in this situation. She was the primary contact for Maureen, and the hospital would have called if she'd taken a turn for the worse in the night. Happy in the knowledge that her grandma was still alive, she got out of bed.

She made breakfast, working as thoughts of her grand-mother and her daughter swirled around in her mind. The problems with Ryan didn't seem so important now. The doctor had told her to get her grandmother's affairs in order. She didn't have the strength for that. Mark would have to be the one to make those calls. After she'd eaten, Amy sat by the window and took out her digital camera. She stared at the photographs of Maureen holding Marie again and wondered how they were only taken the day before. Everything was different now.

She and Mark were at the hospital when visiting began at 9 AM. They went directly upstairs to the intensive care unit—the one for adults, not the one for babies where everyone knew her. A few minutes later, the same doctor who'd seen them first the day before came into the waiting room to speak to them.

"She had a good night," the doctor said. "She's awake and lucid."

"Can we see her?" Amy said.

"Yes," the doctor answered.

Amy nodded in silence. Mark put a hand on her shoulder.

"It's this way," the doctor said. "We were able to move her into her own room earlier."

They followed down the hallway to a door at the end. Amy walked in first. Maureen turned to her, trying to smile. She was propped up on several large pillows. A drip fed clear liquid into her arm, and she was hooked to several monitors.

"Grandma!" Amy said.

"Hello, my dear. I must look a frightful mess."

"No, you look even more beautiful than ever."

Amy leaned in and hugged her, kissing her cold, wrinkled cheek. She stood back, and Mark did the same.

"How are you feeling?" he asked.

"Oh, much better. I'm sorry for creating such a fuss. Collapsing in a café!"

"We're all here for you."

"How's my little girl?" Maureen asked.

"Doing better every day. She's looking forward to seeing her great-grandma again soon."

"Tell her I'm looking forward to seeing her again too," the older woman said. Her voice was softer, more delicate than before. Every word she said was like a precious jewel to be treasured.

"I want to talk to you for a moment, Amy," she said. "Mark, be a dear and see if there are any good books in the gift shop for me. I'm a little bored in here. I didn't have time to pack before I came. I like a good thriller."

"Okay," he said with a smile and left.

"I don't know what tomorrow will bring," Maureen began. "None of us do, but I know now I can't afford to waste another moment. All the time I've been telling you my story I've been afraid of the end. Somehow, I convinced myself I'd never have to tell you, that you'd get bored or something."

"I've never been more enthralled," Amy said.

"But I realize now I have to tell you the end of my war story as soon as I can. The doctors seem to think I'm not going to make it out of here."

"You will, Grandma. If anyone can, you can."

"I don't intend on checking out just yet, but I don't want to leave anything to chance. I need to share what happened, and not just for you, but for those I left behind."

"I don't want you to strain yourself."

"Since when was talking straining oneself? With everything I went through in my life dying from talking seems like an easy way to go. And besides, I don't care what those doctors say. I want to see my little Marie at home. I intend to hold her and see her smile. I'm not finished yet. Do you have your tape recorder?"

Amy reached into her bag and pulled it out.

"Ready?" her grandmother asked.

14

Sunday, November 20, 1943

Maureen was sitting on the park bench reading the newspaper when the woman came. The stories printed on the pages were all about the war but were written to cast the most sympathetic light on the noble intentions of the Germans. Not much had changed since Goebbels took over the Ministry for Propaganda in '33 when Maureen lived in Berlin. The Nazis still controlled the media narrative, shaping the day's news to fit their agenda. The woman, who was about 40, sat beside Maureen on the bench. The Lyon Botanical Gardens were shabby and overgrown, neglected by the invaders who controlled the city now. It was a cold, cloudy day, and few people were in the once majestic gardens. Maureen didn't put down the paper. She counted to 60 in her mind before lowering it to look around. Once she was confident they were alone, she began to speak. The code words came first.

"Winter is better in the south," she began.

"Less snow, but different in the mountains," the woman replied.

Maureen folded up the newspaper and placed it on her lap. After taking one more look around, she turned to the woman.

"What's your name?"

"Manon Ollivon," she replied.

She had green eyes and long brown hair streaked with grey. Manon looked nervous. That reassured Maureen. Spies were everywhere. The Nazis had placed their own operatives in the resistance in the last few months. Many brave men and women had been captured and tortured to death. The murder of Jean Moulin, the first president of the French resistance movement, by Klaus Barbie, the head of the Gestapo in Lyon, had been particularly harshly felt by the freedom fighters left in his wake. Everyone was paranoid now. But was it paranoia when they really were after you? Maureen wasn't going to leave anything to chance.

"Why did you ask to meet me, Manon?" Maureen asked.

"My husband was killed working for the resistance in the Auvergne—"

"I knew him. He was a member of my Golden Horde, a good man. I'm sorry for your loss. The fighting has been exceptionally bitter the past few months."

"The Germans never found out he was fighting for the resistance. I've been living alone in Lyon since he left nine months ago, and I want to do something to help the cause."

"What do you have in mind?"

Manon reached into her bag for a packet of cigarettes.

"Let's walk," Maureen said. She stood up.

Manon lit the cigarette and kept pace with her. An elderly man out walking his dog passed them. The Frenchwoman waited until he'd gone to begin speaking.

"I'm a cleaner. I work for a company that sends us around to various buildings in the city. One of the places we're sent is the Hôtel Terminus."

"Gestapo headquarters in Lyon."

"Yes," Manon replied. "We go in twice a week and clean all the offices. The Gestapo men are relaxed around us. I've heard things, seen things."

"Like what?"

"Like the roundup of those Jews on Rue Saint-Catherine. One of the men mentioned it the day before it happened. I had no idea what to do. My husband was gone. I—"

"Don't blame yourself. There was nothing you could have done. The Gestapo has stepped up their raids this year. No Jew is safe from them now."

"It took me some time to realize how useful I could be, and I spoke to one of my husband's friends who suggested I get in contact with you."

The man Manon had spoken to was someone Maureen trusted. Otherwise, she wouldn't have come today at all.

"How can you help?" Maureen asked.

"I thought I could report anything I hear of interest to you."

"And get yourself killed?" Maureen said. "I've seen it happen too many times. Everyone thinks they're a spy these days. The Nazis don't mess around, and Barbie is one of the most ferocious madmen they have in their ranks."

"I know what he does to those unlucky enough to be arrested. I've heard the screams from the basement. And I'm very much aware of what he's like. I've met the man. He has all the charm of a rabid rat."

"When do you go in next?"

"Tomorrow."

"The Nazis must have vetted you to allow you into their headquarters."

"As far as I know the company I work for handed over all our records, but I've never been questioned or interviewed."

"They're getting sloppy. We'll make sure to make them pay for that. We won't meet again, but if you do have information leave two chalk marks on the back of the mailbox at the corner of Rue Franklin and Rue d'Auvergene."

"I know it. It's close to the hotel."

"Someone will contact you at your house the same evening you leave the marks." Maureen stopped and turned to the woman. "Make sure any information you supply is pertinent and timely. No use telling us what happened yesterday. Tomorrow is what we're interested in."

"I understand," Manon said.

"And please, don't take any unnecessary risks. I don't want to see your body hanging from a lamppost with one of those horrific signs hanging around your neck. Because that's what will happen if you're caught. They don't give second chances."

"I know," Manon said.

Maureen shook the woman's hand and watched her walk away. She waited until she'd disappeared to leave the park herself.

After having her papers checked by some French police-men, she made her way through the city to Christophe's apart-ment. She brought her hat down over her face as she walked. Being in public didn't feel safe anymore. The forest was the only place she was truly comfortable now, but perhaps comfort was the wrong term for what she and the Golden Horde had experienced these last few months. The German assault following the assassination of General Halder on the streets of Clermont-Ferrand had been as swift as it was brutal. But just as the War Office in London had hoped, the conditions in the Auvergne suited her guerilla fighters more than the regular German troops sent to flush them out. The plan to kill the general to lure his soldiers into a conflict they were largely unprepared for had worked, albeit at the cost of dozens of the lives of her men. The tally board was filling. The men she'd trained were flourishing in their new roles as lords of the forest, and the Auvergne was becoming a deadly place for the Nazi invaders.

Chirac had somehow survived being shot on the streets of Clermont-Ferrand and returned to combat two months later. Clerc was still alive also, and now the joint head of the fighting force Maureen had handed back to the Frenchmen who manned it. Her time directing their operations was over. London had ordered her back to Lyon to oversee the resistance activities there.

She relished the prospect of seeing Christophe more often. She had been to Lyon several times in the preceding months, but only for a night here and there. This was a chance to spend substantial time with the man she loved and would one day marry.

He was on the street waiting for her as she arrived. He picked her up in his arms and kissed her, lingering for several seconds before putting her back down again.

He was a shadow of the dandy she had first met in Paris in 1940. His skin and eyes betrayed the stresses of what he'd put himself through for the cause. But that only made her love him more. He could have sat out the war, working for his wealthy father in Marseille, but he chose country above himself and thrust himself into the fight against the Nazis. She couldn't imagine anyone more brave or noble than the man she loved.

He led her upstairs. "It's been too long," he said as they reached the door to his apartment.

"It's been a week."

"As I said—too long," he replied, pushing the door open.

Maureen had come from the forest outside a town called Thiers, where washing was a distinct luxury and was wary of how she might have smelled. "You mind if I take a shower?"

"Not at all," he answered with a smile. He was used to the request—it was the same every time she visited.

Getting the mud and grime of the forest off her body was a pleasure she never grew tired of. A year before, she would never have walked through the streets of Lyon or any other city in anything other than a pristine state, but that was then. She'd been through so much that little things like being dirty in public didn't seem so important anymore.

She spared a thought for Clerc, Chirac, Sella, and the other men she'd left behind as she got out to towel herself down. They were ready to lead the men. She was sure of that. Otherwise, she wouldn't have left, no matter what her superiors ordered.

The sun was setting over the city when she emerged from the bathroom. Christophe was on the balcony drinking wine—one of the few luxuries that ordinary people could still readily obtain and afford. The street below was deserted even though curfew wasn't set to begin for another hour. She sat on his lap, putting her arms around him. He kissed her, but she could tell his mind was elsewhere.

"Things will change, my love. Mark my words. My time in the Auvergne was all about weakening the enemy for the coming invasion. And the men I trained are doing that every day. We suffered painful losses, of course, but the enemy sustained far more. The partisans rule the volcanic region. The Wehrmacht tried to chase us out after we killed Halder, but they fell right into our trap."

"What about you, did you kill any Nazis?"

Maureen stayed quiet for a few seconds before answering his question. "I was the one who hit Halder. I pulled the trigger myself."

Christophe nodded.

Maureen noted the shadow in his eyes. "Have you a problem with that?"

"Just that you're in the thick of the action and I'm stuck in a basement churning out fake papers for the people risking their necks."

"Don't be ridiculous, Christophe."

The look on his face didn't change.

"I've killed, yes—only because I had to. I wish I'd never had to pick up a gun, let alone live in the woods for months on end directing partisan operations. That doesn't make me any less of a lady, if that's what you're thinking."

"It's not that at all. I feel...useless."

"The reason I kill is not to eliminate life but to save it," she said. "That's all I'm trying to do—to get the Nazis out of France so they can't drag innocent Jews from their houses or murder helpless civilians in their villages. How many lives have you saved with those amazing papers you produce?"

"I have no idea."

"Let me take an educated guess. 200? 300? So many men, women and children are safe from the Germans because of what you do. You should feel privileged that you don't have to kill to save lives."

Christophe nodded and took a sip of his wine. Her words seemed to have some effect on him. "You're probably right," he said. "I was always more of a lover than a fighter."

"The best there ever was," she said and kissed him again.

"You always know what to say to cheer me up, don't you?" he said.

"It's a talent."

They sat on the balcony for another hour before he prepared a dinner of vegetable omelets. As he only had two eggs, Christophe used cornstarch and water to thicken them enough to form the omelet. It was a common trick. Maureen didn't mention it out loud, but she almost missed the rations the British dropped into the forest.

But Christophe did an admirable job with what he had, and no one complained these days. Whiners were treated with almost as much severe prejudice as collaborators. There was no room for either in French society.

"I was in Izieu for a visit a couple of weeks ago," Christophe said as he finished his meal.

"You were? How is it now?"

"Since the Italians were pushed out by their German overlords? The area is the same as it is here. Nazi flags, Nazi troops, Jews disappearing."

"What about the houses? Have they had any visits from the Gestapo or the police?"

"Nothing. The locals aren't talking either apparently. It doesn't seem the Nazis are any the wiser to the Jews hiding there. Maybe Izieu will keep working its magic and they'll be able to ride out the war under the mountains."

"I only hope you're right." There was nothing she could do anyway—she'd been ordered by London to stay away.

"You remember the Belmont sisters?"

"The five little girls below the trapdoor in that woman's basement? How could I forget?"

"I'm going to see them in a few minutes. I'm meeting with Celine, the lady of the house, and a few others actively hiding Jews around the city. I thought you'd want to come."

"I'm ready."

Christophe picked up his briefcase and a bag of food and led her out the door to where a pair of bikes were parked on the street outside.

They joined the river of cyclists traveling through the city and didn't see one moving motorized vehicle in the 15 minutes it took them to ride to Celine's house. Celine answered the door in the same suspicious, unfriendly way as before. "She's back?"

Maureen stepped inside. "Yes. Nice to see you again."

Two other women were waiting at the dining room table. In a time when courage had become commonplace, these were the unsung heroes. Maureen felt honored to be among them.

Celine was unfriendly and conservative, but only because she cared so deeply about the girls she was hiding. Celine introduced the other two.

"This is Marion."

A pretty woman with curly brown hair and green eyes stood up to greet them with a smile.

"And Isabelle."

The other woman had short brown hair and was the oldest of the three at about 50. She was polite and pleasant. Christophe knew them both and kissed them on the cheeks. Celine poured each of them a glass of wine. The women all had cigarettes burning.

"How many children do you have in your care?" Maureen asked.

"I have six," Isabelle said. "All boys under 12."

"And I have nine," Marion said. "Aged between 10 and 15."

"How are they?"

"Getting thinner by the day. But their self-discipline is astounding. They're remarkable kids," Marion said.

Both of the other women nodded in agreement.

"You know why I called this meeting," Christophe said. "I think it's time we made plans to evacuate them abroad. It's too risky in the city now."

Celine sat back and folded her arms. "This again?"

"I believe they're in danger," Maureen said. "The Nazis have stepped up their obsession with hunting down Jews lately. Hundreds have been taken from Lyon in the last few months. The rest were forced into hiding."

"Well, that's what we're doing, isn't it?" Celine said. "Leaving isn't a simple proposition, the children can't climb mountains. We have 20 between us. All under the age of 16. How do we get them out? I don't see that we have any other choice than to wait for the OSE to make their move."

"How about a compromise?" Maureen said. "How about

you talk to the children and ask them if they want to get out? Christophe will take the photos and get to work on documents for whoever volunteers to leave first. And the others can follow in due course."

"They can't be expected to make decisions for themselves," Celine said.

Christophe ignored her. "I have some examples of my work." He took out his wallet and laid out his own papers. He then reached into a secret pocket in the blazer he was wearing to show sample Spanish and Portuguese passports he'd made.

The three women took a few seconds to review the documents.

"Impressive," Marion said as she pushed them back across the table to him.

"We can't afford to be complacent," Maureen said. "No matter how well hidden you think your kids might be."

"I'll talk to my children, and see what their feeling is," Marion said.

Isabelle nodded approval. Celine was still sitting back with her arms folded across her chest.

"It's too dangerous."

"Can we see the girls?" Maureen said. "Ask them what they think?"

"Let them know what we're thinking at least," Isabelle said.

Everyone was staring at Celine. "All right, come on."

They went to the basement. Christophe brought the bag of food. He and Maureen shifted the old gas stove to expose the trapdoor. Two minutes later, the girls were out. They were thinner than before but still clean.

"I bring them out to wash as often as I can," Celine said.

"Let the girls eat first," Christophe said.

"Nice to see you again," Michelle, the oldest, said to Maureen. Her sisters Naomi, Celeste, Vera, and Simone were already sitting on a bench eating the bread Christophe had brought. Maureen couldn't help but stare as they ate. Why them and not her? None of it made any sense. She waited until they were done eating to start.

"I'm concerned. The Nazis are closing in, deporting foreign Jews by the hundreds. You might not be used to adults speaking to you like this. It's more traditional to shield children from the evils of the world, but these aren't conventional times. The OSE has done an admirable job here and all over France hiding the most vulnerable, but I'm worried they're not acting with due urgency. It seems they're determined to stick to the plan of hiding out rather than evacuating to a country where the Nazis don't hold sway."

"It can't be comfortable living down there," Christophe said.

"Better than in a concentration camp," Celine countered.

The girls were quiet. None of them had said a word yet.

Michelle, who seemed to be the spokesperson for the group, broke their silence. "What are you suggesting?"

Christophe stepped forward. "I can forge documents for each one of you. It'll take time, but with Celine's permission I could begin soon. With a little luck, we could get you into Switzerland or Spain."

"Where would we go?"

"Likely to a refugee camp. But you'd be safe and in the open air," Maureen said. "You don't have to make a decision today but we wanted to get an idea if you'd be interested or not. Who wants to avail herself of Christophe's kind offer and leave for Switzerland or Spain in the near future?"

Three of the girls put their hands up. Vera and Simone, the youngest two, kept their hands down. Maureen understood why. The easiest thing to do was to stay here, in a place they knew, with someone who would always care for them.

"You're coming with us," Michelle said. "We're not leaving you behind."

"Come on, raise your hands," Naomi said.

"They don't want to," Celine said, but Vera and Simone did as their sisters ordered.

Doubt nagged at Maureen too. She wasn't immune. Doing her best to cast aside the dissenting voices in her mind, she spoke again, determined to focus on the message she believed could save the children's lives.

"Christophe has a camera, so we can take the photographs we need today, and get to work on the passports, or whatever documents you'll need to reach safety. I don't want to scare anyone, but I also need you to understand the danger you're in."

Christophe went to the briefcase for his camera, hidden in a secret compartment at the bottom. He returned a few minutes later and began taking the photos the children would need for their papers.

"We need to figure out what your names will be," he said once he was finished. "You'll need to pose as different people."

Naomi stepped forward. "Will we still be sisters? I want Vera out of the family!"

Her little sister shoved her.

Christophe smiled. "No, you're stuck with each other."

They thanked the three women. Marion and Isabelle promised to ask the children under their care if they wanted to leave and were confident they'd also say yes. Celine wasn't happy, but Christophe smiled and embraced her before kissing her on the cheek.

"Thank you," he said.

Maureen said the same, and they left.

They began discussing what to do with the children when they got back to Christophe's apartment.

"It has to be Switzerland," Maureen said. "I know the border's swarming with German guards but I know some guides who've been walking those mountain trails their whole lives. If anyone can find a way across it's them."

"What if they can't?" Christophe asked.

"Then we'll do something else. But they will. The Germans would need an entire division to close down the border. Getting across will be difficult, but not impossible."

"With winter coming?" he said.

"That's why we don't have a moment to waste. The snow will be thick on the trails within a matter of days. How quickly can you create the documents?"

"Well, if I make them passports, they won't need to traverse the mountain passes, will they?"

"Can you?"

"I can give it a try. The Swiss seem to derive some evil pleasure from making their documents fiendishly tricky to forge, but I'll get something acceptable together. If I can't, we can always revert to Spain."

Maureen walked to the window, looking down at the street. She wondered about the OSE. The humanitarian organization had done commendable work these past few years, but she just hoped they recognized the new dangers the Germans presented. The war was beginning to go against them, and like a cornered animal, the Nazi beast was lashing out against anyone they deemed an enemy. And what easier target did they have than unarmed civilians, innocent of any crime except what they saw as the ultimate failure—being Jewish?

~

Monday, November 21, 1943

They had some breakfast before cycling to the basement where Christophe worked a few blocks away. The first job was to develop the photographs, and he had a dark room in the back for the job. Maureen looked around at the printing presses and the stencils, the pencils and dyes, and wondered how much of his dwindling savings Christophe had spent on this place. His family was still wealthy but didn't give him money. It had always been up to him to earn his living, but it had been months since he'd sold a painting or even tried to.

The basement he rented from a resistance member under a pseudonym was divided into two parts. The main printing area with a door to the street was at the front, with the darkroom at the back. A door separated the two rooms. Each had two small windows at head height; thick drapes obscured the ones in the darkroom, while the two in the main space let in golden beams of much-needed sunlight.

"Thanks for putting everything else to one side," Maureen said as Christophe dipped the first photo into a bin of ammonium sulfate.

"I have two ID's for a resistance man and his wife I need to get to this afternoon, but after that, I'll focus on the passports for the kids."

An hour later, they had developed all ten photographs. Maureen was hanging the last up to dry when she heard a harsh hammering from the front door. They both stopped to listen. The sound of German voices followed.

Christophe whirled around to her, his eyes awash with fear. "They're onto us," he said.

"How?"

"I have no idea, but we have to get out. Do you have anything in the other room?"

"My bag,"

"Get it," he said.

Maureen ran into the main printing area. The door to the street was rocking back and forth on its hinges as whoever was on the other side of it tried to bash it down. She picked up her bag and was back inside the darkroom in seconds.

Christophe was by the window as she returned. "The front door's strong, but they'll be through in a minute or two. I planned for this," he said, pushing a footstool against the wall. He reached up to the window and pulled down the thick black drape. White sunlight streamed in through the translucent, frosted glass. The pounding on the front door continued as he opened the window. It was rigged so that he could slide out the pane of glass. The gap it left was about two feet by three—wide enough for their skinny bodies to squeeze through. Christophe took one last look at his dark room and climbed up through the opening.

Maureen heard the sound of the front door crashing to the floor as Christophe reached a hand down for her. She grabbed on and climbed up and out of the basement to the street outside. Her heart froze as she stood up. Christophe had his hands above his head. A young German soldier stood opposite him, pointing his rifle at Christophe's chest. The Wehrmacht soldier's hands were shaking. He called out, but not loud enough to attract the other soldiers around the corner. Christophe said something, but the soldier told him to shut up in French.

Maureen's mind clicked into gear. "Thank God you're here," she said in German and stepped toward the soldier. "He dragged me down there. He had his filthy hands all over me."

The soldier pointed the rifle at her but then back at Christophe. She took another step and knew her only chance was now. Just as she'd been taught in training, Maureen let her hand scythe through the air, striking the young soldier just below his right ear, where his spine was most vulnerable. She felt the crunch, and the young man dropped the rifle, bringing both hands to his throat.

"Let's go," Christophe said, pulling at her hand.

Maureen looked back as they ran, wondering if she'd killed the soldier. His body was still as they turned the corner. It was 11 a.m., and the city was alive. A tram slid along the street. Without saying a word to each other, they both ran after it. It slowed on the corner, and they both jumped on, drawing several nervous glances from the other passengers.

Maureen looked down at her feet for a few seconds as she tried to slow her breath before she realized in horror that the tram was traveling past Christophe's basement office.

"Don't move," he said as she looked up. "They haven't seen us," he whispered.

The young soldier she'd hit was lying on the street. His body was still, and two other troopers were trying to shake him awake.

She tried to control her fear as the tram rounded the corner. A group of soldiers was waiting outside the office. The door was smashed in, and as they passed, she caught a glimpse of several more Germans inside. Christophe's eyes betrayed nothing. He kept them pointed forward at the road in front. The tram glided on, leaving his now-destroyed office behind.

Neither spoke for the five minutes they remained on board. Once they were well clear, they got off together. Still, neither said a word until they were inside Christophe's apartment.

"How did they know?" Christophe said as he shut the door behind him.

Maureen brought her hands to her face. "An informant, maybe? Who knows? The Gestapo is everywhere. They have their tentacles all over the city. What about Celine's girls?"

"And everyone else I was meant to produce for?" he said. He collapsed on the couch with anguish splashed all over his face. "I'll never get printing presses again. It took me months to source the equipment and put it all together. I'm just thankful we got out of there alive." He stood up and took her in his arms. Maureen put her head on his shoulder, knowing that any hope of getting the children in Lyon over the border legally had been destroyed along with Christophe's forging operation.

Christophe drew back, walked over to the sideboard, and picked up a bottle of wine. He poured a glass, knocked it back, and poured two more. He handed her one, and they walked out to the balcony. The all too familiar sound of an emergency klaxon sounded through the neighborhood.

"You put that soldier down with one chop."

"Just the way we trained to in England."

Maureen looked down at her hand. It was beginning to hurt more now the adrenaline was wearing off.

"We'll have to take them over the mountains," she said.

"Not in winter," he replied.

And with that, a snowflake drifted down from the gray sky outside.

15

Sunday April 2, 1944

The man was wearing a black hat, just as he'd said he would be. The tavern was warm, lit by a roaring fire. The place was almost empty. About ten other people sat around a few small tables, their faces illuminated in gold by the dancing flames. Maureen and Christophe walked over to the contact and, without announcing themselves, joined him. He took a sip of beer before even looking at them. Beer was less common than before the war due to grain rationing, and the man seemed to relish every drop.

"Are you Maxime?" Maureen said.

"Yes," the man replied. "And you?"

He was in his forties and wore a thick black beard flecked with gray. His skin was ridged and weather-beaten.

"That's not important," Maureen said. "But you can call us Monsieur and Madame Dumortier."

"You're not French," Maxime said with a yellow-toothed smile.

"Again, not important," Christophe said. "The important thing is getting our people over the mountains. Can you do it?"

"How many?" Maxime asked.

"A group of children," Maureen answered. "20 of them."

"I don't take kids," the man said and took another sip of his precious beer.

"Perhaps this will change your mind," Christophe said, and threw a wad of cash on the table between them. It was some of the last of his savings. He'd have to go begging to his father for the first time in years soon—something he was loathe to do.

Maxime took one look at the money and put his hand on it, dragging it back over to his side. No one was watching them, and he took a moment to count it under the table.

"They're fit and ready?" Maxime asked once he was done.

"They'll make it," Maureen said.

"Okay, but no one younger than eight. Don't bother sending them along. I won't take them. And don't send any others either. I'll take ten, but no more. I don't usually take more than eight. If you send any more, I'll leave the lot. It's too dangerous up there. The trails are only just opening back up."

Christopher leaned forward. "What about if we pay you double, and the same for any other guide you have to enlist? Will you take all 20 then?"

Maxime hesitated. He shook his head with a wry smile on his face. "Double? And you'll pay for the additional guide too?"

"Yes."

"Okay. I can take them all. I must be crazy, but I'll do it. When do you want to get going?"

"As soon as possible," Maureen replied. "When can you leave?"

The French guide glanced at the door. "As long as the weather holds, we should be good for tomorrow. Let the kids know that I won't wait for any slackers. Are you coming?"

"No. Just the children," Maureen replied. "How long will it take?"

She remembered her trip over the Pyrenees back in '40, carrying the young Bautner boys. It had taken two nights of almost nonstop trekking.

"Two days. We'll stick to the highest trails—less German guards up there. The easier paths are crawling with them these days."

"But you'll get the kids through?" Christophe asked.

"I'll get them into Switzerland. What they do then will be up to them."

"This is only the beginning. If this works out, we'll have more," Maureen said.

"Let's not get ahead of ourselves," Maxime said. "Get your kids ready. I'll see them on the street in Vallorcine at six on Wednesday morning. It's a small village beside the border. I'll be outside the grocer's shop."

"Okay," Maureen said and stood up. They shook the man's hand and left.

The harsh winter had shut down the routes over the mountains into Switzerland to all but the hardiest and most experienced travelers. The children in Lyon were neither of those things, so Maureen had reluctantly agreed to wait until spring to smuggle them across the border.

Her partisan brigade in the forest was forced to disband for the freezing winter months, but under Maureen's guidance, several squads had moved their operations to the cities and towns that surrounded the Auvergne. No one wanted to take the pressure off the Nazis invaders, especially as they showed themselves to be more and more savage as time went on. The raids against the Jewish population, most pointedly those from foreign countries, had become more common as time passed. With some prodding from Maureen, the OSE had woken up to the fact that France wasn't safe for the foreign Jewish children they were trying to hide from the Nazis. Their leadership decided to start shutting down the safe houses they employed all over France. But gradually. The houses at Izieu, due to their secluded aspect, were deemed safe for the time being. Life there continued as it had since Maureen's father bought them, and the first refugees moved in back in '39.

Maureen and Christophe walked out of the tavern in the mountain village of Combloux. The air was thinner here in the French Alps, and the scenery was breathtaking. They stopped at the end of the street to behold the majesty of the mountains slicing into the sky. She'd parked the car outside town to avoid unwanted attention, for the Germans were here. A Nazi flag hung from the pole erected outside the post office, and several off-duty Wehrmacht passed them on their way into the tavern they'd just left. The mountains looked almost impassable. Each was covered in snow like icing on massive cakes.

"Do you think they can make it?" Maureen said to Christophe.

"They won't leave from here," he replied. "It's another 35 miles to the border, unless the kids want to try to tackle Mont Blanc."

"I'm being serious!" she said.

He turned to her and took her in his arms as he always did in moments like these. The feel of him against her calmed her, and her heart rate began to level off.

"They'll make it," he said. "They're young and strong, and you've put the fear of God in them!" He smiled. "They won't lack motivation."

"Good," she replied.

The roads were passable now, the snow having receded a week before, and they could walk the mile down the hill to where she'd left the car with no problems.

The sun was setting over the mountains as they left, splashing the horizon in beautiful red, pink, and purple dashes.

It was enough to make her forget about the Nazis momentarily as she sat in the car with the man she loved.

"You still want to marry me when all this is over?" he said as he started the car.

"More with every moment," she answered.

They drove down the mountain road in silence. She was thinking about a wedding after the war with all her family there. In her mind, all the children in Lyon were there, smiling and applauding as she walked down the aisle. She turned to him and put her hand on his. A voice inside told her to forget the fantasy and marry him tomorrow, but she drowned it out with her other thoughts. Marrying Christophe now made no sense. It was best to stick to the original plan and to let love have its day once all the hatred consuming the world was defeated. It was all the motivation she needed—although she never lacked that.

Christophe spoke with a pensive look on his face. "I'd better begin shuttling the children from Lyon over to Vallorcine if they're to be in place by Wednesday morning. It's going to take three trips back and forth."

"I can't help you. I have a meeting in the city tomorrow."

"I can handle this alone. I'm planning on stopping in Izieu on the way back to try to convince them to take advantage of the same escape route. They're beginning to get worried there."

"Good idea. It's strange that you still visit the houses and I don't."

"Just from time to time. I don't know the kids," he said.

They rode back into the city together. As always, they left the car in the suburbs and parted ways. Christophe went to the 1st Arrondissement to collect the Belmont sisters.

Maureen returned to Christophe's apartment and picked up the coded letter in the mailbox. London knew nothing of her mission with the Jewish children. She doubted her superiors there would have approved. Maybe she was neglecting her official duties as a British operative, but what was more important than saving children's lives? She felt a profound responsibility to help the Jews in hiding. She'd already done so much to weaken the Wehrmacht in the area.

The apartment was empty—quiet as the grave. She took a moment to sit down and go through her messages. The skirmishes in the Auvergne were progressing well. More dead Germans countered by only a few losses among the Golden Horde. A smile spread across her face as she thought about her brave men fighting seemingly insurmountable odds in the forest. She planned on returning to them for a few weeks when this crisis in Lyon blew over. But she also had a lot to do in the city. The recent hits the resistance had taken had weakened it from the powerful force it had once been. While her men might have been winning the war in the countryside, there was little doubt that the Nazis still ruled the cities and towns.

A note from Charles, the wireless operator, sat at the bottom of the pile. He wanted her to check in, most likely to receive and disperse orders from the War Office. Despite her personal desires, she knew that had to be a top priority. After a visit to the bathroom to wash up and apply some makeup, she set out for the apartment he rented a few blocks away.

A secret knock informed him that she wasn't part of a Gestapo raid, and he opened the door to let her inside. He was alone. They sat down to confer about the business of espionage. Charles went through the orders from London first. They were mainly to do with drops and the partisans who would need them.

"I'm getting the distinct impression that there might be something big coming soon," Charles said. "The War Office wants us to hit the Germans' machinery more so than the men. It seems to me like the powers that be are trying to tie the Wehrmacht up here so they can't advance north quite so easily."

Maureen nodded but wasn't quite so sure. They'd been talking about the impending invasion of France for months now. "We'll see, I suppose. We'd be the last people they'd tell."

Wednesday, April 5, 1944

The call Maureen had been waiting for came just after six o'clock. She smiled as Christophe's voice came on. The line was scratchy, and the clicking sound in the background meant that someone was almost certainly listening in. But that was nothing they weren't used to.

"Where are you?"

"In the place from this morning." That meant he was still in the Alps, in Vallorcine. "I had to hike the first few miles to show the guides our friends were up to it. I just got back an hour ago."

"How did it go?"

"It went well. They exceeded expectations. All 20."

Maureen felt a flame of happiness ignite inside her. "I'm proud of you."

"Thanks. I'm off to our other friends in your father's houses now to try to convince them to do the same. I tried calling them earlier but couldn't get through for some reason."

"Good luck."

"I'll see you tomorrow." He hung up.

Maureen knuckled down to some of her other duties as a Special Operations Executive spy behind enemy lines. One of them was to meet with and cultivate informants, just as she had with Manon Ollivion, the cleaner in Gestapo headquarters. As of now, Manon hadn't provided any valuable intelligence, and Maureen was beginning to think she never would when the phone in Christophe's apartment rang again.

It was Charles. "Our friend Manon wants to speak to you. I think she wants to discuss her daughter's schooling."

Maureen recognized the code words immediately—the cleaner had information.

"Tell her I'll meet her outside my uncle's restaurant. What time can she make it?"

"After work, at about seven o'clock."

"I'll be there. Why me?"

"She insisted you're the most qualified."

Maureen hung up the phone.

Her "uncle's restaurant," meant the Botanical Gardens, and seven o'clock actually meant eight. Maureen showed up ten minutes early and sat on the same bench she had last time. She held no newspaper in front of her face this time. The park was almost empty. It was an unusually cold evening for April, and Maureen had brought along her umbrella in case the gray skies above fulfilled what they seemed to promise and opened up. Maureen looked up, hoping the rain would hold off. Informants would often use any excuse not to show up. Rain was a common reason.

Just as Maureen was beginning to wonder if she'd come, Manon hustled around the corner and strode toward her. Maureen didn't wait for her to reach the bench. An instinct told her to stand up. She walked fifty yards to the next bench, looked around, and sat down. The Frenchwoman joined her a few seconds later.

When she was confident the eyes of the Gestapo weren't on them, Maureen began. "It's been a while."

"I didn't have anything pertinent to bring you," Manon said, reaching into her bag for a pack of cigarettes. She took one out and lit it. Maureen declined her offer to have one.

"What did you hear?"

"I'm not sure. I was outside the room, but Barbie was having a meeting with some of his lieutenants—real animals. Jew hunters."

"Do you know them?"

"By reputation. The Nazis don't lower themselves to speak to the likes of me. Anyway, I was outside the office when I heard a word that grabbed my attention—Izieu."

Maureen's blood ran cold. "What else?" she said, barely able to get the words out.

"Not much," Manon said. "I hope it's useful, but they said tomorrow morning—Thursday, April 6."

"Did they say what would happen on April 6?" Maureen asked. She was doing her best to keep her cool, but her insides were churning. She wanted to leap up and run all the way to Izieu to warn them.

"No," Manon said. "That's all I heard. Just the date and the name of the place. Do you know it?"

"I do," Maureen said. "Was there anything else?"

Manon shook her head. "Have I wasted your time?"

"No, not in the slightest. Let me know next time you find out anything. Please excuse me." She stood up and started walking. Once she was out of Manon's sight, Maureen ran to the edge of the park, where she'd parked her bike, and started pedaling. Was the Gestapo coming for the Jews in Izieu? How did they find out? It hardly mattered. The only important thing was warning them. Grisly images of the children being dragged out of their beds polluted her mind until she realized Christophe was there too. They'd take him along with everyone else. But he had the car. He could start ferrying them to safety tonight. He could drive them into the mountains—anywhere.

The streets were close to empty. Curfew was approaching, and it seemed the Germans were becoming even stricter about the little things as the war stretched on. She was sure the Nazis didn't know who she was, but she still couldn't afford to get hauled in. She kept her head down as she went. Fifteen minutes later, she was outside Christophe's apartment block. Her bike clattered against the pavement as she threw it down and ran up the steps. She shoved the front door to the apartment open, almost forgetting to close it behind her in her haste. Her hand was sweaty as she picked up the phone. She asked the operator to connect her to the house in Izieu.

"We should have enough time," she said out loud as the line connected. But then the operator's voice came on again.

"I'm sorry, but the call isn't connecting," she said.

Maureen remembered what Christophe had said about not being able to get through on the phone.

"Try it again," Maureen demanded.

The operator did as she was told but returned with the same answer. Maureen thanked her and hung up. Almost in tears, she tried again but received the same result—the line was dead. The Gestapo must have cut the wires in advance of the operation. She threw the phone down. She had no car and no way to warn the man she loved and the dozens of others with them of their impending arrests. But there were other vehicles in the city. They were rare these days but not unheard of. She'd seen several delivery trucks and vans—powered by coal—on the roads just that day.

Taking a deep breath, she picked the phone off the floor and called Charles. He picked up on the third ring. "Something's come up," she said. The frustration at not being able to tell the wireless operator what was going on without using code almost tore her apart. "I need to take a trip. Can I borrow your car?"

"I don't have one," he said. "My nephew gave me a ride into the city a few weeks ago."

"Have you any idea where I can get one? I'd like to leave as soon as I can."

The line went silent for a second. She was about to speak again when she heard him again.

"I think I know someone."

"Where?"

"I'll be over in a few minutes," he said.

Curfew was beginning in five minutes. The knock on the apartment door came ten minutes later. Maureen greeted the Englishman with a curt nod, and he ducked inside.

"What's going on?" Charles asked.

She took a few seconds to explain her predicament to him.

"And you tried calling again?"

"Twice when you were on your way over here," she answered. "Where's the car?"

"In Parilly."

"That's two miles from here," Maureen said. "How do we get there after curfew?"

"Taking the bikes would be too dangerous. It'll have to be on foot."

"Whose car is it?" she asked.

"A resistance man. It's hidden in his garage. I'm sure he'd let us take it," Charles said.

"He will if he knows what's good for him. So, I have to sneak two miles through the city, then borrow his car. Okay," she said.

"I'll come with you. Easier with two."

Maureen didn't argue. She looked at her watch; it was almost 9:30. It would take them an hour or so to get to Parilly, on the outskirts of the city. Then it was about two hours to Izieu. As long as the Gestapo didn't come in the middle of the night, she'd make it on time.

"You know where this house is? With the car?" Charles nodded. "Let's go," she said and put her jacket on.

Maureen went to the balcony first to check the street for French police or German soldiers. She saw neither, so she motioned to Charles to follow her. They descended to the street. Charles was young and fit, so they jogged most of the way. They were five blocks from Christophe's apartment when they saw three German soldiers on the street outside a tavern. Some of the owners stayed open after curfew to let invaders drink. The three men were visibly drunk, but Charles and Maureen still gave them a wide berth. They had to hide for several minutes from a French policeman and then from more German soldiers after that. A journey that should have taken them an hour took them closer to two. It was time they could ill afford.

"This is it," Charles said as they reached a small house with a garage to the side of it in the suburb of Parilly. "My friend's name is Jean. Let me get him out here."

Charles took a stone and threw it up at the bedroom window at the front. A light went on, and a few seconds later, a man appeared at the glass. Charles called up to him. Jean waved his hand and told him he'd be down in a minute.

Five long minutes later, the front door opened, and Charles and Maureen hurried inside.

"Who's the little lady?" Jean slurred. He was drunk. So much so that he rocked back and forth on his heels as he stood in front of them.

"An operative. My superior officer," he answered. "We need your car."

The man didn't seem to understand what Charles was saying.

"We need your automobile," she repeated.

"It's in the garage," he said and stumbled off. They followed.

A Peugeot 402 sat in his garage, though Maureen had to clear boxes out from in front of it to get it out.

"I haven't taken it out in a while," Jean said.

"You told me you had a working car," Charles said.

"I think it works," Jean replied.

Maureen sat in the driver's seat and started the engine. It coughed like an old man clearing his throat, but the engine turned over the third time.

"I'm coming too," Charles said as Maureen pulled out.

"Make sure you bring it back in one piece!" Jean called after them.

It was midnight. Maureen was tempted to go on the highway, but German military vehicles moved at all times of day, so she took the backroads—not an easy prospect in the inky darkness. She kept Christophe in her mind as she drove.

"Have you lost anyone in the war yet?" she asked.

"Any of my assets?" Charles answered.

"No. I mean, have you lost anyone you loved?"

"My brother flew Hurricanes," he said. "He was shot down during the Battle of Britain. That's why I joined up."

Maureen didn't answer. She just kept staring into the night in front of the car. An hour passed before she saw the blockade on the road. It was a German military truck. The headlights were on, illuminating the scene. Several troops were milling around.

The truck was on the side of the narrow road, and she calculated there was just enough space to squeeze past, but the soldiers would never allow that. Their vehicle seemed to have a flat tire.

"Curfew ended four hours ago. Can you turn around?" Charles said.

She slammed on the brakes about fifty yards short of the German soldiers. They reacted to the sound of her stopping and called out for her to halt. Maureen shifted the car into reverse and put her foot down. The old vehicle creaked and groaned as the tires hissed on the dirt and gravel below. The soldiers dropped to their knees and raised their rifles to the firing position. Maureen saw a place she could turn and backed into it as the bullets came. The rear window shattered, and several more shots hit the doors and the back. Maureen shifted the car into gear and accelerated away but then heard a loud pop, and the car bumped up and down.

"They hit the rear tire!" Charles said.

"We have to get as much distance between us and them as possible," she replied.

She wrestled with the steering wheel, trying to control it as if it was a wild horse to be tamed, but the turn ahead was too sharp, and they flew off the road, colliding with a tree. Charles groaned.

Maureen was unhurt and turned to her colleague. "Are you all right?"

"My leg. I twisted it somehow."

She helped him out of the car. He was limping on his right side and collapsed on the grass. "I don't think it's broken."

Maureen looked around. They were at least a mile from where the German soldiers had been mired, and they weren't following. It seemed like one more country road surrounded by fields, but as she shone her flashlight around, she saw a sign for the village of Saint-Didier-de-la-Tour. It was somewhere she knew. She went back to the car and found a map. It confirmed what she already knew.

"We're about 15 miles away," she said. "It's about five hours until dawn. I can make it on foot from here."

Charles looked at her for a few seconds before apparently realizing he wouldn't be able to talk her out of it. "Okay," he said. "I don't think I'll make it that far cross country."

"You don't have to. I'll go alone."

"Best of luck," he said. "Don't do anything I wouldn't do."

"I already am," she answered with a smile.

He laughed before shaking her hand. Charles fashioned himself a walking stick and limped off in the direction of Saint-Didier-de-la-Tour.

First, she had to ensure she didn't run into the Germans on the road. Maybe they were heading to Izieu, and their comrades had already arrived. Perhaps she was too late. Maureen didn't let the niggling doubts or the voices in her mind telling her to stop and consider her own safety alter her course. She kept Christophe in her mind as she climbed over the hedgerow and into the field beside it.

She walked for 20 minutes before consulting the map. She could get back to the road soon, and then it was just a matter of walking the rest of the way. Tiredness or pain didn't figure in her thoughts. All that mattered were the people in Izieu, the love of her young life among them. She kept on. The Germans would come at dawn. It was a race against time—her against the rising sun.

The darkness was beginning to fade as she reached the River Rhône. Maureen recognized where she was. This was somewhere she'd taken the children on long walks from the houses in Izieu.

"I can make it," she said in English, repeating it like a mantra. The terrain became more familiar with every step. The sun was peeking up from over the horizon in the direction she was walking. Soon, it was casting beautiful colors, but she cursed it.

She passed by farms she'd visited and the school where the children from Izieu had once gone. But she was losing the race. The Germans would be at the houses soon. Something inside her reasoned that since it was already likely too late, she should turn back and hide. She ignored it.

The German trucks were already at the houses when she arrived. Troops were inside, dragging screaming children to the waiting vehicles as the Gestapo masters watched with folded arms and satisfied looks on their faces. Maureen watched some kids scatter, but they couldn't escape the combat-ready troops sent to gather them up. She was about a hundred yards away and hid behind an old shed as the scene unfolded. Frozen and powerless, Maureen looked on in horror as her worst nightmare unfolded before her eyes. She heard something beside her, deep breathing and tears.

"Who are you?" she whispered.

He was a few feet away from her. He looked at her with terrified eyes before realizing she wasn't German. "Leon Reifman. I'm a medical student who helps out with the children."

"What happened?"

"They came a few minutes ago. I was using the outhouse. I hid." Unable to control his sobbing, he let his head fall into his hands.

"I tried to come to warn you," she said in a tiny voice.

Maureen peered around the corner of the shed. The trucks were almost full. It would all be over in a few moments. Her heart collapsed as she saw Christophe dragged out, struggling against the two soldiers holding his arms. A tear rolled down her face as they threw him into the truck nearest her. There had to be some way to affect this. She could still do something.

"Stay down," she said to Leon and got up to her haunches.

The sensible thing would have been to stay hidden. She crawled around to the edge of the shed. It was about fifteen yards to the truck they'd thrown Christophe into. But an old unkempt bush stood halfway. She waited until she was sure the Germans weren't looking and ran out, diving behind the bush as she reached it. It was only five yards to the truck now, and only one man was guarding it—an unarmed soldier who seemed more interested in the cigarette in his hand. Maureen waited until he turned away, then emerged from the bush. She stayed close to the ground, keeping her eyes on the driver. He was still facing away as she reached him, and a well-aimed chop to the side of his neck left him unconscious on the dirt.

The keys were in the ignition. She knew she had only seconds, and the rest of her life would be colored by this decision. She climbed into the cabin and turned the key. The engine roared to life, and she pressed her foot down on the accelerator. Maureen had no idea where she could go or how this escape could ever work. All she knew was that she had to try. She would have rather died than stay hiding behind that shed.

The roars of Wehrmacht troops erupted through the morning air, and one man tried to jump onto the side of the lorry but soon fell off. Shots rang out. Maureen looked in the rear-view mirror as she hit the dirt road that led away from the houses. Two soldiers on a motorcycle and sidecar were speeding after her. One of them fired at her, leaving a hole in the windshield. The other trucks were following now too. The motorcycle sped in front of her. She tried to ram it, but the driver pulled away, and she careened into a bush instead. Maureen backed out, but the man from the sidecar was already in the cabin beside her. She felt the cold steel of the barrel of his pistol against her temple and knew this was the end of her life. She raised her hands.

"Don't shoot," she said in German.

The bullet didn't come.

"Out of the truck," the soldier said.

She stood by the lorry with her hands on her head. Everything was over. All her training was rendered useless. Several Nazi soldiers gathered around, laughing about how the little girl had tried to steal the truck. A tall, muscular soldier picked her up and dumped her in the back with the other prisoners. Christophe's eyes almost bulged out of his head as he saw her. He took her in his arms, tears running down his face.

"What are you doing here?" he said.

"I heard this was going to happen yesterday," she cried. "I couldn't make it here on time. The Nazis cut the phone lines."

He held her tight against him. Five minutes later, it was all over. The trucks moved out. The houses at Izieu were left empty.

16

The internment camp at Drancy, Wednesday, May 3, 1944

The rooms of the former housing project in the suburbs of Paris were crammed with prisoners to be shipped away. Rumors abounded among the people held there. Some said they would be sent to labor camps in Germany. Others spoke with leaden faces of camps in Poland where the prospect of certain death awaited. Maureen kept to herself, doing her best to look after the other people she'd been sent here with. The only saving grace was that the people weren't separated, and she could be with Christophe. The buildings were unfinished, with concrete floors where people slept on straw and whatever clothes they'd had on when they were arrested. Maureen was thankful not to be there in winter as the windows had no glass, and the elements swept through unfettered. It was a miserable, hopeless place, and people left on trains heading east most days. The Nazis never told anyone in advance where they were going, just that they could bring whatever they'd packed before coming here and that there would be a hot meal and honest labor waiting for them at the end of their journey. Some even believed the Nazis.

No one other than Christophe knew who Maureen was. If the guards had discovered she was a British spy, she would have been taken to Gestapo headquarters for special treatment. The thought of dying under torture kept Maureen awake most nights, but she knew Christophe would never tell, and as far as any of the refugees from Izieu were concerned, she was just another concerned citizen. That seemed to be what the Nazis thought too, but Maureen didn't know for sure as she'd never been formally charged with anything—just thrown in with everyone else. The vast majority of the prisoners were Jews, with some political dissidents and troublemakers mixed in too.

Paris was just a few miles away. She dreamed of walking out with Christophe and flinging the doors open for all those behind her. In quiet moments she stared out at the city's buildings in the distance and fantasized about a time when deciding what to wear for dinner was a genuine consideration.

It was early afternoon when Christophe joined her at the concrete frame overlooking the city.

"I thought I'd find you here," he said.

"Just wishing things were different," she said with a smile.

He wrapped his arms around her. His embrace was different than it had been when they first got together. Once, he'd been muscular and strong. Now he was all bones and gristle. And she was the same too.

"The Nazis have taken everything from us," she said.

"Not everything," Christophe said. "Some things they can never touch. What's in our hearts, and the memories that sustain us. Those things will always be ours. No regime can touch them."

She took his face in her hands and kissed him. "If only I hadn't run into that German truck on the road to Izieu," she said. "If I just could have warned you all...."

"You did everything you could. More than most ever would have."

"I failed," she said. "Look at where we are. The kids, they'll be sent to camps in Germany to be killed."

"You believe what people say about "death camps?""

"The Nazis give me reason to believe as much every day. I haven't sensed any end to their depravity."

"I knew the walls were closing in. I should have taken the kids myself and found them somewhere safe to hide."

"With what money?" Christophe said. "Your rich fiancé is gone. You just have me now."

She put her arms around him and smiled. "And I could never want anyone else." She kissed him again.

"The only people to blame for all this horror are the Nazis themselves. Not you. Not me. Not the OSE or the War Office in London. One day soon, a great wind is going to sweep all this evil away, and we'll have our time in the sun."

"You really believe that?" Maureen said to him.

"I have to," he answered with a smile. "It's all that keeps me going. Take comfort in the fact that we got the five Belmont sisters out along with the others hiding in Lyon."

"Maureen Ritter," came a German voice from behind them. It was Schultz, one of the guards. Most were middle-aged, too old, or unfit to operate on the front lines. She had spoken to many of them. Schultz was from Hamburg and had a wife and two daughters waiting for him at home. She'd asked him and his colleagues many questions in her attempts to curry favor for her and her friends, but how can you do this to other human beings was never one of them.

"The commandant wants to see you," Schultz said.

Christophe looked at her with some concern. "What does he want with her?"

"I don't ask questions," Schultz said.

Maureen kissed Christophe on the lips again and let go. "I'll be back soon," she said and walked after the German guard.

Maureen chatted with him in German as they went. She tried to suppress her nerves, but visions of Nazi torture haunted her as she went.

The commandant, an SS man in his early 30s called Alois Brunner, was at his desk when she walked in. He was in the familiar gray uniform. He was dark-haired and almost handsome, but being in his presence made Maureen want to vomit. He gestured for her to sit on the chair in front of his desk. He was writing something and didn't look up for a few seconds.

"You're the American?" he said once he was finished. His eyes were somewhere between yellow and green.

"Yes, commandant," she said. Kowtowing to this man and the other Nazis here was the hardest thing she'd ever done, but she knew her life might depend on it. She'd been trained to kill these men, and there was nothing more she would have liked to do.

"I'm just looking at the arrest records," Brunner said. "You tried to steal a truck full of illegal Jews?" Maureen nodded. Brunner shuffled some papers again. "But you're not a Jew yourself?"

"No, I'm not." She wanted to ask him what difference that would have made but knew that in his eyes, it would make all the difference in the world. She was confident he didn't know who she was. Yet. But that was likely the reason he'd brought her in. Her answers to his questions in the next few minutes would mean either an agonizing death at the hands of the Gestapo or life as a slave in a labor camp. It was up to her.

"I've only just come across your file," Brunner said. "You've been here how long?"

"Around four weeks, commandant."

"What were you doing at those houses in Izieu?"

"My father owns them," she said. "He bought them as a

holiday home when we lived in Berlin. He had a factory in the city. We lived in Charlottenburg for years."

"Is that right?" he said. "But why would you shelter illegal Jews there?"

"They were children, commandant."

"I've heard the same line so many times," he said in an even tone. "All Jews carry the same abhorrent disease. The only hope for civilization is their eradication. What were you doing in Southern France these past few years?"

He was fishing. She had to throw him off the scent.

"I lived in the houses," she said. "I was looking for a husband for so long but I couldn't find one my family would approve of. I've never been one for anything like a career so I thought looking after the children would be a noble pursuit."

"You should have gone to work in an orphanage," the commandant said. "Have you spent time in Lyon?"

"Only on shopping trips, but since the war started there's nothing to buy." She shrugged. She'd made sure to separate herself from any resistance men she'd seen pass through the camp since she'd arrived, but the Germans knew several female operatives had worked in the South of France. This man was acting on a hunch. He had nothing on her. Otherwise, he would have been pulling out her fingernails right now.

"Your family are in the United States?"

"They moved back before the war started. My father made a lot of money supplying weapons to the Wehrmacht. They didn't want to get caught up in the war."

"But you did, apparently."

"I fell in love with a Frenchman who misled me, commandant. I never got involved in politics. I was happy where I was but then travel to America became so difficult. I got stuck. I tried to make the best of my life. I suppose you could say the Jews took advantage of my good nature." Saying those words hurt her, but who else would hear them?

Brunner took a few seconds to ingest her words. He looked up at her with devilish eyes. He seemed to be trying to peer into her soul, to read her thoughts. Maureen had been trained to resist interrogation. The kind that stretched to torture was irresistible, but this, if she could keep it like this, was something she could withstand.

"Do you know how we found out about your houses in the country?" he asked.

Maureen suspected but didn't know for sure. She'd been wracking her brain in the futile attempt to figure that out since coming here.

Brunner continued when she didn't answer. "A concerned citizen informed the local Gestapo of the illegal goings on there."

Maureen hid her anger, playing the role of the dumb woman. It was her best chance to survive this. Perhaps her only chance.

"Who?" she said, knowing he'd never answer. She brought her hands up to her face. "This entire situation is a nightmare." She tried to cry but couldn't. The anger gnashing at her insides wouldn't let her.

"We know everything," he said. "Why don't you just elaborate, and we can see about having you released."

"You can?" she said with a bright smile.

"Yes. You and that boyfriend of yours," he said. "Cooperate with us, and you could be back home in a day or two."

"Of course," she said.

"Where are the other Jews?"

"What other Jews, commandant?"

He leaned forward. "The Jews the OSE are hiding in the area. I know you have the precise locations of where they're being hidden."

Maureen shrugged. "I have no idea. They never told me anything. We had very little contact with—"

"Liar!" Brunner shouted and slammed his fist on the desk.

The tears came now, and Maureen milked them for every lifesaving drop.

"I don't know, I swear! They never told me anything. They were so paranoid about informants. They never said a word."

Maureen knew the locations of several other houses in the region and many others in the west and south. Brunner was just probing. Maureen wasn't going to tell him a thing. And the offer to release her and Christophe was nothing but one more Nazi lie. She would have given anything to reach across and smash his horrible little face into the desk, but she knew that would have meant an instantaneous, gruesome death.

"I don't know," she said. "You have to believe me."

"We know where the houses are," he said. "It's my job to see if you can be trusted. I have on my desk in front of me orders for your release," Brunner said. "But there is a contingency on these pages."

"What is that, commandant?" Maureen asked in her most timid voice.

"That you can be trusted. Rest assured, you can't save any of the Jews hiding around Lyon and beyond. In fact, almost all of them are already in transit here. All I need from you is some information to prove to my superiors that you can be trusted. You're not a Jew. You're not vermin like those you harbored. Perhaps you and your man are worthy of life under the Führer. Now's your time to prove it. Give me the addresses of the houses and I'll see to it that you both will be home in a week."

Maureen stared into Brunner's beady eyes. He was lying. She could tell by how he pressed his lips together and smoothed his hair while mentioning that he'd organize her release. But then, what if she was wrong? What if she and Christophe really could go home? She shifted in her seat and took a deep breath. Could she give him a fake address? No—the delay in her "release" would be while the Gestapo checked them out.

"They told me nothing," she said.

"You see, I don't believe you. I think you're a lot more than you present yourself as. Many of my colleagues underestimate women. They see them as weak, too prone to emotion, and more liable to crack under pressure. Not me. I wonder how many so-called "strong" men could bear the rigors of childbirth, and still carry on while being treated like second-class citizens their entire lives. I can see strength in people and I see it in you. Now, tell me where those houses are and you can go back to your previous life. There's nothing you can do to save the Jews. They're off to the east to work for the German people. Oh, don't worry about them. They'll be rewarded. They'll be far better off than they were in France. But will you be? Imagine sitting in a café with your boyfriend? What's his name?"

"Christophe."

"Christophe. Imagine enjoying life with him again. It doesn't have to be a fantasy. I have the power to grant that."

Maureen was beset with doubt now, and the tears running down her face were real. Brunner smiled. The swine was enjoying this. Perhaps the Jews had already been rounded up, and he was telling the truth. But she would never take that chance. Their lives were worth far more than hers.

"I'm sorry, Herr Commandant," she said. "But I have no idea of the location of any other Jews. I don't even know if there are any more. I would help if I could. Is there anything else I can do to prove myself? I lived in Berlin—went to school there."

Brunner paused a few seconds before picking up a piece of paper. "You'll be moved on from here within an hour," he said. "I'm glad you like Berlin so much. I've decided to send you to somewhere that specializes in prisoners like you. It's near your beloved former hometown."

The Nazi commandant called out, and one of his junior officers paced into the office.

"When's that next train to Sachsenhausen?" Brunner said.

"Leaving in an hour."

"See that this prisoner is on board."

"What about Christophe and the children?"

"Take her away," Brunner said.

The junior officer took her by the arm, but Maureen shrugged him off. The Nazi responded by punching her in the face. She fell backward and was about to attack when she felt her arms taken from behind her. Two more men were holding her back. The junior officer buried his fist in her midsection, and she lost the strength in her limbs. The men dragged her away.

"No, not without Christophe and the others," she whispered. But if anyone heard her, they didn't care.

Maureen felt fresh air on her face and saw a waiting truck with prisoners already loaded in the back.

"You can get in yourself or we can throw you in," one of the guards said to her.

Knowing that she had no choice and no chance of getting out of this, Maureen nodded and climbed in the back herself. She couldn't help sobbing as the engine started and the vehicle rolled out. The loss of Christophe and the others was like nothing she'd ever felt. Nothing in her life had prepared her for the crushing grief that descended upon her at that moment. Several others in the truck were crying with her. Men and women.

A woman beside Maureen put her arm around her. It felt good—a reminder that the callous, evil people were but a drop in the ocean of humanity, and the rest suffered because of them.

It took Maureen most of the 40-minute ride to recover enough to talk to the people around her. The first person she turned to was the woman beside her who'd comforted her at her lowest moment earlier.

"Who are you?" Maureen whispered.

"Sandra Delet," the middle-aged woman answered. "From Cherbourg. The Germans caught me distributing anti-Nazi pamphlets."

Most of the others on the truck were the same. None were Jews. All were French, or from some other Western country the Nazis openly called "civilized." Hitler had a hierarchy of races. Western European whites and Americans were at the top. Eastern Europeans suffered far greater indignities at the hands of a regime that considered them subhuman.

"I heard we're headed to Sachsenhausen," Sandra said. "Do you know anything about it?"

"It's near Berlin, and Brunner said they specialize in people like me. That's all I know," Maureen said.

"What does that mean?" a man sitting across from them asked.

"I don't know," Maureen replied.

"They'll kill us all," the man said.

"Don't be ridiculous," Sandra said. "They're just prisons, not death factories."

"We've all heard the rumors," the man said.

Maureen stayed silent. Her mind was with Christophe and the kids from Izieu.

The truck pulled up, and several SS soldiers greeted the prisoners with angry faces and snarling dogs held back on chains. Maureen wondered if escape were possible. They were at Gare du Nord in the center of Paris. If she could get away somehow, she could melt into the crowd and return to Drancy for Christophe and the others.

But escape was impossible. The prisoners were funneled through a line of guards on each side and, after being separated by gender, were directed into train cars designed for cattle. The smell inside hit Maureen like a fist. Two other women vomited, adding to the disgusting odor.

More people were loaded on from other trucks, and the cars were half full within an hour. With nowhere to sit, the women inside rested on the floor. It wasn't long before the first person had to relieve themselves in the bucket in the corner, and then the dam was broken. Everyone took their turn as the train trundled on. The stench inside the car grew more nauseating with every turn of the wheels below.

Maureen went to the small window to get some fresh air. She had to wait her turn, in the end, pushing past several other women who wouldn't move to catch a mouthful of fresh air. The weather outside was mercifully cool. They would have baked inside the car on a hot day. The window was at head height, about three feet wide and two feet high. Maureen put her hands on the bars. They were rusty. She reached her hand to the base where three iron bars jutted into the wood that comprised the walls of the car and rubbed off rusty dust. It was brown on her fingers. Maureen reached both hands up and grabbed onto the bars. They moved. Not much more than a few millimeters, but they moved.

Sandra was beside her, and Maureen stepped aside to let her gulp in some fresh air.

"We can move those bars," Maureen said when the other woman had gotten her fill.

"What are you talking about?"

"The rust has weakened them. We can bend them enough to squeeze out."

"How on earth....?" Sandra said.

"Let me show you," Maureen said.

She took off her sweater. "It needs to be wet," she said.

The Germans had left two buckets of water in the corner, but Maureen knew better than to touch that. The only other source of liquid was in the other bucket. She held her nose as she dipped the sweater in. The crowd stood back from the window as she wrapped her top around one of the bars. She twisted the material, and soon it became like a tourniquet, just as she'd been shown during her training in England. Once the fabric was hardened and taut, she held onto it, pulling as hard as she could, using her entire body weight. The bar moved another millimeter. She twisted the sweater again and again until all the liquid wrung out.

"Is that it?" one of the women behind her said.

Maureen wasn't nearly as strong as she'd been during training. Months of malnourishment had taken a toll on her body. She put her hands on her thighs and bent over to catch her breath.

"We're not done yet," she replied. "Just let me get my strength back, and I'll try again."

"Let me have a turn," Sandra said.

"You'll need to wet it first. No good otherwise," Maureen said. She pointed over to the latrine.

After a moment's hesitation, Sandra took the now ruined sweater and dipped it into the bucket of human waste to soak it again.

"Show me how," Sandra said.

"It's easy," Maureen replied, twisting the garment around the bar again.

Sandra was smaller than Maureen but had thick shoulders and exerted admirable pressure on the bar for a few minutes until she, too, had to rest. Maureen was ready to go again and took back the sweater. She twisted and pulled at one stage with both feet on the wall until her energy waned.

Another woman stepped forward to help. And then another. Most of the prisoners in the car stood back, washing their hands of the plan.

"What will you do when you jump out? Where will you be?" one woman asked.

"Somewhere better than the camp they're transporting us to," Maureen responded and wrapped the wet sweater around the bar again.

She, Sandra, and three other women took turns for hours, heaving at the iron bars with all the strength they could muster. When night came, most of the prisoners settled down to sleep, but Maureen kept going. The train had only stopped once since they'd left. German SS men had passed in freshwater buckets and shut the doors again without noticing anything unusual. But Germany was getting closer. It was hard to tell exactly how long they'd been traveling, but Maureen knew that jumping out in France would be a whole lot easier than in the country her family had moved to in the 1930s.

After sleeping in the corner for an hour, Maureen began again in the morning. The bars were moving freely within the frame, holding them in place now. It wouldn't be long. It was just a matter of doing it before they reached the camp. Most of the other women were still asleep as she started heaving at the bar again. Her sweater was almost worn out, and when it ripped, Sandra offered hers.

Maureen peered out the window and saw a sign in German; undeterred, she kept on.

It was mid-afternoon when the bar popped out of the frame. Maureen hugged the women working with her but knew they still had more to do. The opening still wasn't wide enough to squeeze through. Even more determined now, Maureen continued pulling at the bar with the help of the others. By the evening, the bar was bent back enough. Maureen stood on Sandra's hand as the other women hefted her up. She maneuvered her skinny body into the gap.

"I can fit!" she said with a smile.

Sandra let her back down into the car.

"Who's with me? We can get out of here."

No one spoke up.

"What?" Maureen said. "You're trusting the Nazis to look after you? Don't you remember how they treated us in Drancy? We're all starving to death. Do you think it'll be any better in the camps in Germany or the east?"

Once more, no one answered.

"I'll go," Sandra said, stepping forward.

Maureen surveyed the rest of the women. "It's just too dangerous," one of them said.

"Going where the Nazis are taking us is the real danger," Maureen replied, but the crowd was unmoved.

After a few minutes of trying to convince more to come, she realized she was wasting her time and walked back to the window. It was hard to know exactly how fast the train was traveling, but she estimated around 40 miles per hour. Jumping at that speed was dangerous. Maureen had been trained how to land from a parachute. She took Sandra aside.

"We're going to have to jump. The train's moving fast. We can try and wait until it comes to a hill, but not too long."

"What difference does it make?" Sandra said. "We're in Germany now. We have been for hours."

"But what if we stop again? If the guards see the bar is bent back, we'll never get out."

"Okay," Sandra agreed.

The image of Christophe's face flashed through Maureen's mind, but she pushed it aside. She had too much else to focus on.

Maureen raised herself up to the window. She saw no towns or any signs of civilization, just fields and trees. The rail track was level with the ground, so they wouldn't have too far to fall.

"We can do this," Maureen said to Sandra. "Now is the time."

The Frenchwoman nodded. "You go first," she said. "I'll follow."

Maureen looked at her for a brief moment before agreeing. Someone had to go first, and if she did, she could help Sandra.

"Get someone to give you a boost up to the window," Maureen said.

"I will," Sandra replied. "Good luck."

The two women hugged. Maureen put her foot in Sandra's hand and climbed up. The train was still chugging along with nothing but fields and trees to be seen. The area beside the carriage was clear, and she pulled herself into the gap she and the others had created. Wrapping one arm around the bar that was still intact, she maneuvered her body around. A ledge at the bottom of the car was wide enough to rest her weight on as she held on. The wind whooshed by as she let go. Maureen hit the ground and rolled, looking up at the train for any guards. She rose to her haunches, checking for pain. But apart from a few bumps and bruises, she was fine.

The guards on the train hadn't noticed, and she saw one man at the back of the last carriage smoking a cigarette. She hid behind a bush, watching for Sandra. The train kept moving.

"Come on, Sandra, jump!" Maureen whispered with her eyes glued to the window she'd jumped from. But Sandra didn't follow. The train disappeared into the distance, and within a minute, Maureen was utterly alone in the land of her enemies.

17

Thursday, May 4, 1944

Maureen stood up once the train had gone, looking around in a forlorn attempt to gather herself and find her bearings. She was sure of two things—this was Germany, and being caught would mean being packed off to the nearest concentration camp. Rumor had it they were dotted all over Germany and Poland, but no one really knew. Almost every effort she'd ever heard of to pierce the Reich and plant spies in Germany had failed. It was too dangerous here. She was unhurt but hungry, and a deep thirst was burning her throat. The ground was damp, but she couldn't find any puddles deep enough to drink from. She wouldn't have had any qualms about doing so. Such was her yearning for water. Everything else faded into the background of her mind. She'd ignored her thirst on the train, determined only to escape, but now that she was out, it was hard to think of anything else. A clump of trees a hundred yards away promised wet leaves, and she tramped toward it. She kept close to the ground as she moved, wondering when they'd notice she was gone. Most likely not until the train reached the camp, and with little idea of where she might be, she doubted they'd send out any search parties. Germany itself was the prison. She was just loose inside it.

The leaves on the trees were still wet from the night's rain, and Maureen took them in bunches, sucking all the moisture off. Once she'd had enough to dispel the ache in her parched throat, she walked to the edge of the trees. A farmhouse lay a few hundred yards in the distance. She spoke the language fluently, but who could she trust in Germany today? She knew from her time living in Berlin that much of the population didn't support Hitler and his policies, but finding those people was the trick. The people she'd known in her time here were probably still alive. Her father's cousin, Helga, was probably still running the factory she'd co-owned with him back in the 30s. Her ex-boyfriend, Thomas, was probably a doctor now, but who knew where? She had to find out where she was first and find someone she could trust, for out here, all alone, she was as good as dead already.

The hunger in her belly and the thirst in her throat drove her toward the farmhouse. It was the only dwelling in sight. Maureen looked down at her filthy hands, covered in blisters and streaked with blood. Her clothes, the same ones she'd been wearing on the day of her arrest at Izieu, were torn and filthy. She could speak the language, but no one would mistake her for anything other than what she was—a fugitive from the Gestapo. It was impossible to know what proportion of the German population would turn someone like her into the authorities, but she guessed, even after five long, hard years of war, the number had to be more than 70%. The German people had been conditioned to fear any enemies of the state and see them as a threat not just to Hitler's regime but to them personally. Still, she had no choice.

She crept past the cows in the field. One offered Maureen

a lazy glance before thinking better of it and returning to chewing the grass beneath her feet. She kept to the fence, moving as quickly as she dared until the farmhouse was about fifty yards away. No sound other than the gentle lowing of the cows and the breeze moving the grass entered her ears. The house was small. Simple but well-kept. Flower-boxes sat outside each window, and the house was colored a cheerful hue of yellow. Maureen noticed no sign of life. She watched and waited but couldn't stay still for more than a minute or two. The pain in her body drove her on. She passed a chicken coop, but none of the birds inside reacted to her presence. Chickens meant eggs, and cows meant milk and cheese. Maureen was sure the authorities would have requisitioned much of the produce for the war effort, but the farmers would still have squirreled enough away for themselves.

She approached the door, still hearing nothing from anywhere. The house's interior was in line with the rest of the farm—well-kept. She passed a portrait of Hitler by the door and stole into the kitchen, stuffing two pieces of bread from the sideboard into her mouth. She chewed twice before swallowing and went to the sink, where clean, glorious water poured from the faucet into a jug she held below it. She didn't bother with a glass, gulping straight from the porcelain container. The water cascading down her throat was the closest she'd felt to joy in longer than she could remember. She panted for breath as she drew it away from her mouth and heard a click from behind her.

"Turn around," a female voice said.

Maureen froze. Images of the Gestapo flooded her mind. The voice from behind her repeated the order. Maureen whirled around. A girl of about 16 with blonde pigtails was pointing a shotgun at her. Her hands were shaking so much Maureen was afraid it might go off at any moment.

"Take it easy," Maureen said in her best Berlin accent. "Don't do anything you'll regret."

"Who are you, and what are you doing in my kitchen?" the girl said.

"I'm sorry. I was hungry and had nowhere else to go. I'm Maureen," she said. "What's your name?"

"Heidi," she said. "Get out of my house."

"I don't mean you any harm. I'll be on my way now." Maureen took a step toward the door.

"Stop!" Heidi said. "My father warned me about people like you—enemies of the state. He'll be back from the market with Mother soon. I can't let you go until then."

"I'm not your enemy," Maureen said. "I'm from Berlin. Just lost."

"Dressed like that?"

Maureen knew better than to lie. She looked around. A knife on the sideboard a foot from her right hand would do for a weapon, but she had no desire to kill this girl.

"Is that your portrait of the Führer on the wall?"

"Of course, not," Heidi said. She was standing about six feet from Maureen, rooted to the spot. "It's my father's."

"I need help, Heidi. If your father turns me in, I'll die. They'll shoot me. So, if you want that, you should just pull the trigger right now. I'm sorry I broke in here, but I had nowhere else to go. I haven't eaten in two days. I promise you I mean you no harm. If you let me leave, I swear you'll never hear from me again. Can you just pretend you never walked in here? I drank some water and ate some stale bread. Nothing more."

"Why were you arrested?" Heidi asked.

"I was trying to save some children from the Gestapo," Maureen said. "But I failed. They caught us all and I'm the only one who escaped."

"My boyfriend was taken away a few weeks ago," Heidi said. Maureen felt the light of hope in her heart.

"For what?"

"He told a disparaging joke about Hitler in the restaurant he worked in. Someone reported him and the Gestapo came the next day."

"I committed no crime, Heidi," Maureen said. Her voice was calm and even. "I was only trying to do what was right. Please, let me go. My life is in your hands."

"You don't even know where you are, do you?"

"No idea. I was on the way to a camp called Sachsenhausen."

"You're not far," Heidi said and lowered the weapon. Maureen let out a breath. "The nearest town is Wustermark but Berlin is less an hour away."

Maureen realized the train she was on was probably arriving at Sachsenhausen as she stood there.

"I'm going to leave now, Heidi."

"My parents won't be back for three hours. Would you like some food?"

"I would, thank you."

"Take a seat," Heidi said. She took the shotgun with her as she walked to the sideboard. Maureen watched as she took out a loaf of bread and cut off two generous slices. She slathered butter and jam over them and brought them to the table on a plate. Maureen tried not to wolf the food down, but her behavior was driven by the voracious hunger within her, and the bread was gone in seconds. Heidi fetched some more and then some vegetable soup.

Maureen was almost finished when she asked the question on her mind. "Do you know anywhere I can hide? Or get to the coast? I can't stay in Germany."

Heidi pursed her lips and took a moment to think. "You can't stay here if that's what you're suggesting."

"Not at all. But what about the local priest or a nunnery?"

"I don't know, but I can try. Whatever we do, it has to be

now. If my parents come home and catch you here, they'll turn me in with you." Heidi stood up. "Come with me."

The evening was drawing in as they walked outside. The young girl led Maureen around the back of the farmhouse to a barn where a single horse was eating hay in the corner.

"Sparkles will make sure you get out of here safely, won't you girl?" Heidi patted the brown horse and brought her out to a waiting cart. Ten minutes later, Maureen was in the familiar position of lying on her back with half a bale of hay piled loosely on top of her. She thought of Christophe for the duration of the journey, fighting back the tears of grief and frustration.

It might have been 30 minutes before the cart stopped. It was hard to tell. Immersed in her own thoughts, she lost touch with the outside world under the hay.

"Stay hidden," Heidi whispered. "I'll be back in a few minutes."

Maureen did as she was told, enduring the heat and discomfort without a word. Another few minutes passed before Maureen heard the young girl's voice again.

"You can come out now."

Maureen pushed herself up through the mess of hay stalks, coughing and rubbing her eyes as she got out. She was in the graveyard of an old church. *Fitting*, she thought to herself. Maureen held an arm over her eyes to block out the sun as Heidi spoke.

"Come with me," she said.

Maureen was completely helpless, utterly dependent on this stranger to save her life. She followed as Heidi brought her into the small church. The temperature dropped as they walked in. The air was thicker. The priest walked down from the altar, ten yards away, and approached them. He was in his late 20s with a thin black beard and dark, piercing eyes.

"I am Father Muller," he said in a deep voice and extended a hand.

"I'm Maureen Ritter. I was bound for Sachsenhausen from Paris before I jumped off the train."

"Heidi tells me you lived in Berlin once."

"For a few years."

"What can I do for you, my child?"

"I need help, Father. I have nowhere to go. The Gestapo will kill me if I'm found."

"They send patrols through every so often, and our local Blockwart is one of the more zealous in the region."

"You have Blockwarts out here?"

"All throughout Germany now."

Things had changed since the 30s. The Blockwarts, the local snitches employed to spy on their neighbors by the Nazi Party, had only been in the cities then.

"But they don't need to know," Father Muller said. "You don't have any papers?"

"I have nothing. No money. No papers. Just my clothes. The Nazis took everything else."

"We need to get you out of sight," the priest said. "Who knows who might come by at any moment?"

"I should get back to the farm," Heidi said and turned for the door.

"Thank you," Maureen said. "I owe you my life."

"Good luck. Father will take good care of you," she said and walked out.

The priest lit a candle and led her through a wooden door and down some granite stairs. The temperature dropped with every step. The walls were hewn from stone, dark and cold. Several old coffins sat in the middle of the dark room.

"This is the crypt," the young priest said. "Few people come down here, and the door is usually kept locked."

Maureen looked around the dark, dingy space and knew it

was here or the concentration camp. If she made it that far at all.

"I'm sorry. It's not much, but it'll have to do until we can organize something better," Father Muller said.

"No, it's fine. But what if the Gestapo comes to search the church? They'll come down here."

"Yes," the young priest said. "The church was built in 1065. The priests had more than Allied bombs and the Gestapo to worry about. That was a time when the barbarians from the east marauded through the countryside." He walked over to the wall. "The old priest showed me this before he left last year."

Father Muller went to the wall and counted out loud until he reached a stone that looked like all the others except that it had a small black hole in the middle. He picked up a metal rod on the floor next to it and inserted it into the spot like a key. The stone came back, revealing a crawl space behind the wall.

Maureen got down on all fours to peer inside. The candle illuminated the space. It was about six feet by eight. "How many of those priests expected to fit in there?" Maureen asked. "They must have been small."

"I've never had to use it thankfully, but you might need to." They both stood up again. "Where did you jump from the train?" Father Muller asked.

"About two miles away."

"They'll come looking for you. It's imperative that you listen out. You can't live in that space, but you need to get in there when they come. And they will."

Maureen nodded. She appreciated his paranoia. The thought occurred to her that he might have done this before with other refugees, but it was too early for questions like that.

"How long can I stay down here?"

"That depends on you. How long will you be able to? It's dark and lonely. The door is usually locked for weeks at a time."

"I'll stay as long as you'll have me."

Father Muller brought her back upstairs, and they found an old mattress and some sheets. They cleared off the floor, sweeping the dirt and dust away before laying it down. A bucket in the corner would serve as her toilet.

"What shall I do with this stuff if the Gestapo comes?" she asked.

The young priest flipped the top off one of the caskets to reveal a skeleton. "I don't think old Father Aloysius will mind too much if he has to share with Father Helmut for a while." He picked out the skull and placed it in the casket beside it. She helped deposit the rest of the bones. They then took to cleaning out the inside of Father Aloysius's eternal resting place. It was clean as it would ever be within a few minutes.

"Oh, and one more thing," the priest said. He bounded back up the stairs and returned about five minutes later. He handed her a book.

"It's banned now, but this was in the room when I moved in."

"Death in Venice, by Thomas Mann," Maureen said. "Thank you. For everything." The young priest nodded and turned for the stairs. "Why are you doing this? Risking your life for me?"

"How could I not?" Father Muller replied. "I'll be back in the morning with breakfast. Get some sleep, but listen out if our friends come calling."

Maureen stood alone as he ascended the stairs. The only light was the candle in her hand. She set up another by her bed and sat on a stone in the corner. It was impossible to tell if it was still light outside. She had the feeling that night and day would be irrelevant to her for a long time.

Sunday, May 7, 1944

The sound of the rats scurrying around her had scared her at first, but she was used to them within a day or so. She kept a tally of the days in the crypt in the back of the book the priest had given her. He established a routine quickly. He came to visit in the morning, leaving her as much food as he could spare for the day. The second visit was after dinner when he'd empty her bucket. He was the only person she'd seen since she'd come here. Her life was in his hands. She'd read the book a little but had mostly slept or lain awake in the dark, staring into nothing, wondering what Christophe was seeing at that moment. He was probably in Germany now, along with the other children from Izieu. Her seething anger gave way to deep mourning in the darkness that enveloped her.

The candles were precious, so she spent most of the time swathed in the inky black of the crypt. Her eyes became accustomed to the lack of light, and she could walk around, but there was nothing to see other than rocks and caskets of long-dead priests. Still, she knew that this was better than any Nazi camp. At least she was alive. The thought that this would end soon sustained her.

"How much longer can the war last?" she said out loud. It was good to hear a voice—even her own. The much-anticipated attack on France hadn't happened yet, but she knew it was only a matter of time. The Allies were bogged down in Italy, but perhaps not for long, and the Russians were making gigantic strides on the Eastern Front. A blind person could see that the war was in its death throes. Perhaps the worst was already over.

"Maybe I'll be back with Christophe by the end of the summer," she said. "Christmas at the latest.

She heard the people come in for Sunday services and then the sound of singing once the congregation was in place. It sounded far off, even though it was only 20 feet above her head. She lay on her bed in the darkness listening to German hymns, letting the music flow through her.

It must have been about 11 in the morning when she heard the sound of shouting. Maureen lit the candle, opened Father Aloysius's casket, and stuffed her bedding inside. The key to the secret compartment was against the wall; she had practiced opening it so many times she could have done it with her eyes closed. The rock slid out. She went for the slop bucket and brought it into the hiding space. She closed it over just as the sound of the door to the crypt opening reverberated down the stairs.

Maureen placed the slop bucket as far from her nose as possible, but the stench was still nauseating in the enclosed space. A tiny gap above the rock served as a peephole, and Maureen watched as two soldiers descended the stairs. Their flashlights scythed through the darkness.

"What is this place?" one of the soldiers asked.

"A crypt, you idiot," the other man answered.

Maureen held her breath as she realized she'd left her book by Father Aloysius's casket. It was on the ground ten feet from where the men were standing.

One of the soldiers picked the top off one of the caskets. It clattered to the floor, revealing the two skeletons inside.

"Did you see this?" he said. "There's two of them."

"What did you expect to find in there? Marlene Dietrich?"

"That would have been nice."

The second soldier walked over to Father Aloysius's casket.

His foot was inches from her book, but somehow, he hadn't seen it yet.

"Anything there?" A voice from upstairs called down.

"No, nothing down here," one of the men responded.

"Then get back up here and let's get moving."

The two soldiers jogged back up the stairs, and the door shut behind them. Maureen let her head drop to her hands as relief surged through her.

～

Thursday, February 15, 1945

The tally marks of days in the crypt were too many for one page now. Maureen organized them into groups of 30. But things were changing. The fighting that had engulfed much of Germany and which seemed about to spread to Berlin had passed them by. Apart from a few random bombs dropped short by Allied fighters and the sound of artillery booming in the distance, she had heard little of the war in the months she'd spent in the darkness. Father Muller still came every day and brought her the newspapers. Even the most Nazi-leaning rags couldn't disguise the disasters befalling the SS and the Wehrmacht on both fronts. The war had dragged on longer than she'd hoped, but the end seemed to be in sight. The nightmare that had begun when she moved to Berlin as a 16-year-old and had taken over her entire life was ending.

Maureen jarred from a restful sleep as Father Muller

walked down the steps. The light of the candle he was holding danced along the walls before he followed a few seconds later.

"Good morning, Maureen," he said. "Sleep well?"

"I did," she replied. "I think I could fall asleep on a cactus these days."

The priest, who was the only person Maureen ever saw, had been jittery these past few weeks. His hands were shaking as he put down the tray of food. His face was lined with worry.

"I have some news," he said.

"What is it? Did someone talk?"

"No, it's nothing like that. It's my brother in the city. He was wounded in one of the last bombing raids. His wife died last year and both his sons are on the Western Front. I'm all he has. I don't think I have a choice. I have to go and look after him."

Maureen's blood ran cold. The relative safety she'd lived in these past seven months was about to be taken away. "What about me? What about your congregation?"

"The parishioners will be fine. No one comes anymore, anyway. They're all too afraid to leave their houses."

"And me? How long will you be gone?"

"Several weeks, I'd imagine. No one will be here to feed you. You're going to have to leave."

Maureen was struggling to believe the words coming out of the man's mouth. It seemed so near the end. Perhaps only a few weeks, but the Gestapo would still kill her in a second if she was caught.

"Where will I go?"

"The city. You used to live there. Surely you know someone who could take you in. It won't be for as long as I kept you here. Both fronts seem ripe to collapse any day now."

"I'll never make it past the checkpoints. I don't have any papers!"

"It's different now. The organization is beginning to collapse. There are so many refugees—people with nothing.

You speak the language. We can say you lost your papers when your house was destroyed in the bombing."

"Is there no one to tend to me out here once you leave?"

"No one I'd trust with your life. People are scared. No one wants to be the last person in the Reich to be executed for harboring a fugitive." The young priest sat down on the edge of one of the caskets. "This has been on my mind for days now. I've been wracking my brain to think of someone who could keep you, but there's no one."

"What about Heidi, the girl who found me?"

Father Muller's face dropped. "I didn't want to tell you this, but she's gone."

"Gone?" Maureen asked. "Where?"

"Taken away. The Gestapo came. Someone reported her for anti-government sentiment. It's an offence punishable by jail-time these days."

Maureen thought about the young girl who'd saved her life for a few seconds, and then Christophe and the others from Izieu. "Does anyone know where she is?"

"I don't know," Father Muller said.

"Is there anyone in the city you could trust? Do you still have family in Berlin?"

Maureen thought of the only relative she had remaining in Hitler's capital. Her father's cousin Helga had been a member of the Party since the early days. They'd parted acrimoniously when he fled before the war started. Her loyalty to Hitler had driven a wedge between them but Maureen still remembered a time when she was close to the family. She'd never married—at least she hadn't when Maureen had last heard when her family left Berlin. Apart from her, her ex-boyfriend Thomas probably lived where he used to, and she had some friends, but she hadn't set foot in Berlin since 1936. Who could she trust with her life after nine years?

"I don't think I have anyone," she said.

"Okay. My brother has a big house in Charlottenburg—where you used to live?"

Maureen nodded and the priest continued. "He's confined to one room. I'll stick you in his basement. If I get the sense he won't approve, I won't tell him. We'll figure something out."

"Okay," Maureen said reassured. "When do we leave?"

"In a few hours. Try and get ready," Father Muller said and left.

She had no personal possessions, so getting ready to leave was just a matter of saying goodbye to the place, and while she was thankful that the crypt had sustained her all this time, she certainly wouldn't miss it.

She washed in a tub he brought her, but still felt dirty even after she'd finished.

Thoughts of the farmer's daughter, the woman on the train, the poor children, dominated her mind as she waited for the priest. The hope that Christophe in particular was still alive had sustained her through the dark times of the past seven months. She dreamed of a shining future with him, always returning to the picture of the two of them back in Marseille, drinking coffee outside watching the undulating azure blue of the Mediterranean as they wasted a blissful afternoon together.

"Time to go," the priest said as he appeared at the bottom of the stairs.

Maureen squinted as she walked outside, even in the dull winter sun. Father Muller's belongings were packed on top of a cart. A sickly-looking brown horse was to lead them into western Berlin. Maureen was thankful it wasn't far, but couldn't help the feeling she was venturing back into the lion's den.

"Are you sure this is safe without papers?" she asked as they set off.

"Perhaps not," he said. "So, I got you these." He handed her some documents. She opened them up. A woman who looked a little like her stared back. "One of my parishioners left them behind last week. I thought they might come in handy."

Maureen stuffed them in her pocket and faced forward. It felt good to be outside, to feel the breeze in her hair.

The first checkpoint was outside Wustermark. Two policemen in their 60s who didn't seem to want to be there looked over her papers.

"I'm so sorry," she said in her best Berlin accent. "The rest were burned up in the last bombing raid.

"Along with everything else," one replied and handed them back.

Father Muller chatted to them for a few seconds before the two policemen waved them on.

"There was no avoiding them, but I figured they wouldn't be too discerning. The checks haven't been nearly as stringent the past few weeks. The Reich as we've known it is coming apart at the seams," Father Muller said once they were out of earshot. "If we take the back roads into the city, we might make it all the way without passing another check."

The day was fading, and Maureen buttoned up the coat Father Muller had given her. Patches of snow were still visible on the ground. Maureen wondered how Christophe had dealt with winter in the camp. She didn't know for sure. Nothing was certain these days, but she surmised he was in the camp they'd tried to send her to. Sachsenhausen was north of the city, barely an hour from where she was. He was that close. She had to dispel futile thoughts of rescue. They would only serve to torture her further, and she had enough to occupy her mind.

They kept on as the buildings grew thicker around them. The scars of the war were visible as soon as the city was. The skyline was fractured and a thick cloud of smoke hung in the air, irritating her eyes and tickling her throat. Houses on both sides of the street were reduced to rubble. As in France, the streets were empty of cars. Berlin had been transported back 50 years. Cars sat unused in driveways as people rode bareback on horses. Almost all, equine and human alike, were thin as greyhounds. They saw no military vehicles, though she was sure the main highways into the city were full of them. The cart continued through the suburbs of Spandau and Westend, toward Charlottenburg, her old neighborhood where her father's cousin Helga likely still lived.

Being back here, where she'd lived for almost four years felt like returning to the scene of a crime. She kept her eyes down, avoiding everyone who passed them.

They spoke little as they rode, but Father Muller broke the silence as they approached his brother's house. "We're almost here," he said.

The small house was on a residential street. It was somewhere she'd passed by dozens of times when she'd lived here, for her father's old house was only three blocks away. She didn't dare ask to go see it. The only thing to do was get off the street as soon as she could. Her luck had held on the journey here, but it might not for much longer.

"Hide around the side while I go and see my brother," Father Muller said.

Maureen did as she was told. The side gate opened with a creak and she hid in the alley beside the house for a few minutes before the priest emerged again.

"I opened the door to the basement around back," he whispered. "Telling my brother is too dangerous. Gustav's a Hitler loyalist, but he can hardly move. As long as you don't make any noise, you'll be safe down there."

Maureen nodded and walked around the back of the house. The priest was good as his word. The door was ajar and she pushed it open to reveal another damp, dark place.

"A little different from the mansion we used to live in," she whispered to herself as she found somewhere to sit among the old garden tools kept there. An old lounge chair would serve as that night's bed.

The door to the basement opened two hours later. Maureen hid behind an old wooden box, but emerged when she heard Father Muller's voice. The priest gave her some food and water, as well as some blankets he'd found. She thanked him and curled up on the lounger. He closed the door behind him and she was alone, back in Berlin.

The rumbling sound of airplanes overhead woke her in the night. The crump of explosions in the distance followed seconds later. The local air raid sirens remained silent, but she knew it was only a matter of time before they sounded and the bombs fell.

18

Friday, February 23, 1945

Maureen was asleep on the lounge chair when the sirens rang. Panic washed through her. The low rumble of explosions in the distance filled the dingy basement. The door was only a few feet away. She didn't know if she should run up to Father Muller or stay put. The priest had come to her once a day since they'd arrived to deliver water and the starvation rations they could spare. His brother still had no idea she was down here. She stood up as the roar of destruction came again, but this time closer. The walls of the basement were thick concrete. The ceiling was the same. It seemed the house was built on a massive stone block. Perhaps she'd be safest here. She heard something from upstairs—the sound of doors opening and shutting again. She walked toward the door to the main house and wrapped her fingers around the handle. Perhaps they needed help. Father Muller had told her not to come upstairs under any circumstance, but this was different. He'd need help getting his brother Gustav to the air raid shelter. Maureen turned the handle and peeked up the staircase to the house. She took one step and a huge bang reverberated through the air. A force tossed her body backward like a massive celestial hand, and she landed against a cardboard box eight feet away. The air was thick with smoke and dust and ash. It got into her eyes and choked her lungs. She tried to get up, but fell to the floor, her ribs aching from where she'd landed. The smoke cleared enough for her to see the door to upstairs was gone and the stairs to the top were blocked with shattered concrete and other debris.

"Father Muller?" she tried to call out, but her voice was lost in the smoke and dust.

She gasped for water and reached for her bottle in a daze but it was smashed. Her head was spinning. Maureen lunged for the door to the back yard. It opened, but only enough for her to crawl through. The garden that had been beyond it was now a mess of debris. The bombs continued to drop. The sound of explosions rocked the air. The siren was gone—perhaps destroyed in the raid. Above her head, huge bombers pierced the night sky, illuminated by searchlights until they disappeared into the black once more to unleash their deadly payload onto the city below.

She stumbled over the ruins of Father Muller's brother's home and turned to look back. A massive gaping hole stood where the lefthand side of the house had been moments before. The next-door neighbor had taken a direct hit which had reduced the entire property to rubble. The second floor of Gustav's house was gone. She was able to see into his bedroom through the smoke and dust.

"Father Muller," she said again. "Are you all right?"

Maureen's side ached, and her throat burned, but she climbed up the loose bricks and concrete all the way up to the second floor. The back wall was gone and she limped into

Gustav's bedroom. His bed was covered in debris. Maureen limped on, almost slipping on broken tiles. The inside wall was still intact and she shoved the door open. The roof was creaking and she knew she had only moments before the entire house collapsed. She tried to push the other bedroom door open, but it jammed after only a few inches. The ceiling had caved in, and as she peered around the door, she saw the bed was broken and covered in concrete blocks stained in her friend's blood.

She didn't have time to mourn. The stairs were blocked. The only way out was the way she came. She turned and walked back into Gustav's bedroom then climbed down to the backyard once more.

Unable to think straight, she stumbled around to the front of the house. A small crowd had gathered.

"Are you all right?" a man asked her.

She recoiled as if he'd tried to bite her. She turned and ran. The bombs were still falling. A house behind her took a direct hit, spewing bricks and smoke into the night. No fire engines came. Only those who hadn't made it to the shelters were on the streets. Many just stood shaking their heads as their homes burned to the ground. Maureen wandered on.

Where can I go? I can't stay out on the street. Her ex-boyfriend and the other friends she'd left behind in '36 had all been living with their parents at the time. She remembered where the houses were but had no idea if the only people who might welcome her were still living there.

She found herself on her old street and walked up toward the house she'd lived in for three years with her family. It was different now. The hedges had been replaced with gates and a Nazi flag lay limp on a flagpole on the front lawn. Maureen pressed her hands against the iron gates, wishing her family was still inside. A voice called in her ear, reminding her of the urgency of her situation. If she was to get out of Berlin alive, she'd have to find somewhere to hide, and fast.

She tried to clear the fog in her mind, to come up with a plan to save her own life. Aunt Helga's house was only a few minutes' walk away. Maureen searched her memories for the way and began to walk. She'd never been there before. Helga had moved into a new mansion with the riches she'd made selling weapons to the Nazis after Maureen had left. But she could remember the address from letters she'd sent years before.

More bombs dropped and as Maureen crested a hill, she could see dozens of little fires in the city below. She looked up at the street sign as a military truck rounded the corner. Resisting the temptation to hide, she kept walking with her head high. The vehicle passed.

She said the numbers out loud in English as she walked. "132, 134, 136." And then she stopped. Allied bombs had ravaged what had once been the grandest mansion on the street. Helga's house was covered in scaffolding but much of that too had wilted and fallen. The bottom windows were boarded up and the silver Mercedes parked out front was a hulking wreck, covered in fallen branches and dust.

Maureen ran up to the door and checked the mailbox—it was empty, and as she peered through the keyhole, she saw a light in the darkness inside. She pressed her ear to the door and heard nothing. Perhaps if she saw some other choice, she might have gone somewhere else. Maureen drew back from the door and ran around the side of the house. Her ribs ached as she climbed the gate and she winced in pain as she landed on the concrete slab beyond it. She could tell by the light of the moon that the backyard was unkempt and overgrown.

Wary of being shot as an intruder, Maureen sank to her haunches and inched toward the back door. It was unlocked and she pushed it open. She walked into a splendid atrium with plants hanging in pots, and plush upholstered couches facing the windows. Another door led into a mahogany-sided hallway. The light of a fire glowed through the darkness. Golden light danced through an open doorway and onto the walls. Maureen walked inside. It was a space fit for one of the masters of the Reich that the once booming armaments industry had created. The ceiling was paneled, with a dozen heavy beams in one direction and another dozen crossing them, forming squares. They were made of beautifully carved dark brown wood, and from them hung chandeliers, each a ring of thirty or so slim white candles with electric bulbs in the tops. But only about half were working. The walls of the room were wainscoted three or four feet high, and above were paintings, several of which depicted the harsh right-angled lines of Nazi art. A great open fireplace with high-backed lounges in front of it was lit at the end of the room. An armchair was facing the fire.

"Aunt Helga?" Maureen said.

Her father's cousin turned around. She was even skinnier than when Maureen had last seen her and her once jet-black hair was now streaked with grey, but other than those things, she looked the same. She still had the same determined, intelligent look.

"Who are you?" she said. "What are you doing in my house?"

But Maureen knew from Helga's tone of voice she knew Maureen wasn't a stranger.

"It's Maureen Ritter. I'm here because I've nowhere else to go."

The fire behind her turned Helga into a silhouette. "Did your father send you? Where is he?"

"In New York. It's just me."

"What are you doing here?"

"I need somewhere to hide," Maureen said and took three

steps toward Helga. "I've nowhere else to go. I was staying a few blocks away but the house was bombed." Maureen looked up at a portrait of Hitler on the wall and stopped herself. "I need food and water. I'll be out of here as soon as I can."

"I haven't seen you in—"

"Nine years," Maureen said. "But you loved us once. I'm asking you to trust in me again. I mean you no harm."

"How long have you been back in Berlin?"

"Only a few weeks. I saw my father's old house. It's different now."

Helga pursed her lips and picked up a glass of wine from the table in front of her. "A banker moved in a year after your father left."

"I have nowhere else to go, Helga. You're the only family I have here."

"Who are you running from?"

Maureen had little to gain from telling Helga the truth. It would only provoke her. "Remember those summers we spent at the lake?" Her father's cousin didn't respond. "That was before all this. Before all this destruction. Before Allied bombs that come in the night and destroy your house and kill everyone you love. Anyone with eyes can see that this will all end soon. The Soviets are coming, and the Americans are only a few hours away. I don't want to die, Helga. Please help me."

Helga stared into her red wine, swirling it in the dancing light of the fire. "I won't lie to the police. If they come asking for you by name, I won't deny you're here."

A dam burst inside Maureen and great waves of relief came gushing through. "Thank you. You won't have to."

"You can hide in the attic until the Allies come. It should be warmer up there."

"Are you staying in Berlin?" Maureen asked.

"Where would I go? This house is all I have left."

"What about the factories?" Maureen asked. "Are you still running them?"

"They were bombed and rebuilt so many times the government gave up on them. They've been closed for six months now."

"And you? What have you been doing?"

"Sitting here, waiting for the end. I won't leave Berlin. Not while the Führer is still here. If I'm to die I want to be near him." She stared into the fire as if she could see Hitler's face in there. "You want some food?"

"Please."

"In the kitchen. Help yourself. The servants all fled last week. My butler, Johann, was the last to leave. I expected better from him."

Maureen nodded and turned for the kitchen. Without taking time to think about her situation she went to the cabinet and found two eggs and some stale bread. She was tempted to crack the eggs straight into her mouth but took the time to fry them after scarfing down the bread.

Helga was still in front of the fire when Maureen returned.

"Am I safe here?" Maureen asked.

"As safe as any of us these days?"

"From the authorities, I mean."

Helga turned around and looked at her. "I won't turn you in. Whatever you are now, you're still family." She stood up and led Maureen upstairs. "You should take a bath while the raid is still going on. No one's coming while the bombs are falling."

Maureen wanted to ask what would happen if the house was hit while she was getting washed up, but held her tongue.

Helga walked her upstairs to the bathroom. "I'd ask what you've been doing all these years, but fear that I might not like the answer," she said.

"Thank you for taking me in," Maureen said.

"You can go to the attic once you're clean. There are

armchairs and even an old mattress under covers. You can use them. I'll be downstairs if you need me, but I suggest you spend most of your time hidden. It's not rare for patrols to pass by and Frau Trundle, our local Blockwart, is the zealous type, even still."

Maureen thanked her again. Helga nodded and closed the bathroom door behind her.

19

Monday, December 4, 2006

Amy stood up from the bed with Marie in her arms. Her grandmother was exhausted and needed sleep. She reached over and hugged the older woman.

"I love you, Grandma," she whispered into her ear.

"I love you too, and little Marie. I love you all. I can't wait to go for dinner in the city. I can see that little baby asleep in the car seat beside me now."

One of the nurses came to the bedside. It was time for Maureen's medication. Amy stood up to leave. She looked over at her grandmother's brother Conor, sitting on the other side of the bed, who had flown over from his home in Florida. He was slim and tanned. His silver hair was still thick on his head. He wore an expensive-looking blue shirt and gray slacks. Getting to know him again these last few days had been a wonderful treat. He took his sister's hand and kissed it, then followed Amy out of the room.

"I never knew," he said. "She never breathed a word about any of it. I knew she was in Europe during the war. I was in the service myself, Michael too, but I had no idea what she went through. It's humbling to hear."

"Maybe we can hear your story next?" Amy said.

Her great-uncle smiled. "My wife's heard mine so many times, she's sick of it! I think she could tell it better than I ever could. And mine's nothing on my brother Michael's!"

They continued down the hallway. Conor was slim and fit for a man of his age.

"It's a blessing that we're all here," he said as they entered the elevator. "I've lost all my other siblings, but if this is the end for Maureen, it's the way she would have wanted to go— surrounded by family."

Amy didn't respond. She couldn't bear the thought of losing her grandmother. Not now. Not ever. Conor's words came as some comfort but not enough. Amy couldn't see the joy or nobility in her grandmother's death. Maureen had lived a fantastic life and had seen so much, but Amy knew her grandmother wasn't done yet. Not in her mind, anyway. The notion that Maureen had to die because she was sick and old was anathema to Amy.

"Excuse me, I have to feed the baby," Amy told Conor. He smiled and patted Marie on the head before letting them go to the lobby. Amy went to a lactation room she knew well and sat down. She took the baby out of the car seat and held her to her breast. Marie's latch was strong, and she was putting on weight now.

"You're a little pig!" she murmured.

Breastfeeding her child felt natural and right. It was comforting to know she could provide for her. It was strange to think how nervous she'd been about this before Marie came— about how scared she'd been to be a mother. Now, it seemed like her natural state. Amy's anxiety over Marie's health had lessened with each day. Her little girl was getting bigger and stronger by the hour.

Normality was heaven to Amy. All other questions about jobs and income and how she'd make ends meet faded into the ether when she looked inside herself. Perhaps she finally knew the keys to her own happiness. Marie fell asleep after she'd eaten, and Amy put her in her car seat and carried it with the handle resting on her forearm.

Her phone buzzed. Ryan had gone home a few days before but had called every afternoon since. She reached for her cell and opened it up. "Hello."

He asked about Marie first, then Maureen. She spent a minute talking about them before he told her.

"I spoke to the kids," he said. "I told them about Marie, and you, and everything that happened."

Amy wondered what kind of a spin he'd put on the story but knew anyone would have done the same.

"They want to meet Marie," he said. "As soon as I told them, they wouldn't stop asking to come and see their new sister."

Amy smiled and nodded her head. "We'll wait until I get back to New York. They can come to the apartment."

She hung up the phone with a wide smile. The person Amy wanted to tell most was still resting upstairs. Her grandmother was stirring in the bed as she and a still-sleeping Marie arrived. The nurse was at her bedside, administering her medication.

"Give us a few minutes, Amy," the nurse said.

Amy nodded and stood at the door to gaze at her grandmother for a few seconds, marveling at what one brave person could achieve, then turned away into the hall. She took a seat and put Marie's car seat down beside her.

There was someone else she wanted to talk to. Mike would have wanted to know how things were with Marie. She began typing into her phone. They hadn't been in contact in a week.

I thought you'd want to know that Marie is doing well.

The response came back seconds later. *That's fantastic news!*

She's a lucky little girl to have you as a momma. I know you'll have a wonderful life together.

She plucked up the courage to say more. *My grandmother had a heart attack, but she's getting better.*

I'm so sorry to hear that. How are you coping?

I'm okay. I'm not sure how long she's got, but every day is a blessing...

I know she must be so happy to have you with her and the baby...Is her family all around her?

A voice inside her chest screamed at her to text him to come over, call him, beg him, but that was all too dangerous. He could break her heart, and she couldn't allow that. She closed the phone instead.

The nurse called her in. Her grandmother was ready for visitors again. She picked up Marie and brought her inside, laying her down where Maureen could see her. Once the baby was situated, Amy took a seat and reached out for her grandmother's hand.

"How are you feeling, Grandma?" Amy asked.

"Better all the time, my dear. Looking forward to getting up out of bed and taking that sweet little girl for lovely long walks in her stroller."

"You will, Grandma," Amy said. "You're that determined."

"We're both determined women. I'm no different than you."

Amy smiled. "I think that could be the biggest compliment I've ever received."

"Just don't make the same mistake I did. Don't let fear or hesitation hold you back from what you want."

"What are you talking about? You were never afraid of anything your whole life," Amy said.

"I was terrified almost all the time during the war years. It became part of me. I lived with it every day."

"But you never let it hold you back. You can't have any regrets."

A rueful smile crossed the older woman's face. "People talk about regret as if it's possible to traverse life without picking up a single one. Everyone has regrets. It's as much a part of being human as falling in love or succumbing to death. I regret not trying to smuggle those poor children from Izieu over the border into Switzerland myself."

"You had no way of knowing what would happen."

"I still have regrets."

"It wasn't your fault."

"I know, and I don't regret that insane stunt in trying to steal the truck that got me caught by the Nazis. In fact, quite the opposite. There is one thing, though...." The older woman trailed off.

"Christophe," Amy said.

Maureen nodded. "How long do you have until she wakes up?"

"I guess we'll see."

The tape recorder was where Amy had left it beside the bed. "Let's finish this," her grandmother said. Amy walked over and flicked it on.

_____

20

Tuesday, April 24, 1945

The shelling began at dawn. Maureen looked out the tiny attic window at the city below. Plumes of smoke rose from a hundred different points, and new explosions came every few seconds. She had little doubt who the honor of taking Berlin had fallen to. The Soviets would soon maraud through the city she'd loved once. She dreaded to think of the terrible revenge the Red Army would exact for the cruelties suffered by the Russian people at the hands of the Nazis. It had been two days since she'd seen Helga, and her food and water were almost depleted. It was time to leave. Hitler's defeat was imminent, but surviving it in this attic seemed impossible. Helga had told her repeatedly to stay put, that they'd escape together when the time was right, but Maureen was beginning to doubt her father's cousin's words. Her behavior had grown erratic and unpredictable over the last few weeks.

Maureen hadn't been downstairs for more than a few minutes in almost a month but pushed the attic door open and walked through. Helga rarely left the house these days either, preferring to sit in her massive living room, listening to the official government radio station as it told the people to hold tight and that the glorious Führer had a plan to get them out of the mess he'd gotten them into in the first place. The sound of newscasts drifted up through the floorboards day after day. It was the only sign of Helga she heard most of the time.

Maureen walked down the wide staircase to the foyer below. More explosions rocked the city center, but these weren't from the sky. No familiar whistling sound had preceded them. These explosions were artillery, and that meant the Russians were close.

The radio was turned up to the maximum extent as Maureen walked into the living room. Helga was in her chair. The fire was full of last night's ashes, and empty bottles of expensive wine littered the floor.

"Maureen!" Helga murmured with a drunken smile. "I haven't seen you in a few days. Do you know what I'm celebrating?"

"The Soviets are shelling the city. Berlin will fall!"

"No, no," she said. Thursday was the Führer's birthday! And today is mine." She gestured up toward the six-foot-painted portrait of Hitler on the wall. Such things were commonplace in people's houses. The despot looked handsome and noble in the picture, not pasty and pathetic as in real life.

"We have to get out now!" Maureen said.

"He turned 56 on Thursday, and I'm 48 today. The man I gave my adult life to is 56. I never married. Hitler was the closest thing I ever had to a husband. And I never met him. Isn't that pitiable?"

Helga stumbled toward the portrait and raised her half-drunk glass of wine to it. "To you, mein Führer. Always, and until the end!"

As Maureen stepped closer, she noticed a revolver on the chair. "What's that for?"

"For the Russians!" Helga slurred. "I'll shoot the first Russki that steps through that door. Right between the eyes."

Maureen had never seen Helga this drunk before. She walked over to her. "We need to get out of here before it's too late. We don't want to be here when the Red Army arrives."

"I'm not leaving. I'm staying here with the Führer."

A diamond necklace was strewn on the couch a few feet away, and a gold pendant sat on the coffee table. The trappings of wealth she'd worked so hard to accumulate meant nothing now.

"You want to go?" Helga said.

She nodded. Christophe had never left her mind. She had to see him. He was so close.

"Yes. Today. If we wait any longer—"

"The SS have pressed old men and boys into a new fighting unit. I doubt any of them have seen any combat before but now they're going to be up against Soviet tanks. Can you believe that? They get to die for the Führer at the very end."

"It's monstrous."

"To give your life for what you believe in?" Helga turned around and picked up the gun. "It's the ultimate honor. And besides, what's to live for now? Everything is over."

"You're wrong," Maureen said. Helga still had the gun in her hand, but it was by her side. "Life will go on once the Reich falls."

"But you want to leave, don't you?" Helga said.

"Will you come with me?"

"No. My place is here. I've lived here all my life and I want to die here."

Maureen walked over to her cousin and embraced her for the first time in nine years.

"I have a bicycle in the shed. Be careful on your way out of the city. No use in being the last traitor to hang in Berlin."

Maureen ran to the shed. She was stepping into the garden

when she heard a bang from inside the house. She ran back. The gun in Helga's hand was still smoking as Maureen arrived back. Her father's cousin was slumped in her armchair in front of her beloved Führer with a hole in the side of her head. Maureen clamped her eyes shut and turned around before realizing that the diamond necklace and gold pendant on the coffee table could mean the difference between life and death. She ran over and snatched them, catching an accidental glimpse of Helga's dead stare, before continuing out the back door. She realized Helga was lying about the gun.

She found the bike and, knowing she'd fade in with the multitude of other refugees leaving the city, cycled onto the street.

She looked back one last time and saw the wrecked facade of Helga's mansion. Everything Helga had believed in was collapsing. Perhaps saving Maureen was the last thing her father's cousin needed to do before the end. Maureen pedaled on.

Hundreds of refugees were on the streets, carrying suitcases and pushing baby carriages. These were not the poor. These were affluent people, maybe those who'd turned a blind eye to Nazi outrages in exchange for a bigger house or a new car. Several soldiers ran past, but none paid her any attention. The shelling came again, only a few blocks away this time.

As Maureen looked back, she could see the center of the city was being pummeled by shells. Hitler and his cabinet were in there somewhere, reaping what they'd sown.

The streets were clear, and with no cars on the road, she joined a stream of bikes. Everyone was moving in one direction —west. The Allies were to the west. The Soviets to the east, and advancing all the time. She had no bags. Nothing other than the gold pendant and the diamond necklace she'd taken from Helga's house.

Several children in ill-fitting uniforms ran out onto the

street carrying rifles. A teenager in uniform roared orders at them, and they stood to attention. Maureen stopped.

"What are you doing?" she asked a blond girl who looked about 14.

"Protecting the city from the Bolshevist hordes," the little girl answered.

"You're a child," Maureen said.

"Stay away from the soldiers," the older boy, who looked about 18, said. "They're front-line troops in training. They'll be protecting you soon."

"You need to go home," Maureen said to the girl. "Please!"

The young officer reached into his holster and drew his weapon. "Stop spreading treason among the recruits or you will be shot!" He raised the pistol.

Maureen looked into the girl's blue eyes and got back on her bike.

~

Berlin receded, and the houses and buildings became trees and fields. Helga's gold pendant was gone. She'd used it to bribe the guard at the last checkpoint leaving the city. Other than the checkpoint she'd passed, the local police and soldiers she'd expected to see were conspicuous by their absence. The downfall was well and truly happening. Perhaps some measure of freedom was returning. Christophe's camp was only an hour north, and she had no idea if it was still in Nazi hands or not. But she had to try. Her legs burned, and she longed for rest, but Maureen didn't stop. Wary of traveling through Berlin, she veered west. Sheer exhaustion forced her off the bike at the town of Velten, just a few miles short of Oranienburg. The Nazis had built Sachsenhausen just north of it. Maureen remembered hearing of the camp in the 30s when she lived in Berlin. It was one of the Nazis' original dirty secrets, one of the first in a vast network that now dotted Germany and the occupied territories.

Avoiding the town, Maureen cycled around it. She asked an old lady in a dilapidated farmhouse directions to the camp. The woman stared at her for a few seconds.

"Please," Maureen said. "My husband's there. I have to see him."

"They evacuated it last night," the woman said. "Huge crowds of prisoners walked west."

"Is there anyone still there? Any German guards?"

"The filthy Poles retook it and let every criminal loose," she said. "It's ten minutes away. I have no idea where they took the prisoners."

The woman walked back into her house, and Maureen got on her bike again. Her heart was racing as she approached Sachsenhausen. Thick concrete walls extended around the perimeter. Several vans were parked outside with the mark of the Red Cross on them. Medical personnel were carrying prisoners on stretchers and depositing them in the back. Several soldiers in Polish Army uniform were guarding the scene. The words *Arbeit Macht Frei* were legible in foot-high iron lettering on the gate.

Maureen threw her bike down and approached the gates. Two soldiers looked up at her.

"Looking for a relative?" one of the men asked in German.

"My fiancé," she said.

"Most of the prisoners were moved out when the Nazis evacuated two nights ago, but there are still several thousand they couldn't move. Ask over there," he said and gestured to a line of people queuing at three desks. "We've taken account of who's left here," the soldier said in a strong Polish accent. "If your fiancé is still here, you can find out over there."

Maureen thanked him and joined the line. The five minutes before she reached the soldier behind the desk seemed to take weeks.

"Can I help you?" he said. He wore round spectacles halfway down his large nose.

"I'm looking for Christophe Canet. From Marseille."

The man picked up a long list and checked it. He put it down and started poring over another. "Yes," he said, and Maureen's heart jumped. "Go to tent 12, just down there."

He pointed to a line of medical tents in the massive court-yard. She thanked him and ran. Her legs ached, but she kept on, past limping prisoners more skeletons than men. Past nurses and doctors carrying bodies and past a pile of fresh corpses.

Maureen arrived at the tent and rushed inside. A dozen beds lined each side, and several nurses were walking up and down. A priest was giving the last rites to a man in the closest bed. Once he was finished, he moved on to the next. Maureen scanned the patients. Each looked like a living corpse.

She grabbed a nurse. "I'm looking for Christophe Canet," she said. "A Frenchman."

The nurse, a middle-aged woman with deep blue eyes and lined skin nodded and took Maureen by the hand. "The men on this ward are our worst," she whispered. "Christophe has typhoid fever. We don't have the medicine. He's too far gone..."

Maureen let the nurse go and ran along the beds, calling his name.

"Maureen?" a voice said. She ran to the end.

"Christophe!" she said.

His face was skeletal and devoid of color. Several of his teeth were missing as he smiled. She took his torso in her arms and embraced him. His body felt weak and delicate, like wet paper. He wrapped skinny arms covered in mulberry-colored rashes around her. She kissed his chapped lips and sobbed as she knelt by his bedside.

"I knew you'd come for me," he said in a whisper.

"I'm so sorry it took so long."

"I looked for you when I arrived," he said. "I wasn't surprised to hear you'd jumped the train. My lioness."

"Where are the children from Izieu?"

"Not here. That's all I know." He turned his head to cough. "Seeing you is like a dream," he said. "Somedays, I wondered if you existed at all or if I was just making you up to fool myself into believing someone so wonderful and beautiful could exist. But now I know it was true."

Maureen gripped his hand, unable to see through the tears. "I love you, Christophe. I'll never stop."

"And I love you, my darling," he said. He gasped and coughed before bringing his eyes back to hers.

"We'll be back in Marseille, sipping wine overlooking the Old Port soon," she said.

"It's not nearly so beautiful as you," he said. He gasped for air. The nurse came down and rubbed a cold compress along his forehead.

"I have a question for you, Christophe," Maureen said once the nurse left.

"What is it, my dear?"

Tears burned in her eyes, and the words almost caught in her throat as she said them.

"Will you marry me?"

"I thought you'd never ask," he said with a smile.

"Here and now?"

He nodded.

"I'll be back," she said. The priest was halfway along the row of beds when she grabbed him. He agreed to her request with a smile and walked down to Christophe's bed.

Maureen took Christophe's hand and turned to face the priest.

"I hope he doesn't care I'm not Catholic," Christophe whispered to Maureen as the priest readied himself. Maureen laughed as the tears rolled down her cheeks.

Several nurses gathered to watch.

Christophe looked into her eyes as the priest recited the wedding ceremony. Maureen kissed him.

"Not yet," the priest said with a smile.

A wonderous joy overwhelmed that horrible place. And just for a few moments, their dreams became reality.

"Are you prepared, as you follow the path of marriage, to love and honor each other for as long as you both shall live?" the priest asked.

They both agreed and moments later were pronounced man and wife. The nurses cheered with tears in their eyes, and Maureen kissed her new husband.

21

Amy's grandmother folded her hands across her chest. Her eyes were dewy. She took a handkerchief from beside her bed and dabbed her eyes. Amy didn't press her. She let her say the words she knew were coming in her own time.

"Christophe died two days later," Maureen said. "I was by his side every moment until he went. We were only married for such a short time, but we loved a lifetime's worth."

Amy wiped a tear from her cheek. The recorder was still on.

"I asked to bring his body back to France but the Polish officers said the risk of contamination was too high. So, I left him there. Hundreds died in the next few days. I stayed to help and did whatever I could to comfort the sick and the dying."

"The Soviets swept through, encircling the city, and choked the Nazi beast to death once and for all," Maureen said. "I was still in Sachsenhausen when it all ended. I made my way back to the American lines. They didn't advance into

Berlin until a couple of months after that. I'd heard what the Soviets were doing to the German population and feared for my safety."

"And then you returned to New York?"

Maureen nodded. "That's it," she said.

Amy turned off the tape recorder.

"You asked me about regret before? I regret not marrying him when he first asked—not giving him what he wanted most. What he deserved from me. I had a wonderful life with Edward. He was everything a husband could ever be, but he wasn't my first love. People talk about the loves of their lives as if you can only ever love one person with your whole heart, but that's just a story—an old wives' tale to make sense of something so complex we could never fully understand it. We grow so much during our lives and our hearts with us. The mistake I made during the war with Christophe was not listening to mine."

"Your heart?" Amy asked.

Her grandmother nodded. "Yes. I let the voices in my mind guide me—the ones telling me to wait, that my family needed to be at my wedding, and that I shouldn't marry because I could die any day. All the logical thoughts that I used when making my decisions led me down the wrong path. And what do I regret about Christophe? Not listening to my heart. Let your heart drive you toward whatever you do and whatever decisions you make. Your brain and even your gut might tell you something else, but let your heart speak the loudest, and when it tells you to do something, listen."

Amy nodded, realizing now what her heart had been telling her all this time and what she'd been ignoring.

"If you know what you want. In this life, you've got to grab it with both hands. Don't wait," Maureen said. "It could be gone tomorrow."

Amy felt something change within her. She knew what she

wanted, what she'd always wanted. Mark poked his head around the door.

"Perfect timing," Amy said. "Can you watch Marie with Grandma for a few minutes? I have to go and do something. I won't be long,"

"Sure," her brother replied.

"Go!" her grandmother said. "I'll be here." She smiled and patted Amy on the wrist. Her touch was stronger, her eyes brighter, more vibrant. Amy kissed her on the cheek and looked up at the clock on the wall. It was just after three o'clock. New York was six hours behind. She took the elevator to the lobby and found the pay phone. Her hands were sweating, and her breath had quickened, but this felt right. The fog in her mind had cleared. She wasn't going to make the same mistake her grandmother had. She dialed Mike's direct line at work.

"Amy?" Mike's voice came back doused in surprise. "What are you calling for? Is everything okay?"

"I wanted to speak to you," she said. "I realized what I did, and the mistakes I made. I'm sorry I doubted you. I didn't think you'd want to be with me because of Marie. I pushed you away because I thought you'd hurt me first. I'm sorry. I love you, Mike. Can you find it in your heart to give me another chance?"

He gasped, and then the line went quiet. He didn't seem to know what to say. A few painful seconds passed before he spoke. "You hurt me, Amy. I never gave you any reason to doubt me, but you dropped me preemptively for something I didn't intend to do."

"I know, and I'm sorry. I was wrong. I'm a broke, unemployed single mother. My best friend is 90 years old, and I'm terrified of getting hurt, but I love you."

"I guess I'm finding it hard to believe you. You really hurt me."

"I know. I'm so sorry. You didn't deserve to be treated like that. You've never been anything but good to me."

He paused again. "I'm in work at the moment. I wasn't expecting this. Can I call you back?"

"Of course. I love you, Mike."

He didn't respond. She hung up the phone, knowing that she'd at least tried.

A text came through on her cell phone. It was from Mark. *Grandma's doctor wants to see us both. I think the test results are back. Meet me in the waiting room.*

Amy's heart dropped.

I'll be right up.

Mark was standing in the waiting room with Conor when she arrived. Marie was still asleep in her car seat.

"The nurse is with Grandma," he said. A knock on the door spun all three around. The doctor entered with a chart in his hand. "We ran some tests on your grandmother's heart." He let the clipboard fall to his side as he spoke. "Her results are astounding for a woman of her age." He smiled. "She's making a remarkable recovery."

Amy's heart soared. She grabbed her brother, who was smiling ear to ear. Conor had his hands on his head, beaming. "She's going to be okay?" he asked.

"We're going to need to keep her in for another couple of days to monitor her, and she'll need to take it easy for a few weeks, but yes, it seems so."

"You weren't expecting this?" Conor said.

"From someone her age? No, we weren't. She's an incredible woman."

"Yes, she is." Amy answered.

She hugged her brother and great-uncle again.

Amy turned to the doctor. "Does she know yet?"

"I just told her before I came in here."

"Can we see her?" Mark asked.

"Of course. Just try not to excite her too much. That's why I brought you in here alone."

Amy picked up Marie's car seat and returned to her grandmother's room.

"When can I get out of here?" Maureen said as they walked in. They hugged her one by one, rejoicing in a life renewed. They spent ten wonderful minutes together before Amy's phone buzzed again. It was Mike. She gave Marie to Mark again, went into the hallway and flicked open the phone. "I didn't expect you to call back so soon."

"Are you coming back to New York?"

"Soon. Can I see you when I get there? Please say yes."

"Oh, God," he said. "I've loved you from the first moment I laid eyes on you," he said in an annoyed tone. "Don't do anything like this again. I can only take so much."

"No chance. I promise. I know what I want now. I love you, Mike." Her heart was complete. She had everything she needed.

EPILOGUE

Thursday, April 3, 2008

Amy opened her eyes and looked at the alarm clock beside her bed. Marie was still fast asleep in her crib in the corner. Mike stirred beside her.

"She slept through the night," he said with a weary smile.

Amy sat up. "Again. She's a good girl."

"Just like her momma," Mike said and kissed Amy on the shoulder.

Mike glanced around the bedroom. Marie's crib and changing table took up much of the space. She'd been in with them the last three nights and would be staying with them until after the wedding.

"I sometimes wonder how we'll deal in this place when the next kid comes," Mike said.

"We'll sort that out after the wedding. We have enough on our plate until then."

Mike got out of bed. "Just nine days away."

"Let's focus on today first," Amy said and got up too. Marie woke up at the sound of her footsteps and was instantly hungry. Amy sat on the bed as she fed her daughter.

Mike went to the window. "Does your grandmother have any idea?"

"None whatsoever. I told her we're going to a book signing."

"She must be excited."

"Oh, yes. She loves getting dressed up and meeting people," Amy smiled.

Mike made breakfast, and they sat with Maureen as if it were a regular Thursday morning.

"Where is the signing today?" she asked.

"Fifth Avenue on the Upper East Side," Amy replied, trying to act as bored as possible. Inside, she was bubbling with excitement.

"Being here, in this apartment with the three of you....it feels like coming home," the older woman said with a smile. Amy's heart melted, and she put her hand on Maureen's.

"We're happy you're here. Thanks for everything you did to bring this one to her senses about me," Mike said.

"My pleasure."

Mike finished his food. "I have to head into work for a few hours, but I should be able to get out for the book signing." He winked at Amy and walked out.

"The first book's still selling well?"

Amy nodded. "Yes. Thanks to you."

"No. You wrote it. This is your time, Amy. I couldn't be prouder of the woman you are."

They hugged again.

Two hours later, they were changing for the "signing." Her grandmother emerged from her bedroom in a stylish white dress with a black belt and matching hat.

Amy dressed the baby in a little pink dress with a matching bow in her blond hair. Amy wore a red maxi dress which she was just about able to fit into now.

They were in the cab on the way to the Upper East Side when Amy turned to her grandmother.

"I'm afraid I haven't been entirely honest with you," she said. "We're not going to a book signing. It's actually a ceremony in the French Consulate for World War 2 veterans."

"What? For soldiers?"

"For those who haven't received the plaudits they deserved in the past. I thought you'd want to go along, but didn't want to stir up anything inside you by telling you in advance."

"It's okay, my dear. Telling you my story was cathartic for me. I'm at peace with what happened now. Any residual pain washed away when you pressed stop on that tape recorder."

"I'm so glad to hear that," Maureen said as the cab pulled up outside the stately grey building on Fifth Avenue opposite the park. Amy got out of the car first. She had Marie in her arms and whispered their names to the Frenchman at the door. He helped her grandmother out of the taxi and led them inside a white function room with a lectern underneath a French flag. About a hundred seats were laid out in front of it. Most were already full. The doorman directed Maureen to her place in the front row, one seat from the aisle. Amy sat to her right while three men she didn't know sat on Maureen's left.

"Where's Mike going to sit?" Maureen asked.

"At the back. He might be a little late."

"Isn't this grand?" one of the men sitting beside Maureen said to her in an English accent. He was about 70 and dressed in an elegant gray suit.

"Yes, it's exciting," Maureen said and turned back to Amy.

A few minutes later, once the room was packed, a French soldier came out and erected an American flag. He then stood to make an announcement. "Ladies and gentleman. Please stand for the President of the French Republic, Nicolas Sarkozy."

"The President!" Maureen said. "I knew he was in New York, but I didn't expect this!"

Amy grabbed her grandmother's hand and smiled as they stood up together. Sarkozy came to the lectern. He asked the crowd to be seated and began to speak.

"It's with profound honor that I stand before you today."

Maureen looked around. "Where are the veterans?" she whispered. Amy just smiled.

"The phrase "the greatest" is often thrown around too easily. We are told about the greatest soccer player or the greatest boxer, but it's my firm belief that with us today sits one of the greatest members of what has come to be known as the greatest generation. It's too often that we ignore the true heroes in our society. Men and women are called heroes because they can throw a ball harder or run faster than others. But that word to me means something different. True heroes to me are those who disregard their own safety to help others, who refuse to lie down in the face of tyranny, and who free us from its bonds."

Amy looked at her grandmother. She seemed to be looking around for who they were to honor.

"We are in the presence of someone who fits that mold. A true hero of both America, and the country she adopted as her own—my beloved France."

Maureen looked shocked. Amy turned around. Mike was smiling ear to ear at the back of the room. Marie called out as if in agreement.

"Ladies and gentlemen, distinguished guests, I give you someone I've read about and who has become a personal hero of mine, the irrepressible Maureen Ritter."

The President started a round of applause that spread through the room. Amy's grandmother looked around, her hand over her mouth in shock.

"In case you don't know what Mrs. Ritter accomplished during those awful times, I could direct you to read her granddaughter's new bestselling book." The crowd laughed. "But for now, I will mention a story of three little boys. Rudi, Adam, and Abel Bautner. Three Jewish orphans who found themselves in a house in the tiny village of Izieu in southeastern France that Maureen was running with some others. Fearing for their safety, and disregarding her own, Maureen brought them through France and carried them, literally in her arms, over the grueling mountain passes of the Pyrenees to safety in Spain where they caught a ship to England and lived out the war together. Maureen asked nothing in return. Her only satisfaction was in their safety. Recently, her granddaughter got in touch with the French embassy, and with her help and that of her fiancé, we managed to track down those same Bautner boys, Rudi, Adam and Abel. And they are with us today."

"They are?" Maureen said.

"It's me, Rudi," the man sitting next to Maureen said with tears in his eyes.

"And Adam," the man on Rudi's left said.

"And Abel," their little brother on the end said.

"Boys?" Maureen said as tears gushed down her cheeks. "My boys?"

The three men stood to embrace her. "Thank you," Abel said. "I owe everything I have in life to you. My children. My grandchildren. Everything."

The three brothers hugged her before taking their seats once more as the President began to speak again.

"But they're not the only people in the crowd today who owe their lives to this remarkable woman," he said. "Could anyone who is alive today because of Maureen please stand?"

Maureen turned around as about 30 people took to their feet.

"As well as the Bautner brothers, we have with us today 11 of the original Jewish refugees from Berlin Maureen evacuated, nine Allied servicemen she helped escape to Spain, and five sisters she and her fiancé, Christophe, smuggled over the border into Switzerland."

"The Belmont sisters?" The five women were standing behind her with bright smiles on each of their faces. Maureen stood and went to them and all the others. They each took a few moments to thank her. The mention of Christophe's name felt particularly gratifying. Amy had insisted on it.

A soldier appeared beside Sarkozy on stage with an open wooden box.

It is my profound honor to present Maureen Ritter with France's highest award for both military and civilian service— the Légion d'honneur."

The crowd erupted into applause as the French President descended from the stage. "Don't get up," he said to Maureen in English.

"Oh, Mr. President, I will," she said, raising herself to her feet. Sarkozy placed the medal around her neck. Amy hugged her again. Adam, Rudi, Abel, and all the others she had saved were on their feet. Maureen looked around at them, smiling as if nothing could check the exultation in her soul.

The End

AFTERWORD

The Children of Izieu

In April 1943, a children's home that provided refuge for dozens of children was established in the village of Izieu, formerly Vichy territory. The home, part of the OSE's network of hiding places, was run by Sabine Zlatin, Jewish nurse and OSE activist. Some of the children who lived there were French, while others had come from Belgium, Austria, Algeria, Germany and Poland. On the morning of April 6, 1944, members of the Lyon Gestapo who had been tipped off by an informant carried out a raid on the children's home in Izieu and arrested everyone there. All in all, 51 were taken that day, including 44 children. Almost all were murdered at Auschwitz. This book is dedicated to their memory.

Eoin Dempsey

July 18, 2023

A NOTE TO THE READER

I hope you enjoyed my book. Head over to www.eoindempseybooks.com to sign up for my readers' club. It's free and always will be. If you want to get in touch with me send an email to eoin@eoindempseybooks.com. I love hearing from readers so don't be a stranger!

Reviews are life-blood to authors these days. If you enjoyed the book and can spare a minute please leave a review on Amazon and/or Goodreads. My loyal and committed readers have put me where I am today. Their honest reviews have brought my books to the attention of other readers. I'd be eternally grateful if you could leave a review. It can be short as you like.

ALSO BY EOIN DEMPSEY

ACKNOWLEDGMENTS

Massive thanks to my family. My mother, Anne, my brothers Conor and Brian and my sister, Orla.

Huge and massive and enormous thanks to the magnificent Carol McDuell and the splendid Cindy Bonner. Also to my fabulous advance readers, Michelle Schulten, Cynthia Sand, Kevin Hall, Ave Jeanne Ventresca, Frank Callaghan, Richard Schwarz, Fiona Grant, Preston Tarran, Maria Reed, Cathi Newton, and many others.

Thanks to my lovely wife, Jill, my ultimate sounding board. And thanks to the most distracting inspirations in the world, my three sons, Robbie, Sam and Jack.

ABOUT THE AUTHOR

Eoin (Owen) was born and raised in Ireland. His books have been translated into fourteen languages and also optioned for film and radio broadcast. He lives in Philadelphia with his wonderful wife and three crazy sons.

You can connect with him at eoindempseybooks.com or on Facebook at https://www.facebook.com/eoindempseybooks/ or by email at eoin@eoindempseybooks.com.

PRAISE FOR EOIN DEMPSEY

Praise for *The Hidden Soldier*:

"A heartfelt trip into two entangled time periods that fans will want to read in one sitting. Engrossing and surprising at every turn, the book is yet more proof that Dempsey is a master of the historical fiction genre."

— LYDIA KANG, BESTSELLING AUTHOR OF A BEAUTIFUL POISON AND OPIUM AND ABSINTHE

"The Hidden Soldier is a poignant page-turner that will leave you breathless. Gorgeously written, Eoin Dempsey carries you back in time and inserts you into the heart of this tragic, pivotal moment in history. Part thriller, part love story, I was completely enthralled from beginning to end."

— SUZANNE REDFEARN, #1 AMAZON BESTSELLING AUTHOR OR IN AN INSTANT AND HADLEY AND GRACE.

""I didn't see that coming! Or that!" I yelled across the house as Eoin Dempsey's wonderful World War II book raced to an utterly satisfying wallop of a finale. His spare, dialogue-driven style, matched with his strong knowledge of the war and masterful ability to dance between two time periods, made for one heck of an enjoyable read."

— *BOO WALKER, BESTSELLING AUTHOR OF AN UNFINISHED STORY.*

Praise for *The Longest Echo:*

"...a chilling page turner that explores a shocking, little-known episode in history and manages to include a touching love story."

— HISTORICAL NOVEL SOCIETY

"A beautiful, heart wrenching novel that captivated me from the very beginning. This is historical fiction at its absolute best, and one of my favorite reads of the year."

— SORAYA M. LANE, AMAZON CHARTS BESTSELLING AUTHOR OF *WIVES OF WAR* AND *THE LAST CORRESPONDENT*

"Based on the true horrors of WWII Monte Sole, this story tugs at the heartstrings while delivering authentic, engaging champions and page-turning scenes that continue beyond the war."

— GEMMA LIVIERO, BESTSELLING AUTHOR
OF HISTORICAL FICTION

Praise for *White Rose, Black Forest* (A Goodreads Choice Award Semifinalist, Historical Fiction):

"*White Rose, Black Forest* is partly a lyrical poem, an uncomfortable history lesson, and a page-turning thriller that will keep the reader engaged from the beginning to the end."

— FLORA J. SOLOMON, AUTHOR OF *A
PLEDGE OF SILENCE*

"There is much to praise in Eoin Dempsey's *White Rose, Black Forest*, but for me it stands out from the glut of war fiction because of its poetic simplicity. The novel does not span a massive cast of characters, various continents, and the entire duration of the conflict. It is the tale of one young man, one young woman, and the courage to change the tide of a war. Emotional, taut, and deftly drawn, *White Rose, Black Forest* is a stunning tale of bravery, compassion, and love."

— AIMIE K. RUNYAN, BESTSELLING AUTHOR
OF *DAUGHTERS OF THE NIGHT SKY*

Printed in Great Britain
by Amazon

30910969R00145